Clover Cottage

Christie Barlow

OneMoreChapter

One More Chapter
a division of HarperCollins*Publishers*
The News Building
1 London Bridge Street
London SE1 9GF

www.harpercollins.co.uk

This paperback edition 2020

First published in Great Britain in ebook format by
HarperCollins*Publishers* 2020

A catalogue record for this book
is available from the British Library

ISBN: 978-0-00-836270-6

Set in Birka by Palimpsest Book Production Ltd, Falkirk
Stirlingshire

Printed and bound in Great Britain by
CPI Group (UK) Ltd, Croydon CR0 4YY

In loving memory of Margaret Jean Ridal,

04.01.31 – 2.11.19

Age 88

Forever in our hearts.

Chapter 1

It was just an ordinary Thursday when Allie Macdonald grabbed her bag and sunglasses, threw her camera around her neck and then waltzed down Love Heart Lane to meet her boyfriend Rory. With a spring in her step she was high in spirits; the sun was shining and with a rare night off from the pub she was going to make the most of her evening.

'Hey,' she shouted, waving at Rory, who was walking towards her.

She tilted her head to one side and looked him up and down, all dreamy-eyed. Rory's bone structure was perfectly symmetrical and there was a softness to his eyes. The sun had caught his face, leaving Allie thinking he looked even more handsome than normal – if that was possible. Allie still got a flutter of butterflies swirling around her stomach every time she laid eyes on Rory. She just knew this man was her happy-ever-after and she loved the bones of him.

The second Rory spotted Allie he sported a huge smile.

She stopped and pointed the lens of the camera at him ... click ... click ...

Rory laughed. 'You and that camera,' he joked, striking a pose.

'Not bad,' she teased, shielding the sun from the view-finder whilst taking a flick through the photographs. 'You should really think about becoming a model.'

Rory rolled his eyes. 'I think you may be a tiny bit biased.'

'Maybe, just a little,' said Allie, pinching her thumb and forefinger together before standing on tiptoe and pressing a kiss to his lips.

'You're in good spirits,' said Rory, taking her hand in his as they began walking.

'I am. Life is good and after all it's a special day,' said Allie, ruffling the golden bristles of Rory's stubble and waiting for the penny to drop.

'Huh, special day – what have I missed?' he asked, pretending to rack his brains.

She halted. The sun caught his eyes as she glanced at him questioningly. 'Stop teasing me!'

His eyebrows arched but much to Allie's relief he recovered his expression with a chuckle.

'Rory! It's our anniversary,' exclaimed Allie.

'Eighteen months today,' he replied.

'Do you remember the first time you asked me out?' probed Allie, remembering the stress of that morning. She had taken an early hike over the mountain pass with her trusted labradoodle Nell to take photographs of the heather-covered glens, when Nell had decided to lollop after a bird over the edge of the crag of the hill and had tumbled a long way to the ground. Allie had never run so fast in her life, stumbling across the uneven ground with her heart in her mouth, and when she'd reached Nell, she'd found her unconscious with a huge gash in her side.

'Over the surgery table,' Rory said, grinning.

Allie had arrived in the village of Heartcross at eight years of age, when finally her family had stopped moving around and had settled in the Grouse and Haggis pub, which they'd run ever since. Even though Allie had known Rory in primary school and they had become friends, it was only when he'd returned from university that she'd begun to take a real interest in him. He was the hot young vet, easy on the eye and just an all-round good guy. Allie had been immediately drawn to him and she was willing to bet she hadn't been the only one attracted to him.

She'd watched him set to work on Nell, dynamic and professional, and had been reassured that her little dog was in the best hands. She'd been mesmerised by the change from the goofy lanky boy he'd once been in the school classroom to the handsome professional man he had transformed into.

'Honestly, it looked like a murder scene! You dressed up in your scrubs, splattered with blood, but you saved Nell's life ... My hero!'

Despite the black mascara tears that had run down her cheeks, right there in his surgery, Rory had plucked up the courage and asked Allie out on a date.

'But I do have a bone to pick with you about that day – I didn't even get a discount on my bill,' teased Allie, swiping his arm playfully.

'I've got a living to make – but you did bag a date with the most eligible vet in Heartcross.'

'You are the only vet in Heartcross, except your dad, of course ... What do you think tonight is all about?' asked Allie. It was unusual to be summoned to Rory's parents' house at such short notice.

Rory had received his call just after four o'clock, as soon as afternoon surgery had finished, whilst Allie's call had been just before three. There was nothing to suggest there was anything wrong except the sudden urgency of the invitation, which had taken them both by surprise.

'I've no idea,' answered Rory, looking at his watch, 'but there's only one way to find out!'

It was an uphill walk across the village green to Rory's parents' cosy three-bedroom cottage nestled at the end of the high street. Alana and Stuart had lived there all their married life and it offered spectacular views of the rolling hills and Heartcross Mountain. For a moment, Allie and Rory took a breather and rested against the wooden fence that adorned the idyllic duck pond, home to a few plump-looking mallards, in the utterly gorgeous village of

Heartcross. Allie pointed her camera at the water ... click ... click ...

They watched the children running along the well-worn gravel paths, their faces flushed with laughter, whilst their mothers sat chatting on picnic blankets under the magnificent green cascades of the willow trees. There was no breeze today; the weather was glorious and the early evening sun hung high in the sky, beaming rays down on them.

Allie shouted over to Hamish and Julia, who were weaving floral-coloured bunting through the railings at the far end of the green. It was a busy weekend for the villagers of Heartcross: it was their annual summer fair, which brought everyone out in droves.

'You are good at all that malarkey,' said Rory, nodding towards the camera before staring out across the park.

Allie had been interested in photography from as long back as she could remember. Even at school she'd been the brains behind the afterschool photography club, always having her camera close to hand. Recently, she'd begun to photograph local events and was amazed when the local newspaper had published her photographs alongside their articles. For Allie's last birthday Rory had bought her a subscription to a national photography magazine which she'd thought was just the best and most thoughtful present anyone had ever got her. Each month she looked forward to the magazine landing on the doormat.

'It's easy. All you do is point and click,' said Allie joyfully, snapping away.

Rory took a look at the photographs through the view-finder. 'They are amazing,' he said glancing at her with respect. 'Have you thought any more about opening up a photography club?'

Recently, the idea had been firmly on Allie's mind, but she was exhausted with the early morning starts followed by the late nights working at the pub and barely got any time off.

'We'll see,' she mused.

Rory watched the concentration on Allie's face as she twisted the lens on her latest Nikon before she leaned slightly towards him and lowered her voice even though there was no one close by to hear. 'You don't think one of your parents is ill, do you?' she said, with an uncomfortable feeling rising inside. It had been the first thing she had thought of when she'd received her call.

Rory's eyebrows shot up and he gave Allie a sideward glance. 'What makes you say that?' he asked. 'I'm not sure I'm prepared for a bombshell like that.'

Immediately, Allie felt a little guilty and summoned a smile. She hadn't meant to worry Rory. 'Or maybe your dad is finally going to announce his retirement. That'll be a huge relief for you. I know you find his old-fashioned ways somewhat suffocating at times.'

'Only at times?' Rory rolled his eyes. He found his father difficult to work with on a daily basis.

Rory had been one of those unique children who had always known what he wanted to do as a profession, unlike

Allie, who had fallen into the job of barmaid by accident – after helping out at her parents' pub one evening due to staffing issues, she'd been there ever since. Lately, it seemed to Rory, she'd lost all motivation to find another job.

Conversely, Rory had been a dedicated student, his time at university taking him away from sleepy Heartcross to bustling London. He'd left university with a first-class degree and big plans. He'd wanted to travel, make a difference and stamp his mark on the world. After his placement at a zoo he'd become fascinated by endangered wild animals and had passionately campaigned to raise money for the sanctuaries that rescued vulnerable animals from appalling conditions where they were confined, exploited or abused. He had been determined to help in any way he could but had ultimately been enticed back to Heartcross by his father on the promise that, one day, he would make him a partner in the veterinary practice. Stuart had sold the opportunity to Rory that they would be equal but in Rory's eyes their partnership was far from equal. Stuart still had the majority shareholding and his decision was final – always. But Rory had ideas and dreams of his own. He wanted to extend the practice, build a brand-new operating theatre with all the latest equipment and technology, alongside an animal hospital. He wanted the Scott and Son veterinary practice to become a household name, further afield than the little rural village of Heartcross. But Stuart had dismissed the suggestion; he couldn't understand why anyone would ever want to expand and become a bigger corporation.

'Look, son, this is a family business, customers know your name, who you are ... It gives them the personal touch. When you start bringing in outsiders, all that is lost, and things get messy. Customers want to know they are seeing you or me, not someone else.'

Even though Rory was eternally grateful for having a secure career it was no secret that his father's working methods frustrated him. Stuart was forever the traditionalist and every time Rory suggested even the most minuscule of changes to the veterinary practice it was always dismissed immediately without further discussion.

'Can you believe we still don't have a computer system to book appointments, in this day and age?' said Rory, cocking an eyebrow whilst shaking his head slightly.

Allie chuckled, linking her arms through his, and rested her head on his shoulder. She knew this conversation off by heart; she'd lost count of the number of times Rory had vented his annoyance to her. His mum, Alana, could never get to grips with a computerised system and, as the receptionist in the family-run business, had kiboshed it within hours of one being set up. 'All we need is an appointment book and a pen. The old ways are the best ways,' she'd said with authority and there was no way she was budging.

Rory had disagreed. Every time he needed to pencil in an appointment or check who was next on his rounds, he had to ring his mother to check the system.

'But ...' said Rory, hesitantly.

'What is it?'

'Lately, Mum ... I thought maybe I'd got it wrong, but her filing is all over the place and sometimes not even in the cabinet. Emails deleted or not replied to, not to mention appointments missed in the diary. I nearly said something but ... Then there's Dad: in the last couple of months he's seemed grumpier than usual,' said Rory, attempting a half-hearted laugh, 'but I suppose sometimes even I go up the stairs and forget what the hell I went up for.' Allie got the impression Rory was glossing over his worries and glimpsed a concerned expression in his eyes.

'Maybe we should live in a bungalow when we are older, then we won't need to go up the stairs,' Allie joked.

'Sounds like a plan. Right, come on,' said Rory, unable to put off the inevitable any longer. 'Let's go and find out what all this is about.'

Enjoying the sunshine, Allie took Rory's hand and swung it gently as they ambled up the lane towards his parents' cottage. On arrival Rory pushed open the gate into the garden.

'Everywhere looks stunning!' exclaimed Allie. Stuart was a keen gardener in his spare time and the front garden was wholly gorgeous, striking in fact, with not a single blade of grass out of place. There was so much colour, blooms bursting from every flowerbed. Allie inhaled the rich scent of the roses that straggled round the old oak-beamed porch. 'Look at these roses, simply stunning ... so pretty,' she said, thinking one day she would love to live in a cottage as quaint as this.

Within seconds Alana appeared from the side of the house with a huge smile on her face. 'I thought I heard the gate.' She fussed round Rory, straightening the collar on his polo shirt before pulling Allie in for a suffocating hug.

'Come,' Alana said with a gesture after releasing Allie and placing a soft kiss on her cheek. 'We are in the garden, the weather is too beautiful to miss.'

'She's in good spirits,' whispered Allie to Rory, thinking that maybe they'd been worrying about nothing. Alana looked happy and relaxed. Maybe the request to visit had simply been an invitation for dinner.

Following Alana around the side of the house, the gravel path crunching underneath their shoes, Rory and Allie were greeted with a splendid-looking afternoon tea.

'This is all very civilised,' exclaimed Rory, casting a glance over the table set out with his parents' best china tea set. Delicately cut finger sandwiches, scones with clotted cream and strawberry jam, sweet pastries and cakes looking extremely scrumptious adorned the floral plates.

Stuart looked up from under his wide-brimmed hat, his glasses balancing on the bridge of his nose, newspaper in hand. 'I'm working like a boss,' he joked, folding up the newspaper and placing it on the table. 'How is everyone?' he asked, standing up and kissing Allie on her cheek and clapping Rory on his shoulder.

'We are all good. It's glorious out here. Summer has finally arrived in Heartcross,' said Allie, pulling out a chair and sitting down opposite Stuart.

'Drink, anyone? There's tea in the pot, homemade lemonade or there's a bottle of wine open,' offered Alana.

'Wine would be great,' answered Allie, looking towards Rory, who craftily pinched a sandwich from the platter. It didn't go unnoticed by Alana.

'Hey,' she said, lightly slapping her son's arm in jest before handing out the plates.

'How was work this afternoon?' asked Stuart, picking up a conversation with his son.

The afternoon had dragged for Rory. 'The same old mundane routine, mostly domestic animals off their food due to the heatwave, and Mrs Green's labrador needs to go on a diet. Goodness knows what she's feeding him.'

Stuart gave his son the parent stare, the one that warned him not to be ungracious. 'That same old mundane routine is a business that has been built up over time, from nothing. Those animal owners trust us, rely on us, which is an honour, as most animal lovers prefer animals to humans.'

Rory had heard the same spiel a thousand times before.

Suddenly feeling a slight tension in the air, Allie looked from Rory to his father. She could understand Rory's frustrations. She had long considered that Stuart was holding off from retirement because he just couldn't let go of the practice, and wanted it to stay exactly the same for ever.

'How about you, Alana, what did you do with your

afternoon off?' she asked, gratefully accepting a glass of wine from her and hoping the change in conversation would lighten the mood.

'I went into town and you'll never guess who I bumped into,' said Alana with enthusiasm, looking directly at Rory, who simply shrugged.

'Clare – Clare Wilson – well, not Clare but her mother.'

Rory sat up straight, 'No way! What is Fiona doing around these parts?'

'Visiting a family friend or something. I had to look twice when I saw her standing in the queue in the department store ... She passes on her best and told me all about Clare. Oh, Rory, she's doing so well for herself.'

Clare Wilson was Rory's ex-girlfriend from university and was practically perfect in every way. Allie knew this because this was not the first time Alana had brought her into the conversation. Despite Allie giving herself a good talking to, that Clare wasn't in any way a threat to her or her relationship with Rory, curiosity had got the better of her and she'd gone searching on Facebook and Instagram until she'd found her. Clare was a natural beauty, even Allie acknowledged that. Her long blonde tousled locks bounced just below her shoulders, her skin was flawless and her piercing blue eyes were captivating. In the last twelve months alone, Clare had travelled to places Allie hadn't even heard of. Everything she did she did successfully and at first Allie had to admit she felt a tinge of jealousy; the places Clare had visited, the charity work she'd undertaken, looked amazing and often left Allie wondering if she had missed out on life.

To Allie's knowledge Rory had dated Clare for over three years, and when he decided to move back to Heartcross on a permanent basis she'd called the relationship off.

'I bet, single-handedly saving the world no doubt!' joked Rory.

'It's funny, really, isn't it—?'

'Funny in what way?' interrupted Rory.

'Because Clare left for Africa a couple of days ago. You were the one who always talked about travelling.'

'Wow! Africa! That's incredible,' trilled Rory, looking suitably impressed. 'Clare was always a go-getter.'

'Apparently, she's working as a travelling vet. It sounded amazing when Fiona was talking about her job, even though I'd rather we stick to domestic cats any day of the week. I'm not sure my nerves would hold up if I came face to face with a lion over the reception counter,' said Alana, giving a little chuckle. 'Have you ever thought about travelling, Allie?'

Alana's question was innocent enough but made Allie's thoughts quickly flick back to her own childhood. Her parents had travelled around a lot when she was younger, due to the lack of job opportunities, and Allie remembered how they had often been struggling for cash, making times very difficult for them as a family. As soon as Allie began to make friends in a new school, it seemed like only seconds later she would be whisked off to the next destination, her parents hoping for a better life but leaving her feeling unsettled and having to try and fit in all over again. She had been eternally gratefully when they had found their forever home in Heartcross and now she was reluctant to stray far away again.

As Allie shook her head and took a sip of her wine Alana passed the sandwiches towards them. 'Tuck in before they begin to curl at the edges.'

Still thinking about her early childhood Allie realised she couldn't ever imagine leaving Heartcross. Everything she needed was right here: her parents, Rory, her job.

Granted, over the years Allie had watched numerous films that featured the bustling cities of New York, London, Tokyo, the sky disappearing between the huge skyscrapers, the traffic, and whilst it had seemed glamorous and exciting, it had also seemed all too manic to Allie, who loved the slow pace of living in the Scottish Highlands, surrounded by the spectacular views of the mountain terrain. Allie knew she would never tire of it.

'So other than the usual spot of gardening, how was your afternoon, Stuart? Did you take a trip into town?' asked Allie.

Silence.

The exchanged subtle look between Stuart and Alana didn't go unnoticed by either Allie or Rory.

'Okay, what's going on?' asked Rory, lowering the sandwich back onto his plate. 'Is something wrong?' Rory leant forward, rested one arm on the table and the other on

Allie's knee. Maybe one of them was ill, thought Allie, but Alana seemed to bloom in an instant, a huge smile hitched on her lips, and Allie noticed Rory relax his shoulders a notch.

Alana folded her arms and leant on the table before nodding towards Stuart to give him the go-ahead to speak.

'It looks like good news with that smile,' said Allie, regarding Rory with one raised eyebrow.

'This afternoon, we've been to the solicitor's office,' announced Alana, tilting her head and smiling widely. 'Go on, Stuart, tell them the good news.'

Stuart cleared his throat; all eyes were on him. 'Everything is absolutely fine, in fact more than fine.'

Beginning to feel impatient, Rory wound his hand round in circles, indicating the need for his father to speed up whatever it was he wanted to say.

'What your father is trying to say is … we are putting the house up for sale.'

Horrified, Rory looked towards Allie. This revelation was not one he was expecting. Turning back towards his parents, he said, 'You can't be serious. Sell this place? Why would you even do that? What about the surgery?'

This house was Rory's childhood home; this was where they belonged. He couldn't ever imagine them living anywhere else or anyone else living here.

'Not this place!' trilled Alana, chuckling.

Rory shook his head, 'I don't understand. What house?'

Allie didn't say a word but tightened her grip around

Rory's hand on her knee. Unlike Rory she had guessed what was coming next.

'The terrace on Love Heart Lane.'

Allie waited and watched Rory. She knew this revelation had taken him by surprise. There was no sharp intake of breath, just a rhythmic blink then the penny dropped. He drained his drink and looked towards the faces turned towards him. His expression was now completely aghast. 'Sorry' – he paused – 'sorry, for a moment there, I could have sworn you said you were going to sell *my* house,' he stated, in a distressed tone, a sick sensation washing over him.

Alana topped up her glass with wine and then Allie's.

'And what I don't understand is why you would even smile about the fact you are making me homeless.' Rory wilted back in his chair and glanced between his mum and dad, waiting for answers. What were his parents thinking? Rory had lived in the whitewashed terrace on Love Heart Lane since graduating as a vet, as he'd found it difficult moving back into the family home after being independent at university. The property was owned by his parents and he knew he was on a cushy number, living there rent- and mortgage-free, but he'd offered to pay his way and they'd refused.

'What am I meant to do? I'm not moving back in with you two – at my age that's ridiculous.' Rory threw his hands up in the air. 'If the house is going up for sale there's a very simple solution – I'll just buy it,' said Rory, feeling satisfied with his decision. 'That's what I'll do. Why am I even worrying about it? I'll buy it direct from you ... that'll save your estate agent bills too. Win–win. I'm not losing my home.' Rory was determined.

'Don't be daft, you don't want to have a mortgage hanging around your neck,' said Alana, 'when you don't have to.' Her voice was upbeat.

'Of course I do,' argued Rory. 'I have a good salary, the business is doing well ... and I'm happy there; it's my home.'

'Unfortunately, buying the house is not an option for the next twelve months,' cut in Stuart.

'Why?' insisted Rory, his voice tight.

'Because we've agreed to rent it out.'

Feeling shocked – even she wasn't expecting that revelation – Allie watched as Rory's cheeks turned crimson.

'You've done what? Why on earth would you do that?' he said, shaking his head in disbelief.

'It's not a bad thing – if you will let us finish. We've signed a twelve-month lease to a man called Flynn Carter,' announced Stuart.

Rory exhaled. He couldn't believe what he was hearing.

Stuart continued, 'He's a property developer looking into this area due to the increase in tourism, or something along those lines.'

Rory was shaking his head in disbelief again as he looked towards Allie then back towards his father. 'You've already signed a twelve-month lease? Without talking to me first? So when are you actually making me homeless from?'

'The first of the month.'

'I don't believe this ... Marvellous, absolutely marvellous.'

Allie placed her hand on Rory's arm to calm him, but she was feeling confused too. She knew Stuart and Alana were fair people and couldn't quite understand why they would do this. Surely there was a reason behind this? But she couldn't quite put her finger on it. Trying to comfort Rory, she summoned up a smile. 'You will be able to stay at mine – at the pub. Mum and Dad won't mind,' she soothed.

'As if we are going to leave you homeless,' said Alana, standing up, still with a smile on her face.

A bewildered Rory and Allie watched as Alana disappeared inside and returned clutching a brown envelope. She sat back down and slid the envelope towards them.

'Let us put your mind at rest. Me and your dad aren't losing our marbles, you know ... Go on, open it,' encouraged Alana.

Rory and Allie locked eyes before Allie took the envelope and opened it.

Both of them stared at the paper in front of them. Allie didn't understand. 'House details? Clover Cottage?' she said, looking at the particulars and passing them to Rory. 'Isn't this James Kerr's old place?' she asked, puzzled.

'It is indeed – and, would you believe, James left it to me in his will,' said Stuart, pouring himself a beer and taking a sip.

'Wow!' exclaimed Allie, 'I wish someone would leave me a house in a will.'

'Well,' said Alana hesitating. 'That kind of is about to happen, except we aren't dead yet.' She chuckled.

'Huh?' said Rory, looking towards his parents.

'We think Clover Cottage would be perfect for you – for you both. It was your dad's idea really but I think it's fantastic too.' Alana smiled towards them both. 'Allie would make the perfect daughter-in-law and we would love to welcome her into our family.'

It took Allie a second or two for the information to sink in then she squealed, grasping Rory's arm, her hands visibly shaking. The excitement wired her body like she was plugged into the mains. She stared again at the details on the paperwork in front of her.

A cottage, their very own cottage.

She was genuinely shocked. 'Oh my gosh, is this some sort of proposal? I'd love to be your daughter-in-law.' Allie looked towards Rory with hope, a swarm of fireflies fluttering around her stomach at a speed of knots. 'Rory, we have a house ... a beautiful cottage ... a place to set up home together.' She barely took a breath.

Excitedly, she read out loud,

Clover Cottage, part of the Clover Farm estate, stands on the outskirts of the picturesque village of Heartcross, freehold detached dwelling

Modernisation needed. Plot circa 5 acres.

Even though the words were floating around in the air, Allie still couldn't get her head around it ... a cottage! Things like this didn't happen to her; they only happened in the movies. This was all Allie had ever dreamt of, to set up home with Rory in such an idyllic setting, just like the one they were sitting in now, and it was right here on the outskirts of Heartcross. Already in her head she'd planned the decor, a new kitchen, roses tumbling around the oak porch and honeysuckle straggling through the hedgerows, the log fire burning away in the winter months.

'Stuart, Alana,' said Allie, looking up, 'I really don't know what to say ... "Thank you" just doesn't seem enough.' Allie's head was in an absolute spin. Her and Rory's home together. This was her dream, cosying up with Rory every night.

'Those particulars are current. We were going to sell the property when Stuart suggested gifting it to you both. We know how hard it is to get on to the property ladder these days and houses in Heartcross don't come around that often.'

It was only then that Allie realised Rory had not said a word. She looked towards him and immediately sensed something was wrong. Rory looked kind of frazzled, like he was about to explode.

'What is it?' she asked, biting her bottom lip. She had a feeling something ominous was about to happen. There had been a sudden change of atmosphere.

Rory took the particulars out of Allie's hand and slid them back across the table.

Feeling bewildered, she watched in dismay.

'Thank you but no thank you.' Rory's eyes were wide and he didn't even look in Allie's direction. Scraping his chair back, he muttered, 'I need some space,' before exhaling, raking his hand through his hair and striding towards the kitchen.

'Rory!' a confused Allie shouted after him but he didn't even give her as much as a glance over his shoulder. What the hell had got into him?

'I'm so sorry,' said Allie, quickly apologising to Alana and Stuart. She stood up and was about to follow Rory when Alana put a hand on her arm. 'I'll go,' she insisted, and before Allie could object Alana was halfway up the path towards Rory, who was leaning against the kitchen worktop with his ankles crossed and his arms folded. Allie sat back down opposite Stuart feeling awkward.

As she sipped her wine Allie felt like all her dreams had come crashing down around her. All her fuzzy romantic feelings about setting up home with Rory were fading fast. Her mood slumped.

Alana and Rory's voices travelled from the kitchen outside into the garden. Rory's was irate. 'How dare you both? I say when, I say where I want to live, and who with. This is typical of you and Dad, always trying to control me at work, and now forcing a home on me. I like living where I am and if I do have to move I would like to choose that property myself. And implying I should ask Allie to marry me. I might not even want Allie to marry me, I may not even want to set up home with Allie. Have you ever thought about that? What gives you the right to do this?'

'We were only trying to help, and don't you think it's time?'

'I'll say when it's time. I don't need my parents pushing me into anything. My life, my choices.'

'But houses don't come up for sale in Heartcross very often. Clover Cottage will be the perfect family home for you both.'

Listening to Rory's outburst, Allie felt numb. Her whole world had come crashing down around her. At first, she'd felt like a child at Christmas, one second ecstatically unwrapping the best present ever, and the next, devastated to find it wasn't actually for her. She knew her mascara was about to run in all directions across her cheeks, and the wretched feeling in her stomach made her feel like she wanted to heave.

Unfortunately, Rory was locked in a heated conversation with his mother, and, feeling sick, Allie had exhausted all avenues of conversation with Stuart. 'I'm so sorry, Stuart, please forgive me,' she said, trying to keep her voice steady, though she couldn't keep the anxiety out of it. 'I feel I need to go.'

She stood up; she wasn't going to hang around any longer. Rory's reaction had hit her hard. Trying to hide her tears, she bent her head low, grabbed her camera and left the cottage feeling downhearted.

Walking back through the village, she dug her hands deep in her pockets of her jacket, her mood plummeting to an all-time low. She paused briefly and looked out over the village green, Rory's words playing over on her mind: 'I may not even want to set up home with Allie.'

Allie was in turmoil, her eyes full of tears. What the hell had just happened? With her head in a spin, she walked around the pond, past the tall rustling reeds, and sat down on the bench under the large oak tree, trying to make sense of it all.

This would be the ideal start for them both, a cottage in the heart of the village where their life was, with no financial burden of a mortgage. As far as she was concerned this was the best thing that could have happened to them. Alana was right; houses didn't come up for sale very often and this cottage would be perfect for them. But after Rory's reaction Allie was beginning to wonder. The only reasonable explanation for his outburst was that just maybe she'd got this relationship all wrong. Maybe she wasn't Rory's happy-ever-after at all.

Chapter 2

Ten minutes later, Allie hadn't moved from the bench. She hugged her knees to her chest and, taking in a breath, she closed her eyes and sighed.

She didn't want to go straight home and face a busy pub along with a barrage of questions from her parents about why her evening had been cut short.

Still close to tears she felt embarrassed by Rory's reaction and didn't like the feeling of rejection at all. Where did they go from here? Tonight could have played out so differently. Right at this moment they could have been celebrating, popping open the champagne, and Allie knew she would have dragged Rory straight round to the cottage to take a look inside. But instead, here she was feeling upset, sitting alone.

Taking a slow steadying breath, she stared at the view in front of her, one of outstanding beauty. It had been a while since she'd hiked to the top of Heartcross Mountain, where the views went on for miles and miles. She closed her eyes, remembering her and Rory's first proper date, a picnic on the mountain. She smiled just thinking about it. The weather had been kind, with a slight breeze as they'd climbed the small incline towards the pass then walked along the rocky path. Around halfway up there was a small brick building, which, as children, Allie and her friends would use as their den during the long summer holidays, and that was where they'd laid out their blanket. Rory had brought the picnic with a little help from Bonnie's Teashop and the whole time Allie had felt a flutter of excitement, too nervous to eat. They'd lain on their backs, their faces towards the sky, when Rory had gently entwined his fingers around hers and leant up on one elbow before kissing her for the very first time.

Ping! Allie dropped her gaze to her phone. Three missed calls and three texts messages, all from Rory. She tapped and swiped the screen and sat with her head bowed reading his messages.

Where are you? x

Please pick up your phone x

Ring me as soon as you get this x

It looked like Rory was desperate to get hold of her, but at this moment Allie didn't know what to say to him. A snap of a twig behind her caused her to spin round, and standing there she saw her friend Felicity.

'I'm jogging! Don't ask, just trying to shift a few pounds and get fit. All those cakes are piling on my waistline.' She patted her stomach but as soon as she locked eyes with Allie her smile faded.

'Bad day?' asked Felicity, narrowing her eyes.

Where do I start? thought Allie, blowing out a breath. 'You could say that.'

Felicity sat down next to her and for a second both women sat in silence, staring at the view, before Felicity spoke.

'What's going on? Do you want to talk about it?' she asked tentatively.

Allie had never been one for tears, and she knew Felicity would be surprised and worried to see her upset. 'You know when you think life is great and then suddenly—' Allie's voice faltered as she wiped away a tear that was sliding down her cheek with the back of her hand.

'Surely it can't be that bad,' said Felicity, trying to comfort her.

'Do you think you will ever move in with Fergus?' asked Allie, looking towards her friend.

'That's the plan,' said Felicity, 'but it's not always that simple, is it?'

Allie knew Felicity's life and relationship with Fergus were complicated. Her heart went out to her friend who had made some brave decisions in the past, including walking away from Heartcross for eight years and living on her own in London.

'Both Fergus and I talk about it all the time and I would jump at the chance of living with him and Esme – they are my life. But the timing and house need to be right. Let's face it, no one seems to move from Heartcross and there aren't many houses going up for sale, are there?'

'That's my point exactly.'

'Huh? You've lost me.'

'If someone gave you and Fergus a cottage in Heartcross, what would you think?'

'Either I'm dreaming or I've won the lottery!'

'I thought I'd won the lottery,' said Allie solemnly, before sharing all the details about the evening so far with her friend.

Felicity blew out a breath. 'I wasn't expecting that. Clover Cottage – wow ... That's amazing! And James left the cottage to Stuart and Alana in his will and they've given it to you and Rory?' she said, obviously happy for her friend.

Allie nodded, 'That about sums it up, except Rory doesn't want it and gave it back.'

'Really? Is he mad? I'd be looking round there right at this second.'

Allie wholeheartedly agreed. She looked at her phone once more. She'd switched it to silent but there was Rory's name flashing away on the screen, trying to reach her again. She knew she should probably pick up the call, but she shrugged off any guilt, knowing she was going to let him stew for a little while longer.

Over the past eighteen months Allie had built up a picture of their future together and this could have been the start of it. She sighed to herself again. She really hoped things were fixable between them.

'Ignoring his calls isn't going to help,' said Felicity, looking at Rory's name flashing repeatedly on Allie's screen.

Allie paused before she answered, and cast her mind back, thinking about Rory's reaction to his parents' offer more and more.

'You know, Rory's never even asked me to move into the terrace with him on Love Heart Lane. Do you think that's strange when he already has a house and I'm living with my parents at the pub?'

'I bet he just thinks it's easier for you to live there, with your early starts. And you know, Allie, sometimes men just need a little push. Talk to him; find out what's going on. There's no point sitting here trying to work it all out without the facts. Rory is besotted with you, anyone can see that.'

Allie shook her head. 'You should have heard him, Flick.'

'It'll all be fine,' reassured Felicity in a soft tone.

Despite her worries Allie knew she needed to talk to Rory.

'Ring him back,' urged Felicity. 'The sooner the better.'

But before Allie could answer and let all her jumbled-up feelings settle, Rory came tumbling towards them both, raking his hand through his hair.

'Thank God, I've been looking for you everywhere.'

Allie looked up. Rory's expression had changed from one of anger and now he genuinely looked deflated and upset.

Allie waggled her phone in front of her. 'I know, I'm sorry,' she said, staring at the ground and avoiding Rory's gaze. 'I just needed to get my head straight.'

'I'll leave you both to it,' said Felicity, standing up and hoping both of her friends would be okay. 'If I don't see you before, I'll catch you both at the summer fair on Saturday.'

Rory waited until Felicity was out of sight before speaking. 'Why did you disappear?'

'Why do you think? Probably overhearing the heated conversation with your mum ... especially the part when you stated you may not even want to marry me or set up home with me. You could have broken it to me gently, Rory.' Allie's voice wobbled.

Saying the words out loud, she did her best to squash the feeling of dread rising rapidly inside her, but she felt her heart-rate quicken.

Since she had been a little girl Allie had always dreamt of the perfect proposal and the perfect wedding, and as far as she was concerned Rory was her happy-ever-after. She felt vulnerable as he perched on the bench beside her. She wasn't sure where this conversation was heading.

'Is it over?' the words were out of her mouth before she could stop them, the comment hanging in the air between them. She braced herself, squeezing her eyes shut, preparing herself for the answer.

'What? What are you going on about?' Rory's eyes were wide. 'I love you—'

Allie looked up. 'But—' she interrupted. Rory exhaled. 'Oh my God, you are saying it's over,' she said, immediately standing up, not giving him a chance to answer. Her eyes were brimming with tears, her heart thumping fast against her ribcage. She couldn't do this; she just wanted to get away.

Rory pulled her back down to the bench and grasped both her hands in his. 'God, I'm sorry. That's not what I'm saying at all. It's just—'

'It's just you don't want to live with me,' insisted Allie.

'That's not what I'm saying either.'

'Then what are you saying, Rory? Because I'm sitting here not knowing what the hell is going on. One minute I feel like I've won the lottery and the next, in the blink of an eye, I feel like I've lost everything.' Allie's voice faltered but she held his gaze.

'Do you not think the decision should be ours? Do you not think our future is our decision?'

'I don't understand, Rory.' All Allie could think about was the cottage that he'd just handed back to his parents. 'Clover Cottage is – was – perfect for us.'

'Allie, I'm not saying it's not perfect for us. What I'm trying to say is my parents always have a hold over my life. I work for them, I live in a house owned by them, they are now choosing where my future house should be and who I live there with! You know my frustrations with Dad; we butt heads all the time regarding business matters. I'm not saying he's a bad guy, and the offer of the cottage is a generous gift, but I just want to make my own way in life. I feel stifled – suffocated – by them at times.'

Allie didn't interrupt but sat listening to Rory, who loosened his grip on her hands now he knew she wasn't going to leave.

'I want to ask my girlfriend to move in with me when I'm ready to ask her. I felt like Mum and Dad were pushing for us to live together, inviting you to be their daughter-in-law. I'm over the moon they think of you in that way, I really am, but I couldn't help feeling this was more about them than us.'

'What do you mean?' asked Allie, confused.

'I think they've decided they are ready for the next stage of their lives – grandchildren. They want to see me, their only son, settled down. But this isn't about them, it's about me ... it's about *us*. I'm enjoying this part of our journey, dating, looking forward to seeing you in the evening, getting ready to go out ... It's a time we don't get back. And what's the rush?'

Allie knew Rory had a point, but she felt ready for the next step. She was tired of living with her parents, waking up and working in the same place. Of course it was convenient but now she too wanted her own space and wanted to move in with Rory. The time was right for her.

'Isn't half the fun viewing properties and deciding where we want to live together?' Rory continued. 'When we are ready, I want us to look for a house together, choose where we want to live *together.*'

'But houses in Heartcross don't come up for sale often. This cottage could be the perfect answer,' Allie pointed out gently. 'And the garden is amazing too; it's a perfect location ...' She bumped her shoulder against his lightly. 'And we wouldn't have to move out of Heartcross. Surely it wouldn't cause any harm to take a look?'

'You are beautiful and persuasive,' he said, dropping a kiss on the tip of her nose. 'But I want to make my own way in the world. Dad convinced me working in the family business was best for me yet I don't feel equal and I'm convinced there's more waiting out there for me.'

'What's wrong with Heartcross?' Allie asked hesitantly.

'Nothing – but there's a big wide world out there to explore.'

'Oh,' said Allie, trying to read Rory's expression before turning back to look at the scenery in front of her. Trying to digest the information, she felt confused, and a small tear slid down her face.

'Please don't cry, I'm just being honest with you. All I'm saying is there is more to life than Heartcross.'

Allie's heart sank. She loved her comfortingly familiar life, surrounded by what she knew, the friends she grew up with. Her home was Heartcross, her life was Heartcross. But maybe she was so caught up in her own little world, she'd never realised Rory didn't feel the same way.

'I don't feel I can stamp my mark on the business until

Dad retires. I want to bring the technology into this century, build a new surgery, an animal hospital. I still feel like I'm living in the dark ages and banging my head against a brick wall. And now I have the added worry of moving out of my home in a matter of days. Everything in my life so far revolves around my parents' aspirations for me.'

Allie knew she didn't have the same frustrations with her own parents, but maybe that was because they weren't as financially secure as Rory's parents or as traditional in their views. And they certainly didn't have more than one house. Money was tight at the pub: some months they barely made a living, but thankfully, due to Heartcross being put on the map over twelve months ago, there'd been an influx of tourists, which had helped to boost the business.

'This isn't about us, Allie, and I'm sorry I made you feel like this. But I do think moving in together should be our decision, not someone else's. We've never talked about living together – it's a major step, a commitment and I don't want to let you down.'

'Are you saying you still want to be with me?'

'That was never in doubt. I always want to be with you.'

A smile crept onto Allie's face, and a feeling of relief swept over her, but at the same time she was still feeling a little disappointed about the cottage. She nodded her understanding, but she wasn't about to give up. Rory had admitted it was down to timing, and surely if his father retired Rory would think differently. He could run the business just the way he wanted. Rory might think Clover Cottage wasn't the place for them but how would he ever know if he didn't go and look? Allie was certainly intrigued by what Clover Cottage might have to offer.

Rory leant forward and kissed her tenderly on the cheek. 'Thank you for understanding.'

Even though Allie hoped this was just a waiting game she felt a tiny niggle begin to fester inside her. What if she and Rory did want different things in life?

Chapter 3

On Saturday morning Allie was up with the lark. Usually she'd clean the pub once the drayman had arrived, but today it was the summer fair on the green and already her parents were bustling around with the other villagers erecting the tents for the day ahead.

She set to work dusting down the bar, putting out clean bar towels and restocking all the fridges. As she cleaned the lines and reconnected the ales and lager and made sure they tasted okay, her mind was firmly fixed on Rory. She hadn't crossed paths with Stuart and Alana since Rory had refused the cottage, and she was hoping there would be no awkwardness between them today. She wondered what Rory was going to do. The clock was ticking and he had to move out of Love Heart Lane in a matter of days, but as far as she knew he hadn't even started to pack up his things.

She picked up her untouched cold mug of tea and leant against the bar thinking about Rory. When he'd refused the cottage she'd doubted his intentions, but Rory had been his usual attentive self since then and had confirmed to Allie that refusing the cottage was nothing whatsoever to do with their relationship, thus putting her mind at ease. Of course, she understood his frustrations with his father, but she still couldn't shake the feeling that a cottage in Heartcross was a unique opportunity for them. She was surprised Rory wasn't in the tiniest bit curious to take a look inside.

Wandering into the kitchen to make a fresh cup of tea, she hummed along to the radio then heard the door of the pub opening. She quickly popped her head into the hallway and saw Isla standing in the bar frantically looking for her.

'Allie! Allie! Where are you?'

Allie appeared and locked eyes with Isla. 'What's wrong?'

Isla flapped her hand in front of her. 'Nothing, nothing whatsoever ...' The smile stretched across her face. 'You'll never guess what ... honestly, I couldn't believe it when I saw him.' Isla pulled out a stool at the bar and perched on top.

'Saw who?' asked Allie, intrigued. She hadn't seen Isla this excited since she decided to buy a herd of alpacas for Drew's last birthday.

Isla took a deep breath. 'Zach Hudson!'

'Don't be ridiculous – where the hell would you see Zach Hudson? Have you had a bump on the head?' But Allie had to admit Isla looked radiant this morning and didn't look like she'd been bumped on the head.

'I kid you not, he's staying at the farm – in one of my vans!'

Allie laughed. 'There is no way Zach Hudson is slumming in a caravan in the village of Heartcross.'

'Hey! Don't be cheeky; those vintage vans are the bee's knees!' said Isla, pretending to be insulted.

'You know that's not what I mean!' Allie laughed at Isla's expression. 'But Zach Hudson is a celebrity. Why the hell would he be staying in one of your vans?'

Isla looked like the cat that got the cream. Since she'd opened Foxglove Camping, Isla had been doing a roaring trade. Julia at the local B&B had helped to spread the word, along with her Facebook page, and with the increase of tourism to the area they were both fully booked.

Zach Hudson was an actor in one of the most popular Netflix series, in his late twenties, and just the sound of his name made nearly every girl on the planet swoon.

'I didn't know it was him at first because he'd booked in under a pseudonym – Todd Jones.'

'Obviously so no one would know it was him,' interrupted Allie.

'And when he arrived with the most adorable dog, Sydney, I just kept looking at him and then I asked him outright, was he Zach Hudson. Honestly, I couldn't believe it. I felt like pinching myself. He's filming a documentary about the Scottish Highlands and chose Heartcross as he'd heard about us all when the bridge collapsed! Zach Hudson has heard about us!' Isla flapped her hand in front of her face.

'Isla, this is amazing for you, for Foxglove Camping. This catapults you right up there, puts you on a different level ... celebrity clients ... Just think of the publicity this could bring to your little business. What you need is a photograph – Zach with Sydney outside one of the vans. And I know just the girl to take that picture.' Allie nudged Isla's elbow playfully.

'I was thinking exactly the same and Drew has convinced him to judge one of the dog shows this afternoon alongside Rory!'

'No way! This is going to be brilliant! I'm taking photos for the local paper too, which obviously means I am going to need an introduction.'

'Without a doubt!' said Isla, glancing at her watch. 'I'd best get back to the farm. Drew and Fergus are in charge of the hog roast and I need to go and put the gazebo up. And I've left Finn and Esme bathing Mop the alpaca. Finn is convinced she's going to win best of show, especially if Uncle Rory is judging. The pair of them are so excited and I keep reminding them it's a dog show, not an alpaca show, but they don't seem to be listening to me!'

'They are in for a fun afternoon. I'll see you later on the green and make sure you look glam. I'll get the camera at the ready!'

A couple of hours later Allie set off to meet Rory with her camera slung around her neck and a smile on her face.

The sun was shining and the trees along the lane swayed lightly in the breeze.

She was bursting to tell Rory all about Zach's arrival in the village and as soon as she saw him shutting the door of his house she hurried up the lane. Before Rory had even clapped eyes on her she sneaked up behind him.

'You'll never guess what,' she said, causing Rory to jump out of his skin.

'Christ on a bike, are you trying to give me a heart attack? Where did you spring from?' he asked, spinning round as he locked the front door.

'Sorry, sorry ... but you'll never guess what,' enthused Allie, bursting to tell him the news.

'What?' he asked, narrowing his eyes and slipping his arm around her shoulder as they began to walk along the lane.

'Zach Hudson – *the* Zach Hudson – TV celebrity Zach Hudson—'

'I think I get the picture. What about him?' chipped in Rory.

'He's here in Heartcross.'

Rory laughed, 'Have you been on the sherry already?'

'He's filming a documentary in Heartcross and is staying at Isla's – honestly!'

Rory let out a low whistle. 'I've been watching some of his latest documentaries. I know you ladies like him in his TV series but some of the more serious stuff he does is actually quite good.'

'You can ask him all about it because Drew has talked him into judging the dog show with you. And guess who'll be taking photos for the local press?' Allie waggled her camera.

'Really? This will be great for you and Isla.'

'I know. Every year it's a good day without fail – but I am a little nervous.'

'About what?'

'About seeing your parents after ...'

Rory slid his arm from around Allie's shoulders and squeezed her hand. The last forty-eight hours at work had been tense for Rory; to say there was an elephant in the room would have been an understatement. Rory had kept everything on a professional basis, but the tension had rippled between him and his father.

'I've been thinking ...'

Allie stopped and locked eyes with him. 'What about?'

'The cottage – but I'm making no promises.'

Allies eyes widened with anticipation and she could barely contain her excitement. 'Are you saying you're going to view the cottage?'

Rory smiled. 'There's no harm in looking.'

These were the words Allie wanted to hear. She let out a squeal then flung her arms around his neck, giving him a suffocating hug.

'Rory, you are the best!' Pulling away, she took his face in her hands and kissed him all over numerous times.

'Get off me, woman,' he joked.

Allie was ecstatic. She knew once she got Rory to see the cottage he'd fall for her persuasive powers. 'What made you change your mind?'

'To be honest – you,' he said, taking a sideways glance at her as they began to walk. 'You were right; houses don't come up for sale very often in Heartcross, but the last time I visited there it wasn't pretty ... I think you're expecting it to all be kitted out with mod cons. The only thing I remember it having of any use was a roof!'

Allie stopped walking. 'Are you saying it's derelict?' In her head she had visions of a shabby-chic kitchen with an island decorated with vases of beautiful blooms, vintage crockery, floral home furnishings and one of those posh stand-alone baths in the middle of the bathroom.

'I'm saying James Kerr lived a very basic life. I think the pigsty was in a better condition than the cottage.'

Allie cocked an eyebrow. 'So it's a project?' she asked, always up for a challenge.

'An expensive project ...'

'An expensive project,' Allie repeated. 'How much of an expensive project?'

'I'm thinking it would be cheaper to knock the whole thing down and start again.'

'It's that bad? But that would cost a fortune,' she mused, raising an eyebrow. She never managed to save a penny from her wages from the pub. How could they ever afford to do this?

Even though her dream was tarnished slightly she wasn't giving up hope.

'It's going to cost a fortune no matter what.'

'But ... it still has a gorgeous name,' chipped in Allie dreamily. 'Clover Cottage.'

'There's nothing Laura Ashley about it, believe me, and if I remember rightly it wouldn't be somewhere you could move into straightaway. There weren't even any carpets on the floor and, let's face it, if there were they'd probably need ripping up.'

'But that's half the fun, making somewhere your own. A renovation project. Vintage furniture can be sourced cheaply these days from lots of online stores and charity shops.'

Rory wasn't convinced there was anything fun about a renovation project. He remembered vividly the stress of returning from university in his second year to discover his parents had ripped out the bathroom and were installing a new one, and the dust was immense. His mother was stressed up to the eyeballs, especially with the endless cups of tea she was making for the builders all day long.

'Mmm, let's just take a look first. But no promises,' said Rory in a firm tone, but he knew by the sparkle in Allie's eye and the smile on her face she didn't care what state it was in. She'd already got them moved in, alongside a couple of kids and no doubt numerous pets. He wasn't one hundred per cent as convinced as her, and, if he was truly being honest with himself, he wasn't sure if this was really what he wanted at this moment. He loved Heartcross, but he knew he still had ambition outside the small village. Hearing about Clare had ignited his old ambition to see more of the world while he had no ties. If he began to renovate the cottage and move in with Allie, he knew that would most probably mean children soon after – and how would he ever manage to escape to fulfil his ambition then? He was certain Allie was his future but the timing for him wasn't quite right now, especially with his current workload. The cottage would be a mammoth task – and could they even afford it? He knew he was more of a realist than she was: he ruled with his head whereas Allie followed her heart. But he could see how important it was to her, and there was no harm in taking a look.

'What about the grounds surrounding Clover Cottage?' Allie was intrigued. The particulars Stuart and Alana had shown them indicated that the cottage came with numerous acres, outbuildings and even another small property.

'I never even thought to ask. I'm assuming James Kerr left it all to my father, but maybe not. That's something I need to check with Dad. We don't want to be living next door to just anyone.'

Allie agreed. 'And what's the plan? Are you moving back in with your parents? There's room at the pub.'

Rory shrugged. 'I've not even thought about it but I suppose I best had since the clock's ticking. Maybe I should have a word with Isla – if one of her vans is good enough for Zach Hudson ...' he said laughing.

All along Love Heart Lane and the High Street, triangular coloured bunting was woven between the lamp posts and flapping in the light breeze. The weather was perfect, not too hot, the sun was shining and only a few clouds dotted the cobalt sky.

Allie and Rory followed the makeshift cardboard signs hammered into the grass verges that pointed to the village green. This afternoon Allie had offered to man the Pimm's tent alongside her mum whilst her dad looked after the pub.

Allie loved this event; the mood was always jolly and it was so much fun to catch up with everyone. As they turned the corner the village green was unrecognisable. Small coloured tepees lined the edges, alongside trestle tables selling jams, chutneys and homemade jewellery and trinkets. There was something for everyone.

Alfie and Polly were standing at the entrance jangling their buckets for charity donations. Throwing a handful of coins into the bucket Allie and Rory stepped onto the green. There were Finn and Esme parading Mop the baby alpaca around the field on her lead like it was the most natural thing in the world.

There were jugglers, stilt-walkers, balloon sellers and a bouncy castle. Families were sprawled out on their picnic rugs enjoying their day. Over at the far end of the green there was a live band playing on a makeshift stage with hay bales doubling as seating. Hamish was accompanying them on his fiddle. Children were running and squealing between the candyfloss and sweet stalls. There was a great stir of excitement all around. Isla was plodding along with one of the Shetland ponies from the farm, providing rides for the youngsters. The whole field was a medley of sights and sounds.

Felicity and Rona's stall was stacked with the most delicious-looking pastries and cakes and had a queue a mile long eagerly awaiting their turn. Allie waved at Felicity, who was busy slicing cakes and popping them into paper bags.

'I need one of those flapjacks before they sell out,' said Allie, pulling Rory towards the queue. 'I swear Flick could win awards for her baking.' Felicity must have read her mind and quickly passed a bag over the tops of heads as Allie mouthed a thank you.

They carried on walking and spotted Fergus and Drew manning the hog roast, each with a beer in hand. Rory started walking in their direction until Allie tugged at his sleeve and nodded towards a multicoloured tepee with a makeshift bead-fringed curtain.

Allie laughed. 'That's hilarious,' she said reading the sign out loud. 'Have your fortune told today with Mystic Martha – £2 a go.'

'Since when has Isla's gran been a fortune-teller?' asked Rory with a chuckle.

Allie tugged at his arm. 'Come on.'

'You cannot be serious. Since when has Martha had any sort of psychic powers or predicted any information about a person's life?' challenged Rory.

'You're not scared, are you?' teased Allie, rummaging around in her bag to find her purse. 'This could predict our future!'

'Don't be ridiculous!' But before Rory could object any more Allie had pulled him to the entrance of the tent.

'Keep an open mind – this could be interesting!' she whispered, parting the curtain to reveal Mystic Martha sitting at a small round oak table, running her hands over a crystal ball that doubled as an upside-down glass ball lampshade.

Rory stifled a giggle and Allie shot him a warning glance. He couldn't quite believe she was taking this all so seriously.

As they stepped inside, Martha looked up. She was hunched over, rubbing her hands slowly over the crystal ball, creating a mystical atmosphere. She was barely recognisable as Isla's grandmother, and Allie was taken in by her appearance. Her hands were wrapped in fingerless gloves, her wrists laced with bangles and her bony fingers stacked with silver rings. Draped around her shoulders was a black shawl and from her tiny waist hung a black skirt edged with gold crescent moons. There was no denying she played the part well.

She stretched out her bony hand and gestured towards the empty chairs. Both Allie and Rory sat down in silence.

Martha hadn't faltered in her role once, and never acknowledged who they were.

Still rolling her hands over the crystal ball, she nodded towards the bowl on the table which was already filled with coins, so it looked like Allie and Rory weren't her first guinea pigs of the day.

Allie placed the money in the bowl and looked towards Rory, who arched an eyebrow. She didn't have to be a psychic to read his mind. He was wondering why he was even entertaining such a farce.

Not looking up from the ball Mystic Martha began to gaze with deep concentration. Her voice was low, eerie, causing the hairs on Allie's arms to stand on end.

'Just remember, your future is never set in stone ... you are in charge of your own destiny.'

Rory gently kicked Allie under the table but she didn't react, her gaze firmly fixed on Martha.

Then for a split second Martha stopped rolling her hands and a fleeting look of worry spread across her face, but quickly she composed herself.

'What is it?' asked Allie.

'Changes, there are huge changes ahead ... I see brand-new opportunities for you both in completely different directions.' Martha gazed up at Rory. 'I see a whole world out there and you are settling for something else ... I see fame ... I see travel ... places afar.' Martha's eyes were drifting in and out of focus. 'An extravagant gift divides you. And for you, dear girl' – Martha now turned towards

Allie – 'I see upset. Don't let opportunities slip through your fingers. You need to overcome your fears ... Be brave,' and with that Martha stopped stroking the ball, stood up and disappeared behind another section of the gazebo.

When Allie looked towards Rory he was rolling his eyes. 'What an absolute load of codswallop,' he muttered.

'She'll hear you,' mouthed Allie bringing her fingers up to her lips to shush Rory.

'It's only Martha!' exclaimed Rory, perplexed that Allie was taking this seriously. He parted the beaded curtains and blinked. He hadn't realised how dim the tent had been until he stepped out into sunshine. Already there was a queue forming outside the tent, which took Rory by complete surprise.

'Where to next? The hog roast to catch up with Drew and Fergus ...' It was only then he realised by the look on Allie's face that her mood had slumped. 'Whatever is the matter? Please don't tell me you believe a word that Martha said?' he asked in disbelief. 'This is Martha we're talking about. She's made it all up as she's gone along.' He hoped Allie was going to burst out laughing, but she didn't crack a smile.

'Martha thinks you're going to break my heart. Does she know something I don't?'

'How have you deduced that from that conversation? You must be seriously winding me up. And that's not what she said anyway. She said brand-new opportunities in different directions.'

'"An extravagant gift divides you."'

'Allie, you are being really silly. I'm not even having this conversation,' Rory said, pulling her in for a hug and kissing the tip of her nose. 'You are just being daft,' he said with a chuckle.

'Don't laugh at me. You can't mess around with psychic powers.'

'Mystic Martha has a lot to answer for. I can't even believe you are letting her get to you. Martha is no more a fortune-teller than you or me,' insisted Rory. 'Now come on, let's go and get a drink. I think I'm in need of a pint after that.'

Allie knew she was being daft and Rory was talking sense but somewhere in the back of her mind was a niggle about what Martha had revealed. The words *settling for something else* were etched on her mind. Did that mean Rory was settling for her?

Noticing her mood wasn't lifting, Rory gave her a long-suffering look, 'Stop thinking about it, otherwise this day is going to be ruined.'

Allie fixed a smile on her face, 'Okay, okay ... but you would tell me if you weren't happy?'

'Of course I would, but we don't need this conversation because I am happy. Now not another word about it,' urged Rory, tilting Allie's face towards him and kissing her firmly on the lips. 'And ...'

Allie's stomach lurched. 'And what?' she asked, her voice faltering.

'I've already agreed to go and see the cottage. I'll talk

to Mum and Dad today and apologise for my outburst. I'll eat humble pie and all that.'

Allie tried hard to repress the wide grin that was about to burst on to her face at any second. 'Are you sure?' she quickly added, trying not to sound too keen, though there was no denying she was secretly glad he was coming round to the idea, or at least had changed his mind about viewing it.

'I've said I'll go and have a look – but remember, there's a whole bunch of factors to consider including the cost of it all. Now come on, let's enjoy our day,' he insisted, taking her by the hand. 'Mystic Martha knows nothing,' he said reassuringly, pressing a swift kiss to her cheek.

As they walked Allie felt better, but she thought again about what Mystic Martha had said. Even though she knew Martha had led a colourful life, she had no recollection of Isla ever telling any stories about Martha's psychic powers. Allie had never queried her and Rory's future together until his reaction over the cottage, and now Mystic Martha's prediction was firmly on her mind.

'I see upset.'

Of course, Allie wanted to think the stupid reading had no bearing on their relationship. She was passionate about their future and hoped she was overreacting, but after Rory's outburst at his parents' house she couldn't deny that slight niggle. It just wouldn't disappear from the back of her mind.

Chapter 4

Allie and Rory found themselves heading towards the hog roast, where Drew and Fergus were both in a cheery mood. Next to them Baby Angus was sitting up in the pram, shielded from the sun under an umbrella attached to the hood of his pushchair and bashing the hell out of a green T-Rex dinosaur. Flitting her eyes around the green Allie found herself scanning the area for the superstar Zach Hudson. As she looked towards a small group of giggling girls gathered at the far end of the green, she knew he couldn't be too far away – and she was right: there he was, being pulled along by an over-excited black labrador that seemed to be attracting a crowd all by itself. Allie couldn't help but stare in his direction. Even from a distance she was impressed with Zach's physique and good looks, and her heart gave a little flutter.

Zach Hudson had seemed to catapult to fame overnight. He had the ability to light up the screen and make every girl swoon after him in a matter of seconds. He appeared on the cover of magazines, his likes on Instagram were off the scale and his tweets were instantly retweeted all over the world. And here he was, walking around the green in a tiny village in the Scottish Highlands, taking it all in his stride.

Allie prayed she wouldn't make a fool of herself like the last (and only) time she met one of her idols. She and Isla had been poised by the computer patiently waiting for 9am, when the tickets went on sale for their favourite band, Take That. They'd spent the next five minutes refreshing their browsers, and after successfully buying two tickets, the day came for them to travel to London, spend the night in a swanky hotel and watch their favourite band. This was the only time Allie wished she'd ordered anything off the menu other than a spinach pizza. When they literally bumped into Gary Barlow in the lift, she had been star-struck, lost for words, and all she could do was smile from ear to ear, though Isla was frantically shaking her head at her. Allie had two floors to pluck up the courage to speak to him and as they trundled towards the ground floor a babble of word vomit spilt out as she shakily held her phone up for a selfie. It was only when he stepped out of the lift and she looked at the treasured photo that she saw the terrible smile of green teeth – not a photo she would be uploading to social media any time soon.

Thinking back to how mortified she had been, Allie was not about to make the same mistake again. She quickly turned towards Rory. 'Check my teeth,' she said, slightly panicking.

Rory's eyebrows shot up as Allie clenched her teeth together and prised her lips open wide in some sort of weird, twisty grimace.

'What are you doing, you absolute loon? You look like some sort of constipated chimpanzee,' said Rory, his eyes drawn towards Allie's mouth. 'Not that in the whole of my career have I ever had the pleasure of treating any constipated chimpanzees.'

'Green! Is there any green?' Allie pointed at her teeth.

'There's no green,' he finally confirmed, 'and please stop pulling that face. You look in pain.'

Rory was still none the wiser why Allie was even asking, until a group of girls suddenly went screaming past him, nearly knocking him clean off his feet.

'Aww,' he said with amusement written all over his face, 'spinach teeth, I get it now ... and there he is' – Rory nodded towards Zach – 'he's heading this way ... Are you going to go all giggly on him?' He playfully tickled Allie's stomach and made her jump.

'Get off me,' ordered Allie laughing, straining to look over Rory's shoulder to see how far away Zach was.

Word was spreading like wildfire around the summer fair, and the villagers were overcome with excitement. Zach now looked like the Pied Piper, accompanied by a long line of fans skipping behind him encouraging each other to pluck up the courage to speak to him. Allie anticipated the headlines in tomorrow's newspaper, and her own excitement was building, knowing she was the official photographer at the event today. Not only were her photographs going to appear in the local paper but being able to photograph Zach was going to be a fantastic opportunity. She just needed to rein in her inner fangirl.

Rory lightly slapped Drew on the back as they approached the hog roast stand. Spinning around, Drew automatically handed them both a beer. Fergus was by his side but was busy handing out hog roast buns, dripping with homemade apple sauce from Bonnie's Teashop, to the long line of people standing in front of him.

They all stood to attention at the sound of a loud high-pitched squeal and listened as Hamish's voice came over the crackling Tannoy announcing that the dog show would commence in the middle showring in approximately ten minutes' time.

Almost immediately the villagers began making their way over to the hay bales scattered around the edge of the ring in readiness for the beginning of the show.

Feeling a tug on the back of his shirt, Rory looked down to see Finn and Esme beaming up at him with Mop the alpaca at their side. Allie angled the camera towards them and the pair of them struck a pose. Click ... she took their photo.

'Not bad,' said Allie, showing the picture to the children. 'Let's see if we can get you in the local paper.'

'Daddy,' announced Esme, 'we are going to be famous.'

'Let's hope so,' replied Fergus, smiling fondly at his

daughter. 'You can look after me and Felicity in our old age!'

'Just so I know,' said Rory, turning back towards Finn, 'what breed of dog have you got there, Finn?' he asked, smirking, 'because we need to log that information on your entry form.' Rory cocked an eyebrow.

'Well, Uncle Rory' – Finn sounded matter-of-fact – 'Mop is a very special breed ... so special that's there's only one of its kind.' For a second Finn looked deep in thought. 'Pacapoo.'

Rory grinned. 'A pacapoo, one of a kind. I'll remember that.' Mop, the chocolate-coloured baby alpaca, who was all legs and resembled Bambi, was standing still on her lead looking adorable. Her mass of brown corkscrew curls bounced on the top of her head as Rory gently patted her.

With a cheeky smile, Finn nudged Esme for her to get on board. 'Uncle Rory ... we need to tell you something.' Finn's eyes were wide as he looked towards Esme, who nodded her encouragement.

Finn gestured for Rory to come closer. Rory did exactly that and bent down while Finn cupped his hands around his mouth and whispered into Rory's ear, 'There's no such thing as a pacapoo.'

Everyone fell about laughing.

'But Daddy reckons she doubles as a standard poodle and no one will notice,' said Finn, all knowledgeable, looking up at Rory.

Drew threw his hands up in the air. 'Hey, don't bring

me into this!' he said, tickling his son's tummy, causing him to giggle.

'I'm sure a pacapoo will become the next big breed and this is where you heard it first!' exclaimed Rory, admiring Finn's dedication to Mop.

Once more the sound of Hamish's voice came over the Tannoy. All competitors needed to make their way towards the tent at the side of the showring immediately.

'That's us!' said Esme excitedly, pulling on Finn's arm. 'Come on!'

'I'll see you in the ring, Uncle Rory!' said Finn with a cheeky grin before leading Mop away with Esme hot on his heels in her yellow wellingtons.

'On the upside, if they come first, they win a month's supply of dog food, which you can have, Allie, for Nell,' said Isla appearing from nowhere and looking all glam. She tied a Shetland pony to the fence next to a hay bale and handed Rory a clipboard. 'I'm not sure a pacapoo is on the list of breeds so I've added an extra box on the form.' Isla winked at Rory but they were distracted by Drew's low whistle.

'You've got changed. I've not seen that outfit before,' he observed.

'Oh, you have, it's been in the wardrobe for years,' replied Isla, brushing aside the compliment, but the shirt looked new and matched her white skinny jeans perfectly.

'And that smell,' said Drew, leaning towards her and inhaling the aroma. 'You are wearing your best perfume.

Mmm, we all know who you are trying to impress,' teased Drew, giving his wife a peck on the cheek. 'Should I be worried?'

'Don't I always look this good?' she asked, knowing full well she was usually dressed in overalls, her battered old wellies covered in dung.

Everyone could see Isla had gone to great lengths to get the outfit just right. This would be the perfect opportunity for publicity to rocket her little business, especially if Allie's photographs were used in the paper and seen online.

'So you've heard?' said Isla, her mouth hitching up at both sides and turning towards Rory.

'Heard? I've never seen Allie so excited before! You women, all excited about a TV star – they are just normal people, you know.'

'There is *no way* Zach Hudson is just a normal person,' objected Allie, and Isla nodded in agreement.

At that moment they all turned to look towards a commotion happening on the green. Zach was surrounded by a group of teenagers clutching their mobile phones, huge beams on their faces, waiting patiently for their chance to take a selfie with him. Even from this distance Allie was smitten with his impressive good looks and physique. He was handling the crowd well, chatting away and having his photo taken along with his trusted furry friend.

'Remember when the girls used to flock around us like that?' said Fergus grinning, watching in amusement. 'Girls used to hang on our every word too.'

Isla laughed. 'Really? Considering most of the women living in the village are standing right here.'

But Fergus didn't have time to object as once more Hamish's voice rang out over the Tannoy. Rory had precisely five minutes to make his way over to the judges' table.

'That's my call,' said Rory, clutching his clipboard and looking towards the queue of contestants lining up at the side of the showring. 'Look,' he said chuckling, nodding towards the line.

Amongst all the breeds of dogs stood Mop the pacapoo, sticking out like a sore thumb. They watched as Esme gave her a cuddle and high-fived Finn, the pair of them beaming with pride. Esme took her seat on the front row of hay bales and gave the thumbs-up to Finn, their eyes firmly fixed on the bright red rosette pinned on the front of the judge's desk, sporting a shiny gold number 1.

Since the baby alpaca had been born at Foxglove Farm, Finn and Esme had fallen in love with the adorable creature. The three were inseparable and had become the best of friends. Finn and Esme had spent every spare moment training Mop, leading her through rows of old walking poles that hikers had left behind in the teashop, jumping her over the small coloured poles in the fields. Isla had been amazed and impressed by the dedication of both children, who had taken the training very seriously. Every weekend without fail, rain or shine, they were out in the fields encouraging Mop to be the best she could be for this summer show.

Just as Rory was about to head towards the showring, he felt Allie leaning her chin on his shoulder. 'He's coming this way,' she said, unable to hide the excitement in her voice.

Noticing the women were quivering wrecks, Drew rolled his eyes and took control. He waved Zach over. Immediately Allie observed he was much taller in real life, but was still slim, good-looking and unnervingly familiar.

As he approached, Drew stretched out his hand. 'Zach, this is Rory, local vet and fellow judge for the dog show.'

Allie noticed that Rory appeared starstruck and she smiled to herself.

Rory held out his hand. 'You are setting the cat amongst the pigeons. I'm a huge fan of your documentary series.'

Zach smiled a boyish smile. 'Thank you,' he said shaking Rory's hand.

'And this is Allie, local publican and photographer – Isla's best friend and Rory's girlfriend.'

'Pleased to meet you both,' he said, now shaking Allie's hand.

'And this is Sydney.' Zach looked down at the plump Labrador who had begun to wind herself around Allie's legs. As soon as she went to pat her, she rolled over, exposing her tummy for a tickle.

'She's a good judge of character,' said Zach with warmth.

Allie continued to tickle Sydney's tummy. 'Such a softy.'

'She is, and the star of my latest documentaries. It's a joint effort; that's why we are here. It's a beautiful place you live.'

'Thanks,' said Allie, standing up, 'we love it here. I can't imagine ever living anywhere else.'

'This place has a good community feel about it. We like that, Syd, don't we?' Syd sat and looked up at Zach and cocked her head to one side, as if she was really listening to him. 'With this job, we kind of forget where home is, especially when it's non-stop filming.'

'I bet,' replied Allie, admiring the bond between Zach and his dog.

Isla noticed Hamish waving to them and tapping his watch. Hamish was always a stickler for time and he was the mastermind behind the village show. Everything always ran like clockwork.

'I think you're wanted.' Isla touched Rory's arm and he cast an eye over his shoulder.

'Yep – that's our cue. Are you ready?' Rory looked towards Zach, who nodded.

'A quick photo for the press,' said Allie, not missing her chance and whipping off the lens cap and organising Rory and Zach to stand next to each other with Sydney sitting at their feet.

Click … click … click …

Allie scrolled through the pictures. 'Perfect. Now, Isla, could you stand next to Zach?'

Without hesitation Isla positioned herself next to him while Allie took a photo.

'You're okay with us using the photos in the paper and online, aren't you, Zach?'

'Of course,' he said without hesitation.

'Now go,' ordered Isla, stepping away, 'Hamish is about to burst a blood vessel if you don't hurry up,' she said, grabbing the handles of the pram and smiling down at Angus, who'd fallen fast asleep.

Leaving Drew and Fergus still serving up the hog roast the rest of the gang began walking towards the showring. Rory couldn't help but feel amazed at the crowd following them. 'Is it like this everywhere you go?'

'Pretty much,' replied Zach, taking it all his stride.

'How do you put up with it?' asked Rory, 'I kind of feel like royalty!'

Zach laughed. 'Part of the job. After a while, you kind of switch off and forget they are there, but if it wasn't for them I wouldn't get to do the job I do. It's when they stop following me I have to worry.'

'I suppose it's all part and parcel of the brand,' chipped in Allie, thinking it would drive her mad if she could never walk anywhere without being followed.

'That's why some of us are cut out for fame and others prefer a quiet life,' added Isla.

'I do a job I absolutely love, always wanted to be an actor, went to drama school ... It's a tough competitive industry and for me it was the right place at the right time. Of course I would like to go out to the pub and have a quiet meal, and I get absolutely sick to death of hotel rooms – they all look the same. Still, I wouldn't change it for the world. And this time I get to bring my best friend on my adventure too.' Zach looked down fondly at Sydney and patted her head as she walked at the side of him.

'Such an adorable dog,' said Allie, quickly snapping a photo.

'So, Heartcross – have you lived here long?' Zach looked over towards Rory and Allie.

'All my life,' answered Allie proudly. 'My parents own the Grouse and Haggis pub at the heart of the village. I'm a barmaid and Rory's the partner in his father's veterinary surgery here.'

'And you've never thought about travelling or venturing out into the big wide world?' asked Zach, locking eyes with Allie.

For a split second Allie wondered how she was feeling about that question. It was the second time she'd been asked the same thing in the past couple of days. Zach seemed generally surprised she'd never left Heartcross.

'Never. Heartcross is everything I've ever wanted,' she said, thinking once more about the upheaval in her early childhood and how relieved she'd been when her parents had finally settled down and she felt like she belonged somewhere.

'And a photographer,' he probed, pointing to the camera hanging around Allie's neck.

'Mainly just a barmaid with a tendency to take a good photo – or so I'm told,' Allie quickly added, not wanting to sound big-headed.

'Very good photographs,' chipped in Rory, sliding his arm around Allie's shoulders and squeezing.

'So what's getting in the way? You could travel the world taking photographs. There are so many amazing places to visit out there. You should think about it,' said Zach with such passion Allie took note.

'I've been telling her that for years.' Rory gave Allie a knowing look. 'There's so much more to your talents – not that I'm denying you pull a bloody good pint too.'

'I've had lots of practice,' she said smiling.

'You should think about voluntary work for a charity, especially if it's your passion,' Zach said.

'I've had a few photographs published in the local press, nothing major ... It's just more of a hobby,' answered Allie, suddenly thinking of her mum and dad. 'And anyway, I work alongside my parents in the family business. What would they think if I suddenly said, Hey, guys, I'm off to travel the world?'

'I'm sure they'd be happy for you,' said Zach.

These days, Allie knew her parents were relying on her more and more for the early morning shifts while they covered the late ones. It was hard work to cover both and they weren't getting any younger.

'I'm a Heartcross girl through and through,' she said, but Zach's words had registered on her mind and even she thought her reasons for staying in Heartcross suddenly sounded lame.

Zach rummaged around in his pocket and handed Allie

a business card. 'Here, take this,' he said as they approached the judges' table. 'Please feel free to send me any photos from today and I'll upload them to my social media, but just make sure any photos of me get my good side!'

Feeling excited by the gesture Allie steadied her hand as she took the card from Zach and slipped it into her bag. 'Thank you so much,' she replied.

Applause began to ripple from the villagers sitting on the hay bales as the Morris dancers took a bow and jingled their way out of the ring. Standing on tiptoe, Allie kissed Rory on his lips before shooing him towards the judges' table and wandering over to take a seat alongside Isla and a sleeping Angus. She pondered the conversation with Zach for a moment. Had she ever really thought of travelling and leaving Heartcross? The longest time she'd ever spent in one place before her parents settled in the pub had been just over twelve months in a small town called Colewell, just north of Dumfries. Their end-terrace had been next to a stream flanked with stepping stones that led to the back garden of a girl called Emmy. They'd become close friends and every night they'd rush back from school to hang out together. Allie had felt like she'd made a true friend and for the first time had felt content and settled – until she was called into the living room and faced a look from her parents she knew only too well. The look that meant they were on the move again. 'We are sorry, Allie, but your father has been made redundant and the landlord has increased the rent, so we can't afford to live here anymore, but we have good news – Uncle Alf has a contact in the brewery and there's a pub available that we can manage and we can live in too!'

'Still in Colewell?' asked Allie, with her fingers firmly crossed behind her back.

Her mum cast her eyes down and shook her head. 'Unfortunately not. We are heading to Heartcross, a small village in the Highlands.'

Feeling a wrench in her stomach Allie burst into tears and ran to her room. She didn't want to go anywhere; she wanted to stay right where she was, right where she was happy with her best friend living only five stepping stones away.

Still, all these years later Allie knew she didn't like change. She was settled and had everything she wanted, including friends just like Emmy. Maybe working in the pub had become the easy and safe option, surrounded by the people who loved her and had never let her down … It was what she knew. From the outset of their relationship, Rory had definitely had a confidence-boosting effect on Allie. She would describe him as her rock; he always praised her pictures and with his encouragement she'd submitted some to the local paper, which snapped them up immediately. But for a split second Allie questioned if she was truly happy. Did she want more than Heartcross? What would it be like to travel to all the amazing places out there in the big wide world? Allie just didn't know if she was brave enough to find out.

She gave herself a shake. Of course she was happy, she told herself. She lived in the most beautiful village with the most spectacular scenery and tomorrow she and Rory were going to view Clover Cottage, the place in her mind where she was going to set up her future with the man she loved. Heartcross was her life, *their* life. Her heart gave a little skip.

'Penny for them,' asked Isla, noticing Allie had slipped into a little world of her own.

'When your parents emigrated to New Zealand, did you ever consider going with them?' Allie asked. Isla's parents had moved when she was in her late teens.

Isla narrowed her eyes and parked Angus's pram next to the hay bale and sat down. 'Where did that come from?'

Allie attempted a smile. 'Just that conversation with Zach. He seemed surprised I'd lived here most of my life and had no intention of venturing out into the big wide world.'

'Each to their own, I say, but of course I miss my parents, it was a heart-wrenching decision ...' Isla's voice wavered and tears sprang to her eyes.

'I didn't mean to upset you,' said Allie, feeling awful.

'It's not you. I miss my parents and they aren't getting any younger, and this one' – she squeezed Angus's chubby leg – 'as well as Finn have never met their grandparents in real life, only on Facetime. Dad's not well and we just haven't got the money to visit. I just pray ...'

Allie placed a hand on her friend's knee; she knew exactly what Isla was thinking.

'Heartcross was where Drew was; he was my future, the guy I wanted to set up home with, have my family with. It was one of the hardest decisions I've ever had to make, believe me.' Dabbing her eyes with a tissue, Isla smiled. 'Look at me getting all emotional.' She wafted a hand in front of her face. 'But Heartcross is where Drew is, and the farm, and I chose him. If one day Drew decides he wants to up and leave then that's a different story.'

'But what about your ambitions?' probed Allie.

'I've got my own little business, the alpacas, and I've got Gran too – who'd have thought she'd stay around this long? Heartcross seems to have tamed her.' Isla let out a laugh. 'So what is it you want to do, Allie Macdonald? What are you thinking?'

Allie shrugged, 'I'm not entirely sure what I'm thinking. It just seems everyone is off travelling the world. Rory's ex is currently working in Africa as a vet and I think it's made him think about travelling again. And look at Zach, travelling all around making documentaries. Even Polly left London after losing her job and is still here.'

'We've definitely converted her into a country girl.'

'It's just ... and I know it's all a load of nonsense ... but when Mystic Martha predicted my future—'

Isla interrupted. 'Do not let Gran hear you say it's all a load of nonsense. She takes her psychic powers very seriously.'

Surprised, Allie pulled back her shoulders and sat up straight, 'What do you mean?' she asked, then swallowed hard.

'My gran is an absolute tool, but back in the day, people paid good money to have their fortune told by her, and mark my words, more often than not her predictions came true. She even travelled with the circus and at one time had her own hut in some seaside town. The stories she could tell you.'

Allie's eyes widened. 'Now I know you're winding me up.'

'Honestly, I'm not!' exclaimed Isla, carefully manoeuvring the umbrella attached to the pram to shield a now awake Angus from the sun, before putting her hand up to her chest as if saying an oath. 'I swear it's not an act; Gran is psychic.'

That was not a revelation Allie had been expecting.

'What did she say? Because you're obviously rattled.'

There was an awkward pause as Allie tried to get her thoughts in order.

'Come on!'

Allie spilt the beans while Isla gave a small chuckle and placed a perfectly angelic-looking Angus on his bum on the ground in front of them.

'That could mean anything. Like Gran said, you are in charge of your destiny. I definitely think you and Rory are meant to be together, so stop fretting, woman ... Mystic Martha wouldn't want you to worry. It's meant to be a bit of fun, not a game-changer!'

Allie nodded. 'Okay,' she said, breaking into a smile even though around her friends it was always hard to hide her true feelings. 'It's probably the time of the month and I'm being supersensitive. And Rory has agreed to take a look at Clover Cottage tomorrow.'

'There you go then. What is meant to be will be.'

Allie began to relax. Isla was right and she was just being silly.

She turned to look at Hamish and Julia hovering by the judging table, making sure Rory and Zach had enough refreshments before they began. They were in deep conversation as they looked over the entry forms, Zach's trusted Labrador lying at his feet without a care in the world. Pinned to the front of the table were the winning rosettes.

Everyone looked like they were having a good time, and the chatter was noisy until Hamish blew into the handheld megaphone and silence began to sweep through the crowd. Allie studied Rory, who looked relaxed and was laughing alongside Zach as Hamish stepped into the middle of the ring. She knew the next couple of weeks would be stressful. At some point they were going to have to pack up all his things and move them from Love Heart Lane and put them goodness knows where. Allie was crossing her fingers that quaint little Clover Cottage was going to lure Rory in from the outset and they were going to live there happily after ever.

'Budge up – I can't miss this for the world,' said Felicity grinning and gesturing for Esme to come and sit with them. But the little girl flatly refused. She was determined to support Finn and Mop from the front row.

Allie had never seen so many people interested in watching the dog show at the summer fair but she knew why this event was suddenly so popular today.

The best photographs were going to be taken from the front of the ring where Rory and Zach were sitting, so Allie stood up and made her excuses. She worked her way along the line of contestants, taking photographs of each one alongside their dog, including Finn and his pacapoo, who was already the winner in Allie's eyes. Walking towards the judges' table she stood beside Zach, who seemed to be taking his role as judge very seriously.

'So, which one of us is Simon Cowell?' asked Zach jokingly, with a confident air about him. 'And do we have a red buzzer?'

Allie looked at Zach, with his foxy good looks and bright blue eyes. He was wearing a cobalt blue shirt, the sleeves rolled back to reveal his tanned forearms, a black waistcoat and a pair of skinny jeans. 'Mmm, don't go buzzing it on Finn's turn otherwise we'll have an upset on our hands,' said Allie, pointing the camera at the competitors as they began to walk into the ring.

They all held their dogs on a short tight lead as they pranced them around the makeshift arena before taking their places behind the white taped line opposite the judging panel.

Zach watched as Julia from the B&B began parading

her blue roan cocker spaniel, which sported a red polka-dot bowtie, followed by Esme's aunty Jessica who walked a Chihuahua on a sparkly pink-sequinned lead.

'They are all taking this super seriously,' exclaimed Zach, looking along the line of dog owners standing there with their perfectly groomed animals.

'You'd better believe it,' chipped in Allie, continuing to angle the camera and take photographs.

'It's a major event, and this village show has been running for decades,' said Rory, pouring them all a glass of water from the bottle placed in front of them.

As Zach cast his eye along the line, he stifled a giggle and leant in towards Rory. 'Fourth boy along – that's Finn, isn't it, from the farm I'm staying at?'

'It sure is,' answered Rory, looking over towards Finn, who was standing up straight and beaming towards the judges.

'But that's not a dog!'

Rory's face was deadpan, 'That, my friend, is a pacapoo!'

'A what?' asked Zach, his mouth falling open.

'A pacapoo! Half poodle ... half alpaca.' Rory didn't crack a smile.

Zach did a double-take then gave Rory an incredulous stare. 'Are you serious?' The disbelief was written all over Zach's face but Rory had him believing it was possible.

Zach blinked slowly, and was rendered speechless,

Allie and Rory exchanged knowing looks and smiles. Then Zach spotted the twinkle of mischief in Allie's eyes.

'Stop winding me up! You actually had me there for a minute!'

A wide grin spread across Rory's face. 'Sorry, mate, I couldn't resist,' he said, dissolving into laughter.

'A pacapoo,' said Zach, looking back across the ring. 'So how does this work, can an alpaca really win a dog show?'

'Technically, no, but as this is Heartcross and I know Finn and Esme have worked so hard training Mop from the outset I think they deserve to win best alpaca in show.' Rory slid a special rosette from the back of the clipboard across the table. 'Isla made them their very own rosette. We have everything covered.'

'That's good, as I wouldn't want to reduce any kids to tears. Could you imagine the news headlines?' said Zach, giving a little chuckle and patting Sydney, who was now stretched out in the sunshine at his feet.

After Hamish introduced the dog show and explained the timed obstacle course the crowd applauded and Jessica was first up against the clock, navigating her dog around the course. As soon as she finished, the crowd applauded again, and she took her place back in the line.

Next up was Finn. Esme was bouncing from foot to foot, giving Finn a thumbs-up. Finn beamed at his best friend then stepped forward and took his position at the start, his determination showing as he pushed up his sleeves, his alert gaze concentrated on the obstacle course in front of them. Then he bent down and pressed a kiss on Mop's nose. An admiring murmur spread through the crowd. Standing up straight Finn patted Mop on the top of her head and gave a nod to Hamish, acknowledging he was ready to begin, whilst unclipping the lead from Mop's collar.

Hamish held the megaphone to his lips and looked at the stopwatch in front of him as he counted down from three then waved the flag.

A fast stride took Finn and Mop around the course in record time, taking the crowd completely by surprise. Everyone watched in amazement, and Allie couldn't help but smile at Zach's reaction, his rapid blinking followed by open staring and a slow disbelieving shake of the head. He was clearly mesmerised by Finn and Mop's performance. Within seconds it was all over.

As soon as Mop romped over the line the crowd were up on their feet clapping. Amazed, Hamish clicked the stopwatch and asked both Zach and Rory to verify the time. They confirmed Finn and Mop were in the lead.

'Well, that's one pacapoo!' exclaimed Zach. 'That kid and that alpaca are unbelievable.'

Finn took a small bow towards the audience before clipping the lead back on to Mop's collar. A proud Isla closed her eyes and pulled in an expansive breath. Her lips pressed together and her chin quivering slightly, she got to her feet with Angus in her arms, swiping at a proud tear that slipped down her cheek.

Esme ran into the ring to congratulate her best friend,

and squealed as she high-fived Finn. They began to jump and down in excitement before Hamish ushered them to the side of the ring. Finn handed Esme the lead and hot-footed it towards the judges' table, taking Rory and Zach completely by surprise. Finn stood on tiptoe and offered them both a firm handshake before running back towards Esme.

'A very passionate little boy,' exclaimed Zach, amazed at Finn's confidence.

Twenty minutes later Hamish took his position in the centre of the ring. Esme was standing next to Finn and grabbed his arm as Hamish placed the megaphone to his lips. Allie was ready to take the photographs as Rory stood up and passed the all-important results to Hamish, who quickly scanned them before stepping forward. The crowd hushed. Rory and Zach strolled down from behind the table and joined Hamish, clutching the rosettes.

'In third place ... Julia and Woody.' The crowd applauded as a beaming Julia stepped forward with her cocker spaniel and shook the hands of the judges. Rory handed over the rosette whilst Allie took a photograph. Zach manoeuvred Julia to one side of him whilst the runner-up was announced.

After the second place had been announced and the photographs were taken, all eyes were on Hamish. Taking a deep breath he looked down at the paper.

'In first place—'

Esme let out a tiny squeal in anticipation and Finn clutched her arm.

'In first place,' repeated Hamish, as the onlookers stamped their feet, 'Jessica and Gloria!'

The crowd erupted into applause and rose to their feet. Jessica scooped up the tiny chihuahua and placed her under her arm like a clutch handbag as she sprang towards the judges.

'Thank you, thank you,' she said accepting the rosette from Zach and shaking Rory's hand before posing for photographs.

'Gloria – great name!' said Zach admiringly, patting the little dog on her head.

'Named after Gloria Gaynor, the queen of disco – "I Will Survive" – She was the runt of the litter and abandoned by her mother ... hand reared,' said Jessica with warmth. 'I couldn't imagine my life without her.'

As soon as the photographs were taken, Hamish ushered Jessica to stand next to the other winners. Allie grinned at Rory and both turned back to face the crowd. She'd already registered Finn's crushing disappointment; his shoulders lowered, his eyes closed, he had let his head fall back as he slumped on to the hay bale. But Allie knew there was a special award.

For the last time Hamish silenced the crowd.

'We have one last trophy to give out today, but firstly, can we all put our hands together for our fantastic judges, Rory Scott, our local vet, and Zach Hudson, actor and explorer!'

Both took a bow as the applause rippled all around them, together with a handful of wolf whistles.

Once the clapping had died down, Hamish spoke again. 'Today, we have a very special judges' award. This goes to a young contestant who, with his best friend, have put all their love and effort into training a delightful pacapoo. Mop, our local baby alpaca, the first to be born at Foxglove Farm, raced around the course in record time, not putting a foot wrong. So today it gives me great pleasure to announce that our special judges' award ... goes to Finn Allaway and Mop!'

Finn looked up and stared disbelievingly, before a slow smile began to spread across his face as the words registered. Esme gasped as they locked eyes and threw their arms around each other, bouncing on their toes, before Esme pushed Finn forward. As he led Mop into the ring he looked across towards his mum and dad and shared a look of admiration. Drew slipped his arm around a teary-eyed Isla's waist as they watched Finn punch the air.

'Huge congratulations,' said Hamish, 'How do you feel, now that you have just won the special judges' award?'

'On top of the world,' replied Finn, clutching his fist to his chest, his voice choked with tears. 'I don't believe it.' He shook his head repeatedly. 'This is just the best!' He waved at Esme to come and join him and she bounded towards her best friend without hesitation.

'We did it, we did it,' shrieked Esme throwing her arms around Mop's neck then high-fiving Finn.

Mop was oblivious to all the commotion and was snuffling around on the ground and swishing her tail from side to side. Zach bent down in front of her and patted her head.

'So this is what a pacapoo looks like?' he said with a grin, pinning on Mop's collar a bright red rosette sporting a gold shiny number one.

Rory had the honour of handing out two further badges to Finn and Esme, with a £5 voucher attached to spend at the sweet stall.

As they posed for photographs, the charmingly quirky-looking Mop tilted her head and looked like she was grinning.

'You've definitely got a winner on your hands. Where to next, Crufts?' joked Zach, looking at Finn, who was biting his lip.

The boy suddenly looked worried, and his gaze flitted around the ring as he began to bite a nail. 'I need to tell you something,' said Finn, his voice wobbling.

Zach knelt down. 'What is it?'

'There's no such thing as a pacapoo. Mop isn't a dog, she's an alpaca!' With a trembling chin Finn held out the sweets voucher in front of him, his head bent low, his eyes looking up.

'I'll let you into a little secret,' whispered Zach in his ear. 'I know. But as judges we can award that rosette to whoever we want and you and Mop are our winners!' Zach pushed the voucher back towards him.

'Really – I can keep it?' asked Finn, his eyes wide.

'Really – and honesty is always the best policy. You pair'

– Zach turned towards Esme too – 'will go far. Mark my words!' he said, pulling them in for a picture.

After high-fiving Rory, Finn and Esme squealed and vigorously waved their vouchers in Isla and Felicity's direction before skipping off to the sweet stall with Mop trailing after them.

'Well, you've made a couple of kids very happy,' Allie said as she stood beside Rory and Zach and watched Finn and Esme disappear amongst the crowd.

'I agree,' joined in Hamish, giving Rory a light slap on the back and Zach a nod of appreciation. 'This one,' said Hamish, patting Rory on the back once again, 'always steps up to the mark. We couldn't manage without him. A pillar of the community.'

'Never mind dog shows, you could be a judge at Crufts or maybe a new TV show – dogs that have talent!' chipped in Zach.

Allie could see the excitement flickering in Rory's eyes. Zach had his full attention, 'Really? Now that sounds like some sort of plan.'

'Yes, I agree, you are destined for bigger things. Wasted on local village fairs,' said Hamish with a chuckle.

'You should definitely think about the bigger picture,' Zach continued. 'You have such charisma, such warmth with people, and on screen you would be a natural.'

Allie was watching Rory closely. He was hanging on to Zach and Hamish's every word.

'But also not forgetting how important you already are

to our community, the local vet. Everyone knows who you are here,' chipped in Allie, linking her arm through Rory's. 'My own superstar.'

'Well, there is that,' replied Rory, but with less enthusiasm in his voice.

Allie looked up at him but didn't catch his eye. He was staring out over the green, deep in thought. She could tell something was bothering him. Maybe it was her imagination but he didn't seem quite happy.

'I think your public awaits.' Hamish tilted his head towards Zach, who spun round to discover a long queue of admirers hoping to have their picture taken with him.

Instantly putting on his dazzling smile, Zach went to work, his charisma and presence putting the starstruck fans at ease.

Allie took the opportunity to pull Rory towards her and slipped her arms around his neck. 'Are you okay? You look kind of distracted all of a sudden,' she probed gently.

He seemed to hesitate. 'Me? I'm absolutely fine.' Rory looked down at her. Even though he was smiling Allie knew he was still thinking about something else, but this wasn't the time or the place to push it further.

'What a fantastic day this is turning out to be. Finn and Esme need to be bottled. I think pacapoos could become the next big thing.'

'I remember when a mongrel was just that, a crossbreed, and now people pay ridiculous amounts for them.

And how are you feeling now?' asked Rory, his eyebrows drawing together. 'You seem to be in a brighter mood, thankfully.'

'Well, why wouldn't I be? It's fabulous weather, and I'm surrounded by all our friends and family. I love days like this, don't you?' Allie knew she was testing him slightly to see his reaction.

'Absolutely,' he replied on cue yet Allie still had a tiny inkling that something was bothering him.

'And would you believe Mystic Martha really does have psychic powers, according to Isla, and has made a living out of it in the past?'

Rory looked at Allie astonished.

'But don't worry,' she quickly interrupted. 'Isla's talked some sense into me and she's made me realise I'm in charge of my own destiny.'

'Thank God for Isla,' said Rory, looking relieved, and pressed a swift kiss on the end of Allie's nose.

'And tomorrow we will go and look at Clover Cottage. Shall we go and find your mum and dad now and see how the land lies?' asked Allie, pushing for the commitment.

'Yes, come on,' said Rory, taking Allie by the hand.

'And then I'd better find Mum and pull my weight at the Pimm's tent,' she said, noticing Stuart and Alana chatting to Rona and Aggie at the side of the cake stall.

As they walked towards them, Rory called out cheerily, 'How's everyone doing?'

'All good! It's such a fantastic turnout. We can't believe

how many people are still flooding through those gates! It must be down to that famous chappie milling about,' exclaimed Alana, leaning towards Rory and kissing his cheek. Thankfully, everyone seemed chilled and in good spirits, thought Allie, smiling at Alana and Stuart.

'And we are just making our way over to the stage. Bill is playing with his band in a moment. Are you pair joining us?'

'Absolutely!' replied Allie, waggling her camera. 'It'll be an ideal opportunity to take some photos.'

'See, that was Martha who instigated that situation; she's all about the happy-ever-after,' whispered Rory in Allie's ear.

Allie couldn't help but smile, remembering the time Martha arrived in the village. Within only a few days of being reunited with her old friends over one too many gins, she had set a horrified Rona up on a dating app and before she could object she'd been matched with the man of her dreams, Bill. The relationship was still going strong.

Allie leant into Rory's shoulder as they walked towards the stage. Even though Martha's reading had made her a little jittery, the day was panning out perfectly. Rory pulled her in close and whispered, 'I do love you,' setting the butterflies swirling around Allie's stomach. Then he pointed to the crimson chequered picnic blanket laid out on the grass under the old oak tree. Alongside a wicker hamper there was a bottle of wine chilling inside an ice bucket.

Allie marvelled at the sight in front of her. 'Is this for us?' she asked, amazed at the effort Rory had gone to.

'It is. I thought after this morning and your wobble—'

'I wasn't wobbling – well, not really – okay, maybe a little.' Allie pinched her thumb and forefinger together. 'It's just ... I don't know ... Maybe I'm just being daft, but I've got this feeling that something isn't quite right. You seemed in a world of your own before, like you had something on your mind, and then with what Martha said —'

'You're right.'

'Have I got something to be worried about?' Allie ground to a halt, her eyes wide.

'You're right; you are being daft.' Rory shook his head despairingly. 'How can anyone predict the future? In my book things happen for a reason, what is meant to be will be, and this is meant to be. I thought you deserved a fabulous lunch and a glass of wine while we listen to the band ... Enjoy it, Allie.'

'How did you organise this so quickly?'

'I have my sources.' He grinned, not giving any more away.

'I don't think I could love you any more if I tried,' said Allie, feeling she needed to tell Rory exactly how she felt.

'That's good to hear,' he said, taking her hand and kneeling beside her on the blanket.

She took a peep inside the basket. 'And my favourite sandwiches too! You have pulled out all the stops. This day couldn't get any more perfect,' she said dreamily, finally feeling settled. She passed the wine to Rory, feeling foolish for hanging on to Mystic Martha's every word.

'Here's to us,' she said, raising her glass in a toast after Rory had poured the wine. Just as they were about to clink their glasses together they heard screaming behind them, making Allie sit up straight. They turned to see a commotion on the road adjacent to the green.

'That's Felicity,' said Allie, recognising her voice and scrambling to her feet. She looked into the crowd. Her stomach lurched, her heart pounding against her ribcage, as she clocked Felicity running towards them, looking terrified and shouting for Rory at the top of her voice.

Out of breath, Felicity stopped in front of the picnic blanket. Close to tears, she stumbled over her words. 'Rory, you need to come, there's been an accident.'

Rory leapt to his feet and followed Felicity towards the road, where a crowd had gathered. Pushing his way through the villagers he witnessed a grief-stricken Zach and, lying stretched out in the middle of the road, Sydney, his trusted Labrador. She'd been hit by a van.

'Bloody hell,' said Allie, gasping for breath as she arrived at Rory's side.

'Rory, help her – please help her.' Zach's voice cracked as his pleading eyes locked with Rory's.

Rory understood the urgency and spun round towards Allie, 'Allie, I've not got the surgery keys. Go and find Dad and tell him to meet me there immediately.'

Allie turned quickly and ran back through the crowd of people to find Stuart.

Chapter 5

The second the surgery door was unlocked Rory gently placed Sydney onto the operating table. Her eyes were droopy and the rise and fall of her chest was low. After quickly pulling on his white scrubs Rory sterilised his hands. Stuart joined in while Alana busied herself making strong sweet tea for everyone.

Allie was standing next to Zach, who was clutching Sydney's lead with all his might. 'Don't leave me,' he was muttering under his breath. There was nothing Allie could say or do that was going to make the situation any better. All they could do was watch and hope Rory could work his magic.

'I just don't know what happened. One minute she was by my side and the next ... All I heard was a screech and a thud.' Zach's voice cracked. 'She never runs off. Never.'

Out of the corner of his eye Rory could see a crowd had gathered at the surgery gates. People were standing pointing their cameras towards the surgery window.

'Dad, can you shut the blind please?' ordered Rory with authority. 'The last thing we need is an audience.'

Stuart hurried over to the window. 'There's press out there and a TV camera! My God, word spreads quickly,' he said, immediately shutting the blinds and switching the lights on.

'Vultures,' murmured Zach, his eyes firmly fixed on Sydney.

Alana appeared and handed Zach two drinks, a mug of hot sweet tea and a small glass of whisky.

'Here, drink this. It's good for shock and will take the edge off,' she said, handing him the whisky glass, which Zach gratefully accepted. He swirled the liquid around before draining the glass, wincing as the amber liquid burned his throat.

'I keep a bottle in my desk, because you never know when someone might need it,' Alana said softly, taking the empty glass and handing Zach the mug of tea.

Rory and Stuart had already set to work on the primary survey check. After examining Sydney's vital functions and airways Rory shone the pen torch into the dog's eyes to assess responses and pupil size.

'We need to administer pain relief.' Rory looked at his dad, who nodded his understanding and opened the drugs cabinets.

'Methadone or Fentanyl?' asked Stuart, waiting for Rory's response.

'Methadone – it's stronger, and we need fluids. Can you set up the IV cannula too?'

'Yes,' replied Stuart.

Zach was staring vacantly at Sydney, his eyes teeming with tears, as he began to ask questions, trying to gain a better understanding of what was going on.

Rory spoke slowly and calmly. 'We are getting Sydney stable. She's been hit with some force but from the initial checks it looks like it's her back legs that have been hit. I need to assess her visceral organs and carry out an ultrasound to rule out fluid in the abdomen and check the chest for a pneumothorax, followed by an x-ray to check for fractures.'

Zach looked like he was about to crumble. 'But she's going to be okay, isn't she?' Eyebrows raised, he offered a questioning gaze, muttering *please* repeatedly under his breath.

'I'm going to do my very best, but Zach and Allie, I'm afraid we need to ask you to step outside and take a seat in the waiting room.'

Zach couldn't speak; his face was pallid, his hands jammed into his armpits as the tears slipped freely down his cheeks. He took a step towards the table and bent and kissed Sydney's head. 'I love you, buddy.'

Allie's heart was breaking as she led Zach out of the surgery. She swallowed a lump in her throat. 'Come on,' she whispered, touching Zach's elbow.

Zach exhaled and kissed Sydney one more time before shutting the surgery door behind him.

Over an hour had passed and all that had cut through the eerie silence was the tick of the waiting-room clock. Zach had not moved a muscle, as he sat on the brown plastic chair with his elbows resting on his knees and his head in his hands, hoping that the surgery door would open sooner rather and later.

Allie was sitting next to him glancing down at her phone. The word had not only spread around the village but across all social media channels. She couldn't quite believe how quickly a story could hit the news headlines. Within minutes of arriving at the surgery the phone had rung constantly with news reporters trying to get hold of Zach, but now the receiver was lying on the reception desk, off the hook.

Finally, Rory stepped into the waiting room.

'Hey,' he said softly, causing Zach to lift his head.

Rory took a step closer, drying his hands on a towel. Zach let out a slow steady breath and stiffened. All eyes were on Rory.

'I think you'll find someone wants to see you.' Rory said softly, a smile touching his face.

Zach exhaled, tears filling his eyes. 'Really?'

'Really!' confirmed Rory.

Relief was carved in Zach's face, as he pressed his palms to his eyes to control the tears before tipping his head back and looking towards the ceiling. 'Thank you,' he said with sincerity. Standing up he thrust his shaky hand towards Rory. 'Honestly, I can't thank you enough,' said Zach, beaming.

'Anytime,' said Rory. 'But I need to tell you that at the minute Sydney is heavily sedated. She's stable and has fractured her leg, but I've applied an external splint to the limb for temporary support.'

Zach nodded.

'But our facilities here are too small – we can't house Sydney overnight and we need to keep an eye on her, so I've arranged for her to go over to the veterinary hospital in the next town. It's run by a good friend of mine, Molly McKendrick. Sydney will be well looked after and I'll pop across later to check on her.'

Zach nodded. 'Can I see her?'

'Of course. Dad's in with her at the moment.' Rory took a step to the side and gestured towards the room.

Standing up, Allie wrapped her arms around him. 'You are a lifesaver,' she gushed, squeezing him tight.

'I am, but sometimes my job is made difficult by the lack of space here.'

Allie detected something was niggling at Rory. 'What's up?' Taking a step back she raised her eyebrows.

'This is why we need bigger premises, but Dad won't listen. I don't want to be shipping animals over to Molly's. It makes me feel inadequate that we can't take full care of the animals we treat. We need to look for bigger premises, but Dad is having none of it.'

Allie felt his frustration. 'It is difficult, but this place hasn't the room for expansion.'

'And then there's this.' Rory took a key out of his pocket and opened up the drugs cupboard.

'I'm not sure what I'm looking at. There's barely anything in there,' admitted Allie, staring into a nearly empty cupboard.

'Exactly, there's a lack of drugs and treatments, which I'll need to chase up. Mum usually takes care of all this.'

'She's probably snowed under and has forgotten. It will be easily fixed.'

'Sometimes, I just feel like everything is left on my shoulders.' He blew out a breath and took a quick peep through the blinds. 'Jeez, have you seen how many people are out there?' he said, amazed at the crowd gathered outside. Then, turning round, he saw his mum walk back behind the reception desk.

'We've had to take the phone off the hook. The press are ringing every two minutes asking for an update,' said Alana, placing the receiver back. It immediately rang again. 'See!'

'Poor Zach, the joys of being famous.' Rory rolled his eyes. 'I suppose they aren't going to disappear until some kind of statement is made,' he said, hearing his phone ping. 'That's Molly – she's on her way but I'm not sure it's going to be a good idea to try and manoeuvre Sydney through that many people.'

Allie followed Rory back into the surgery and for a

second watched a very smiley Zach leaning over Sydney, stroking her gently. 'I thought I'd lost her there for a minute ...' Zach didn't look up, his voice faltering. 'I'm going to spoil her rotten when I get her home.'

'And where is home?' asked Allie.

'London – but we travel around a lot, it just depends where we are filming. Sydney comes on set with me and everyone loves her.'

'I kind of got that feeling. Goodness knows how the news got out, but Zach—'

'I know, social media has gone berserk,' interrupted Zach.

'It has indeed – and I'm not sure how the accident got out so quickly.' Allie sounded surprised.

'That's the joys of mobile phones – nothing stays private these days. One tweet, one Facebook post from someone who thinks it's their job to tell the world ...' Zach shook his head gravely. 'This is when the job I do gets out of hand.' Allie picked up on the sad tone of his voice. 'The last thing I want to do is step out in front of all those people, but they won't go away until either they've seen me or I've released a statement.'

'What do you want to do?' asked Rory, once more parting the blinds and creating an immediate frenzy.

'I'll have to show my face,' sighed Zach.

Stuart shook his head in disbelief at the crowd gathered outside. 'We've directed Molly to the lane at the bottom of the garden. Can I suggest that when she arrives you go out to the front of the surgery and we will transport Sydney out the back entrance?'

'Good idea, Dad. Is that okay with you, Zach?'

Zach nodded and glanced at his mobile phone, then let out another sigh. 'Filming has been cancelled tomorrow but it's only to be expected. I can't make the documentary without Sydney. She won't be up and running any time soon.'

Molly arrived in less than ten minutes, and parked the ambulance in the lane at the back of Stuart and Alana's garden. She gently rapped on the back door and Alana let her in.

'What's with all the cloak-and-dagger stuff? Why the back entrance?' asked Molly, confused.

'A road accident,' said Alana, leading the way towards the surgery.

'But why the back entrance?' she repeated.

Stuart parted the blinds and Molly witnessed the crowd gathered outside.

'Huh? What's with all those people?' asked Molly, bemused, before looking at the man standing at the side of the table. She narrowed her eyes and peered closer.

'Do I know you?' Molly tilted her head to the side.

Zach, who must have dealt with this situation umpteen times in his life, hitched a friendly smile onto his face and held out his hand towards her.

'I'm Zach and I believe you're going to take the best care of Sydney tonight,' he said with warmth.

Allie stifled a giggle and watched the look on Molly's face change as the penny dropped.

'Zach – Zach Hudson,' she stuttered, looking towards Allie, whose head was bobbing in confirmation.

'And that's the reason we've sneaked you in the back way. We can't transport Sydney through the crowd.'

'So, what's the plan?' asked Rory, realising it was the middle of the afternoon, he was famished and his stomach was rumbling for Scotland.

'I've got to face them some time,' confirmed Zach, looking at his mobile. 'I'm trending on Twitter. The rumours are Sydney's been killed in a hit and run ... They won't give up until I make some sort of statement or show my face. Fancy facing the music with me?' he asked Rory.

'Me?' answered Rory amazed.

Allie sensed he was feeling a little shy. 'Go on, it'll be great publicity for the surgery,' she encouraged. 'And whilst you're out the front distracting everyone we can move Sydney to the ambulance and wait for you.'

Rory began to peel off his scrubs. 'What are you doing? Keep them on,' insisted Allie, thinking about the photo opportunity.

'It's not me that's the heart-throb,' he said, rolling his eyes.

Feeling proud, Allie gave him a gentle push. 'Go on, your public awaits,' she teased.

Hearing the commotion outside, a nervous Rory followed Zach towards the front door. Taking a deep breath he pulled the door open and Zach stepped outside. Almost immediately every mobile phone in Heartcross seemed to be angled in their direction, with a barrage of questions thrown at them.

Zach threw up his arms and the crowd fell silent.

'Firstly, thank you all for showing such concern,' he started before composing himself. 'Early this afternoon my trusted friend Sydney was hit by a car, but this man, Rory Scott' – Zach placed his hand on Rory's shoulder – 'saved her life. This man, in my opinion, is the best vet. In fact, he's an absolute supervet. Everyone here at the surgery, Rory, Stuart, Alana and Allie, has shown me so much compassion. What a wonderful family business to have here in Heartcross. I'd travel miles to bring my pets to this magnificent establishment. Sydney is nursing a fractured leg but is comfortable. Thank you, everyone, for your concern.'

Zach nodded his appreciation towards the crowd. The atmosphere had changed from one of worry to one of elation and excitement buzzed through the charged air.

'As you can imagine I want to get back to my girl so has anyone got any questions before we disappear back inside?'

The journalists outstretched their microphones.

'Hi, I'm Aidy Redfern, BBC Scotland. What will happen to the documentary you were filming here in Heartcross? Will it still go ahead?'

'Unfortunately, it will have to be postponed for the time

being until Sydney is up and running, no pun intended, but on the bright side I get to come back to this wonderful place again.'

Zach nodded towards the next journalist. Rory watched in awe as Zach controlled the crowd and kept them in order. He answered the questions swiftly and with great professionalism.

'Hi, I'm Lucas – *Glensheil Herald*. What's next for Zach Hudson?'

'I'll be travelling to Africa and filming a wildlife series at one of the sanctuaries that rescue lions. I'm a great supporter of these centres and all the time we are striving to improve lion conservation by monitoring lion populations and supporting research. These sanctuaries rescue, rehabilitate and, wherever possible, release the lions back into the wild but sadly many of the animals they rescue have been too damaged by captivity to return, so we are focusing on providing them with the best possible lifetime care at the sanctuary. I'll be there for the next twelve months, so it's going to be an exciting time!'

Rory's jaw dropped open and he gave a slow shake of the head. He couldn't believe what he was hearing! This trip was everything he'd dreamt of and planned with Clare all those years ago.

'Will Sydney be travelling with you?' Asked Lucas.

'Not this time. She'll be having a rest from a busy filming schedule and will be staying at home.'

Zach answered a few more questions before it was time

to call a halt, as he wanted to get back to Sydney. 'Again, I'd just like to say another thank you to this man; he is the best. You have a fantastic community here and thank you for making us feel so welcome.'

Once more the crowd applauded and Rory was genuinely grinning. As he followed Zach back inside the surgery the crowd began chanting, 'Rory the supervet.' Rory couldn't help but feel the buzz – he'd never experienced admiration like this before.

'So that's what being famous feels like?' said Rory, raking his hand through his hair. 'Is that amount of attention a daily occurrence for you?'

'Some days are a little more manic than others,' answered Zach, waving one last time towards the crowd before shutting the surgery door.

Rory was shaking his head slightly while smiling in disbelief. 'I really quite like it!'

'I can't actually thank you enough.' Zach stretched out his hand and shook Rory's.

'I'm just sorry we have to move Sydney. We really need to expand, but the surgery is here and there's just no room.'

'Have you looked to move premises?'

Rory rolled his eyes. 'I can't even get Mum to use an electronic booking system, never mind move the surgery.'

Zach laughed. 'I bet your mum was as proud as punch when you followed in your dad's footsteps. Can you imagine when I said I wanted to become an actor? The disappointment was written all over my parents' faces when I didn't want to follow in Dad's footsteps. "You need stability ... a proper job," said Zach, mimicking his father's voice. 'Sometimes you just have to do something that isn't the norm for them to take notice, and stand by your beliefs.'

'But never mind that ... Africa.' Rory blew out a breath. 'Zach, that's something I've always wanted to do. Field conservation, captive animals, education, rescue and care – it's all so important.' Rory was reeling off a long list with enthusiasm. 'No creature should be killed for its scales, fur, tusks. Wildlife should be just that, wild, uncontaminated by humans and protected as far as we can.'

Zach looked at Rory speculatively for a moment. 'So come with us.'

'Don't tempt me,' said Rory, with a fixed look of concentration then a swift look to see if anyone was listening. 'I'd snap your hand off.'

'So do it then.'

Rory suddenly felt as though he was on a rollercoaster of emotions. 'Seriously? It's not that easy though, is it? When everyone relies on you and expects you to do the right thing.'

'And what's the right thing?' probed Zach.

'To turn up for work every day, because that's what I do and that's what people expect me to do.' Rory's thoughts turned to his dad; he wouldn't be happy working with agency vets for twelve months. And then of course there was Allie ...

'But could you be tempted?'

'Of course I could be tempted – I am tempted – more than tempted.' Rory gave a deep, heavy sigh. There were just too many factors against him, what with the business and Allie. He knew she had her heart set on Clover Cottage and setting up home, and he loved her and wanted to make her happy, but Africa had been a dream of his for so long. Would she understand how much this meant to him? It wasn't as if he was saying never to the idea of living together, and twelve months would pass in a flash. But would Allie feel the same way?

'It's okay for you – you're Zach Hudson and can travel the world and do what you want, that's kind of expected,' he continued. 'But I'm good old dependable Rory Scott, local vet. Everyone relies on me.'

'Your experience would be invaluable. Attached to the sanctuary there's an education centre which allows the local children to learn about the wildlife and the importance of conservation. It would be brilliant to have a vet on board with all your knowledge.'

Rory felt excited but apprehensive. This conversation had put a fire in his belly. Africa. He'd be up close and personal with animals he could only dream of working with.

'Food for thought,' said Zach, following Rory back into the waiting room.

'What are you pair talking about?' Allie appeared in the doorway and narrowed her eyes. 'You look as thick as thieves.'

A strangled laugh came from Rory. 'We were just saying we may well be in a need of a pint, and I'm famished. We never did get our lunch,' he said, flustered, diverting the conversation whilst sliding his arm around Allie's shoulder. The last thing he needed today was Allie thinking he was going to up and leave for Africa after just one conversation with Zach, but he knew he'd have to have a conversation with her about it sooner rather than later. He couldn't help but think the timing was perfect.

'Sydney's in the ambulance and comfortable, Molly's waiting for you out the back and Drew is going to bring you back in about an hour if that's okay with you?' Allie looked towards Zach.

'Perfect,' he answered before thanking Alana for all her help and the glass of whisky to steady his nerves. 'And where's Stuart? I need to thank him too.'

Alana gestured towards the surgery and Rory opened the door to find Stuart peeling off his scrubs.

Zach strolled towards him with his hand outstretched. 'I'm just off. Thanks for everything you've done today,' he said.

'All in a day's work. You can always rely on Scott and Son. We never let anyone down and we open when we need to. Isn't that right, Rory?'

'Absolutely, Dad,' Rory replied automatically, but feeling guilty as the conversation with Zach was still very much on his mind. He knew he had some serious thinking to do.

'Molly's waiting,' called Alana, leaving Zach thanking

Stuart and Rory once more before he disappeared down the garden path towards the ambulance parked on the lane.

'What a lovely man. So down to earth despite his fame.' Stuart opened the blind. Thankfully everyone seemed to have dispersed back towards the summer fair.

When the ambulance pulled away Rory turned towards Allie. 'Come on, I'm in need of some food, even though the wine will be warm and the birds may have pecked at our lunch. I think hog roast buns and a cold beer are on the menu,' he announced.

'Sounds like a plan,' agreed Allie. 'And thankfully Aggie stepped in to help Mum on the Pimm's tent. I bet she was cursing me for my no-show.'

Hand in hand they walked back towards the green, which was still a hive of activity. Mystic Martha was making a fortune as well as telling them, Drew and Fergus were still serving up beers and sandwiches, while the cake stall was empty, leaving Felicity and Rona enjoying a nice chilled glass of Prosecco, sitting in deckchairs in front of the stage being entertained by the local dance troupe.

Rory was in a little world of his own, still trying to process Zach's proposal. Africa. How, actually, could he afford to go? That was something he would have to seriously consider, especially as he wouldn't be getting a wage for the twelve months he would be volunteering, and then there was the accommodation. There was so much more he needed to know.

Clover Cottage

'I can't wait for tomorrow,' announced Allie, resting her head on Rory's shoulder as they walked. 'Whilst you were outside talking to the press I had a good chat with your mum and dad about the cottage. They knew you'd come round, said you were stubborn, but that once you'd thought about it they knew it'd be an offer you couldn't refuse – prime position, beautiful spot, handy for work ... and maybe one day soon we could think about starting a family ... Of course, not right away, but maybe in a couple of years?' Allie knew she was babbling and looked up at him. Rory's expression was fixed and Allie swiped his arm playfully, wondering what he was thinking.

But Rory's mind was obviously elsewhere.

'Earth to Rory, are you listening to me?'

She waited.

'Rory!'

Rory jolted out of his reverie and realised he hadn't heard a word Allie had spoken. 'What did you say?'

Allie tutted and rolled her eyes. 'Clover Cottage. What are you thinking about?' she urged. Her phone pinged in her pocket and she reached for it.

'Oh my God!' she exclaimed, before Rory could answer.

'What is it?'

Allie now had Rory's full attention.

She spun the phone towards him. 'It's you and Zach, you're all over the news. The TV crew filmed you – you are plastered all over the internet!'

Chapter 6

The day after the accident, Rory sat hugging his morning coffee whilst staring at his iPad in disbelief. Ten thousand new followers on Twitter in twenty-four hours. How could that even be possible? All this attention gave him a flutter of excitement, a snippet of what it was like to be in the public eye, and he quite liked it.

At first, he'd begun to respond to people's comments, but soon he couldn't keep up, there were just way too many of them.

The video of him and Zach standing outside the surgery had gone viral and once more the little village of Heartcross was plastered all over the news.

'Zach Hudson hails Rory Scott as supervet.' Rory said the words out loud. They gave him a fuzzy feeling inside. That tweet alone had thousands of retweets and the surgery's Twitter account, which had barely been used over the years, had exploded into a life of its own.

It might be Sunday morning, but Rory logged on to his

emails. He stared in amazement and sat back in his chair as his inbox downloaded mail after mail.

There were emails from newspapers, magazines and radio stations, all wanting to interview him regarding his new-found fame. He was going to need a PA at this rate. Even though he was bowled over by the attention, he couldn't forget Zach's invitation to go to Africa, and the more he thought about it, the more appealing it became. It wasn't as though he was unhappy in Heartcross, far from it, but he wanted to experience more within his field and this would add more strings to his bow as a vet.

He thought back to yesterday, and a part of him still felt disappointed that Sydney had had to be transferred to Molly's surgery over in Glensheil. He wanted to expand the premises and provide care for the animals he treated here in Heartcross, but unless his dad agreed to the idea it wasn't going to happen any day soon. Maybe Zach's offer would make his dad stand up and take notice? Perhaps it would make him realise that Rory had his own ambitions and didn't want to be in his father's shadow continuously. He had a voice and wanted to be listened to. At times Rory had felt as though he was taken for granted. All he knew was that at this moment his career felt stagnant. He needed new challenges and something to stretch him and excite him.

Shutting down his emails, Rory opened up Facebook, clicked on Clare's profile and browsed through his ex-girlfriend's latest uploads. She was currently working near Etosha National Park in Namibia. The images were incredible: it was one of southern Africa's most beloved and most easily accessible wildlife sanctuaries, home to over a hundred mammal species and three hundred bird species. Flicking through the posts only jolted him into craving this opportunity even more.

Clare looked like she was having the time of her life; she was doing exactly what they had both talked about doing at university. Rory remembered researching areas and even pricing flights but it never came to fruition after his dad convinced him to stay in Heartcross. But maybe this was his time? He needed to take the bull by the horns and get more information from Zach.

Suddenly, hearing footsteps, Rory spotted Allie through the window. She was right on time. He leapt into motion and shut down Facebook, knowing he needed to talk to her about how he was feeling. But as the door swung open and he was greeted by an excited-looking Allie, he didn't have the heart to burst her bubble. It just wasn't the right time.

'It's today! It's today!' she squealed, clapping her hands together like a demented sealion. 'Come on, come on, get your shoes on,' she ordered, oozing excitement and giving Rory a gentle push to hurry himself along. 'I'm dying to take a look inside the cottage.'

She beamed into his eyes and Rory couldn't help but give her an upbeat smile, even though inside he felt awful.

'Okay, okay,' he answered, standing up and popping a kiss on her cheek. 'I'm coming.'

'You're lucky I'm even here on time,' she said, handing him his jacket and phone. 'It's taken me nearly fifteen minutes to walk up Love Heart Lane, you know.'

'Huh, why?' he asked, puzzled, walking towards the window and taking a look outside. The lane was deserted.

Allie couldn't control her giggles. 'All those Rory supervet fans waiting outside for autographs.'

'You are hilarious.' He shook his head in jest before pulling on his trainers. 'Not that I'm letting it go to my head or anything but—'

'But what?'

'Over ten thousand followers on Twitter overnight and numerous requests for newspaper and radio interviews!'

'Christ on a bike!' Allie exclaimed in amazement. 'Scott and Son will rocket into the public domain.'

'That Zach Hudson really does have some clout,' said Rory, holding open the front door before locking it behind them.

Five minutes later they were standing at the gate of Clover Cottage. Overhead white cotton clouds sailed across the clear blue sky. The old flagstone path was overrun with wild flowers and grasses dancing in the light breeze. For a moment they stood and stared. Rory couldn't help thinking this place looked like it should be condemned, never mind being suitable for raising a family. It had money pit written all over it. He observed that Allie still had that dreamy romantic look about her.

'Doesn't it look perfect,' Allie murmured as she reached for his hand and pushed open the gate.

At one glance she knew the cottage was in need of some tender loving care but she also knew she was the woman to transform this place into their happy-ever-after home.

'I'm already in love,' she murmured and Rory knew that look in her eyes – determination. What Allie wanted, Allie usually got, and in almost every situation she knew how to wrap him around her little finger. If he wasn't careful, she'd have them both moved in by the end of the day.

They stumbled across the overgrown front garden and Allie stopped in her tracks, making Rory bump into her. 'Just imagine roses tumbling around the door, Rory,' she said dreamily.

'There's lots of work to be done, especially in the garden, and with our busy lives – you at the pub, me at the surgery ...'

Allie wasn't daft, she knew that, and she was aware this would be a financial struggle, but surely there were ways and means. 'And when it's all pruned to perfection we will be sitting out relaxing with a nice glass of red, living our best life,' she said, painting a blissful picture and hoping to entice Rory into the same train of thought.

'And when did you win the lottery?' asked Rory.

'Surely we could get a mortgage or a loan. Other people do it and we are both working.'

Rory took out the bunch of keys from his pocket, placed one in the lock and gave the stiff front door a budge. Allie stared wide-eyed as the door slowly opened. She took a long breath. She had to admit it wasn't exactly how she'd built up the picture of this cottage in her mind. Inside it was dark and musty and the smell hit them both straightaway. Allie stepped forward and pulled back the curtains to let in some light, only to find the rings snapped and the curtains flapped, and a cloud of dust danced before her eyes.

'They've seen better days,' said Rory, staring around the room. 'In fact, I think everything has seen better days.'

'Okay, I have to admit you were right, there's nothing Laura Ashley about it right this very second,' admitted Allie, feeling a little deflated.

She took a swift glance around the room, which was empty except for a battered old sofa, a small table and a couple of chairs, an upturned crate and a dusty oak sideboard that housed an empty whisky bottle, a chipped glass and a photograph.

Allie picked up the dusty photo frame and wiped it with the sleeve of her jacket. She squinted and realised it was a photograph of a young James Kerr with his two sons standing on each side of him.

'I wonder why James didn't leave the cottage to his sons?' said Rory.

'My guess is because of their criminal lifestyle. Maybe he feared they would sell it to someone who would upset the quiet peace of Heartcross,' replied Allie.

'Maybe.'

'They actually look happy,' said Allie, placing the photograph back on the sideboard. 'But how could anyone live like this?'

Rory shrugged and walked back into the hallway.

'Do you think they are stable?' asked Allie, cautiously looking towards the staircase.

'I'll go first,' said a gallant Rory, holding on to the shaky banister, which had numerous missing spindles.

Proceeding with caution he stepped on the first two stairs. They creaked but seemed steady enough. Carefully, Allie followed him. At the top was a small landing with four further doors.

Rory pushed open the first to reveal a grim-looking bathroom that housed what seemed like the entire spider population.

'Eww, that stench.' Allie wrinkled her nose, staring at the avocado-coloured bathroom suite in dismay.

'Surely that will come back into fashion one day,' Rory said, relieved to shut the door firmly behind him.

The other three rooms were bedrooms, all a good size with oak wooden beams running across the ceiling. Allie walked over to the window and looked out at the land that rolled for miles and miles, a great quilt of gold, brown and green squares divided by walls of mossy grey stone.

'But what a view. Imagine waking up to that every day. It feels so calm ... This would make a lovely nursery,' Allie said, transfixed by the beauty.

'Nursery? This place needs to be condemned.' Rory frowned deeply, thinking this was the last place he'd let a baby sleep.

Allie waved a hand dismissively. 'Obviously I don't mean in this state,' she said, slipping her arms around his waist and staring into his eyes. 'I think you'll make a good dad.'

'You aren't trying to tell me something, are you?' he asked nervously.

'Of course not! But one day ...' she said.

'One day,' he repeated, feeling relieved. Even though Rory knew he wanted children one day, he didn't want them right now, and he'd thought Allie had felt the same way. He guided her back downstairs and they walked into a kitchen that housed a free-standing cooker and a chipped Belfast sink with a dripping tap. Next to the kitchen was a dining room, equipped with a coal fire, and off that room was a small office.

As they stepped back into the living room, Allie's body tingled with excitement. 'I think it looks promising,' she said in a bubbly tone.

Rory rubbed at his brow as he stared around the room.

'We can transform this place exactly how we want to,' continued Allie.

Rory had a fixed look of concentration on his face and was taking regular deep breaths.

'This place needs to be invested in heavily,' he said and began listing the problems. 'Allie, there's no central heating, most of the walls need plastering, it needs a new kitchen, bathroom, boiler, rewiring ... Which bit looks promising? This is going to take a hell of a lot of time and money to put right.'

'But it's got potential – huge potential. Look at all the outside space and those views! And those outbuildings could be the next stage of Scott and Son. It may take time and money but think how perfect it could be in the end.'

Allie had a good feeling about this place. She could see past all the hard work, but Rory was shaking his head. 'I think this is way too much for us to take on.'

'But think about it,' she began to argue. 'Houses don't come up for sale often in Heartcross, even you agreed that. We can take our time with this project. Let's talk to Alfie. He knows fantastic contractors at reasonable prices. Surely it's worth an ask?'

Rory didn't answer. He stepped outside and walked around the side of the cottage. Allie followed.

'Rory, talk to me. What are you thinking?' she urged once more, willing to move the conversation on. Even though she was feeling positive about this ramshackle cottage there was a small part of her that felt a tiny bit disappointed at the state of the place. She knew it would be a massive commitment for them both – emotionally, physically, financially – but surely it would be worth it in the end? But it was plain to see that Rory didn't seem keen at all.

Rory stopped and turned towards her. 'Have you ever

wanted more from life, Allie?' he asked, looking out over the landscape. 'What's your dream?'

For a second, Allie was taken back. 'What do you mean, what's my dream?' she asked, confused.

'What's your dream now – this second?'

Allie had a sinking feeling. 'Health, wealth and happiness ...' She stared at him. 'This isn't what you want, is it?'

Rory didn't answer her question. 'Surely there's something you want to do, something on your bucket list, a dream job, something a little more exciting than pulling pints? Your dream is not to be a barmaid for the rest of your life?'

Allie had no idea where this conversation had even come from but immediately felt defensive. 'And what's wrong with being a barmaid? It's a living that's kept a roof over my parents' heads for as long as I can remember. I like my job. Most days I get to see my friends, I get to chat to all the interesting people that frequent Heartcross ... I enjoy it. We can't all be rocket scientists or vets. My parents aren't like yours, Rory.'

'And what's that supposed to mean?' Rory met her gaze, the tension bubbling under the surface.

Allie couldn't believe how the promise of the day had turned so sour. They had the perfect chance of building their happy-ever-after home and Rory seemed hell-bent on throwing it away.

Trying her best to remain composed and not escalate

things between them, Allie took a deep breath. 'My parents work ridiculous hours and they have no inheritance to hand down to me or my children if I ever get round to having any. What you see is what you get. My parents didn't have the money to send me to university; it would have crippled them financially, but we look after each other no matter what.'

Rory absorbed what she was saying. 'So you're saying I get everything handed to me on a plate?'

'Pretty much so,' Allie replied, unable to hold back. 'You continuously moan about how your dad—'

'Moan? Moan?' Rory raised his voice. 'I thought I was sharing my thoughts with my girlfriend.'

'Okay, that came out wrong. Your dad frustrates you, I get it. You want to have an all-dancing surgery, you want to be able to look after more animals on the premises, so do something about it.' Allie flung her arms open wide. 'Look at this land, look at those outbuildings. Turn those into your animal hospital. You'll be right here on the premises in charge of it all. That' – she pointed – 'could be your new state-of-the-art surgery. What's stopping you?'

Rory remained quiet.

'All this – for nothing. You don't know how lucky you are.' Allie barely came up for breath; she knew she'd been bottling this up since Rory's reaction on the evening his parents had handed over the particulars for the property. 'And here's you not happy with your lot. Sometimes you don't know a good thing when it slaps you in your face.

As a kid my parents dragged me from pillar to post. I never fitted in anywhere or stayed in a place long enough to call it home or make real friends until we finally settled here in Heartcross. It was tough and they struggled for money, but for my family, our future family, I don't want that. I want a place where they are settled from the start, a place they know is home, a place they can put down their roots. Sometimes you can be so spoilt, Rory, and stubborn, and can't see the bigger picture.'

'Well, maybe I don't want to. Maybe I want to do what's right for me before life ... opportunities slip through my fingers.'

Allie stared at Rory. 'Life? Opportunities? What the hell is going on with you?'

Rory took a deep breath, 'Zach—'

'Oh my God, a few thousand followers overnight and it's gone to your head. Tomorrow you'll be yesterday's news. You need to get back to the real world. You're a vet, not a TV star.'

'Exactly, and there's more to life than Heartcross.'

Allie narrowed her eyes, suddenly perplexed.

'Allie, you need some fire in your belly. It's like you are stuck in a timewarp. Surely you want more out of life? There's a whole world out there, a world to be explored, and you want to stand behind the bar pulling pints.'

Now not only was Allie angered by his comment but she was hurt. 'Because that's what I do, Rory, and I do it well. And because it's my parents' business and we are a family and we look after each other. And why am I explaining myself to you?'

This discussion was getting heated.

'But surely we all have choices? Look at you – your face lights up every time you take a photograph. Why don't you want to embrace that? Get your name out there, be someone.'

Allie's mouth fell open, and for a second she was speechless. 'I am someone. I am Allie MacDonald, barmaid at the Grouse and Haggis, and bloody proud of it.' But Allie knew, even though she sounded convincing, that this wasn't all she wanted from life. Of course she had dreams, but her parents relied on her. How could she leave them running the pub on their own? They *needed* her to stay in Heartcross and help. And so Allie's dreams would have to wait.

She took a deep breath before carrying on. 'If my parents gave me this opportunity' – she gestured towards the cottage behind her – 'I'd be jumping at the chance of setting up home with the person I supposedly love. Or are you too good for me now you've hit the headlines?'

Rory shook his head. 'Don't be daft.'

Allie knew this wasn't like Rory; he wasn't one to spoil for an argument. 'What's really going on here, Rory?' she asked, sensing there was something bigger bothering him.

'All this – the cottage, moving in together, it's too soon ...' There was an air of finality to his words, one that shocked Allie to the core.

They stared at each other.

Allie had never rowed with Rory on such a scale and she was hurt and upset by his unusual attitude. She had no idea where any of this had come from, and lashed out. 'If that's what you think then maybe we aren't destined to be together,' she finally said, determined not to cry in front of Rory, but feeling as though the tears were bubbling just underneath the surface.

Rory threw his hands into the air, turned around and stormed off.

And as he did so, she felt the hot, frustrated tears slip down her cheeks.

'Damn you,' she bellowed after him.

Chapter 7

A llie closed her eyes and tried to process what the hell had just happened. This was meant to be a happy moment, a moment to remember, looking around your first house with your boyfriend, excited about the future. But now she didn't even know if she had a boyfriend.

Surrounded by an unfamiliar silence, she sat on the arm of the old battered sofa and heaved a long sigh. She couldn't remember a time when she and Rory had ever argued like that. She had a horrible feeling inside and she didn't like it. She finally managed to calm her rapidly beating heart and fixed on Rory's words. 'Your face lights up every time you take a photograph. Why don't you want to embrace that? Get your name out there, be someone.'

But it wasn't that easy though, was it? As much as she would love to spend her life taking photographs, to have her pictures printed in the newspapers or displayed on walls, people relied on her, her parents especially. And after all the trouble and uncertainty they'd been through, Allie was determined that she would be there for them.

Finding herself still sitting in the cottage thirty minutes later, she wearily stood up then pulled the front door shut behind her. Setting out for Heartcross, she found herself walking towards Foxglove Farm, in need of a chat with Isla, her sensible friend and calming influence. Isla would help to put everything into perspective.

But there was no sign of Isla when Allie rapped on the front door, so she took her chances and wandered around the back of the farmhouse. She heaved a sigh of relief when she spotted Isla whistling away whilst pegging out the washing.

Hearing the stones crunch, Isla spun round. 'Oooh, I was just thinking about you. Help yourself to some lemonade and tell me all about the cottage.' She nodded towards the wrought-iron table and chairs in the courtyard. 'I can't wait to hear all about it.'

Still feeling bewildered Allie sat down and poured herself a drink. Isla had the picture-perfect life, husband, children, a beautiful home – not to mention a mad grandmother living with them. And Isla seemed so happy that Allie was a little envious. Even after her parents had settled in Heartcross, there had been times as an only child that Allie had felt lonely when she was put to bed and her parents were working in the bar until the late hours of the night. She remembered writing to Santa Claus asking for a baby brother or sister, a partner in crime, a playmate and a best friend. It was only years later she'd discovered that her parents had tried for more children, but it just didn't happen for them. It made her sad thinking that she would never be an auntie, and after all the heartache her friend Felicity had suffered, Allie had been thinking more and more about having children and knew she wanted a large family. After meeting Rory she had hoped that he would be the man to raise those children with, but after today, she wasn't so sure anymore.

Once the washing basket was empty Isla walked over towards Allie shaking her head. 'Honestly, they all take me for granted. This is meant to be my day of rest but no, good old Isla has to wash, clean and cook whilst everyone is out enjoying themselves.'

'Where is everyone?'

'Finn is out playing in the stream with Esme, Angus is having a nap and Drew has taken Zach over to Glensheil. Apparently Sydney had a good night and can be brought home today. Obviously home is the caravan.'

'And Martha?'

'Martha is over at the teashop keeping Rona company while she tries out some new recipes. So come on, I want to hear all about Clover Cottage.'

Allie took a sip of her drink then pressed her lips together, feeling her insides suddenly tremble.

'It didn't go very well.'

Isla gave her a quizzical look. 'Why not?'

'I'm beginning to think Martha really can see into the future.'

Allie confided in Isla about her argument with Rory,

thankful she could vent her frustration to her friend. She was maddened by Rory's behaviour and even more so that he'd stormed off. She blinked away more tears.

'I'm not entirely sure what is going on with him. I know it sounds daft but it seems like there's something else on his mind. And since the incident with Zach he's checking his social media every two seconds – he's becoming obsessed! I can see him smiling to himself. Honestly, you'd think he was the famous one.'

'To be fair,' said Isla, 'every time I scroll through my phone the press have gone to town on the story. The journalists are currently hanging outside Molly's surgery hoping for a glimpse of Zach collecting Sydney. It would drive me insane being followed everywhere I went. Oh, and imagine always having to look your best. That really wouldn't go in my favour.' Isla indicated her clothing and made Allie laugh. Isla hadn't even managed to get dressed yet today – she was sitting there in her PJs and a pair of wellies. 'Some people are cut out to be famous. Unfortunately I'm not one of them.'

'Rory even hinted that my job as a barmaid wasn't a worthy one and surely I wanted more out of life. How dare he?'

'Rory said that?'

Allie nodded.

'And do you want more out of life?'

Allie had to admit she'd been thinking about the argument with Rory more and more. It wasn't as though she had no ambition whatsoever; a small part of her would like her to try something else, to pursue her skill as a photographer in some way. But she also had a job she actually enjoyed. Every day in the pub was different; you didn't know who was going to walk through the door, and she met some interesting people.

'I'm happy – well, I was happy until this morning. Granted, the cottage needs work, a hell of a lot of work, but isn't that half the fun, doing the place up together, making it your old little piece of paradise? I mean, look at you.'

'Me?'

'A family, your own home and beautiful surroundings.'

'I'm not sure you could call this place paradise. It always stinks of cow manure, but I suppose you get used to it after a time,' Isla said with a chuckle, trying to lighten the mood.

'He said the cottage was too soon ... so I suppose that's that, if he doesn't want to move in with me.'

'Has he said he doesn't want to move in with you? Or did he just say that the cottage was too much, too soon? Sometimes with men you have to cajole them a little bit. It may just take a little time with Rory. At first he didn't want to view the cottage. You've actually got him there now.'

Allie knew that she and Rory usually managed to communicate without the conversation escalating into a row. Somehow this felt different.

Isla reached over and squeezed her friend's hand. 'This is Rory we are talking about,' she said reassuringly. 'He's besotted with you. Anyone can see that.'

Hearing the drone of a car engine Isla stood up and peered around the corner. 'It's Drew and Zach.' She took another look. 'And Rory's in the car with them.'

Allie exhaled. 'Well, this is going to be awkward.'

'Paint a smile on that face. Everything will be okay, trust me.'

'Come on, girl,' Zach's voice rang out as the car door slammed behind them.

Their voices were getting louder as they walked towards the farmhouse. Allie felt herself bristle.

Sydney came sniffing around the corner and as soon as she spotted Isla and Allie she trundled towards them, lifting her broken leg in the air. Allie bent down to stroke her as her tail wagged from side to side. 'Well, you do seem brighter,' she said, ruffling the dog's ears.

The three men walked around the corner in jovial conversation. 'I can't thank you all enough,' said Zach with sincerity.

'And what an opportunity for this man,' chipped in Drew, slapping Rory on the back. 'My mate, a TV star.'

'I wouldn't go as far as that,' replied Rory. His smile dropped as he clocked Allie and did a double take.

'Sometimes you just don't know what's around the corner,' continued Drew, oblivious to the sudden change of atmosphere.

Allie stared at Rory unblinking, watching his face. He seemed happy at whatever proposal they were talking about, in fact very happy.

'What's all this?' queried Isla before Allie had a chance to ask what was going on.

Allie's heart was hammering against her ribcage as she waited for Rory to speak.

Rory looked over towards Zach but he was in full throttle, moving next to Rory and putting his arm around his shoulder. 'You know when people cross your path for a reason,' Zach began.

'I thought that once,' muttered Allie under her breath.

'This man saved Sydney's life.'

'I wouldn't go that far, it was just a broken leg,' objected Rory, playing it down.

'Nonsense, you opened up your surgery, gave us your time, your expertise. I've never encountered such kindness before. That dog is not just any dog' – Zach looked lovingly towards Sydney, who was now lying at Allie's feet – 'that dog is my best friend and I couldn't imagine or don't want to imagine life without her.'

'I'll be handing out the tissues in a minute,' said a teary-eyed Isla, coming over all emotional and flapping her hand in front of her eyes.

'So, even though my filming schedule is up in the air, my producers came up with an alternative.' Zach grinned at Rory. 'Because the publicity and social media had gone through the roof, they've suggested we film a reality show.'

'A reality show – like the Kardashians?' asked Isla, sitting up, knowing that brain-numbing TV was a must at her time of life.

'More like the Karcrashions, no pun intended, after what happened to Sydney,' joked Drew.

Zach rolled his eyes. 'It's a good job I've got a sense of humour! My producers have put forward a proposal and Rory has agreed in principle. Obviously we need to get agreement from Mr Scott senior, but we are going to film Rory – Supervet – in his surgery, capturing the highs and lows of working in a veterinary practice. We are going to explore the power of unconditional love between humans and their animals. With Stuart and Alana's agreement we are going to rig up cameras in the waiting room and behind the scenes. We want to capture the drama, the raw emotion, plus scenes from the operating theatre and powerful interviews with everyone that uses the practice.' Zach sounded passionate about the whole project.

Allie was gobsmacked and felt a tiny pang of jealousy that she was the last to know. Suddenly, Rory's life seemed to be taking a direction that she had no involvement in whatsoever. This was news she wasn't expecting at all. Overnight Rory was going to become a TV sensation. Allie was fully aware of Zach's following and she already knew the ratings would be sky-high.

'Congratulations,' she said, standing up and kissing Rory's cheek without making eye contact. She didn't really know what to say or how to react. She didn't even know how she felt. It all seemed to be happening so quick. All she could think about was their argument. Things were changing fast and there was no denying Allie was feeling unsettled. She was used to making decisions *with* Rory but that seemed to be changing too. She was beginning to think he was slipping away from her.

And then there was Martha's prediction. Allie's mind was awash, Martha's words swirling uncontrollably in her mind. "There are huge changes ahead. I see brand-new opportunities for you both in completely different directions. I see fame ... An extravagant gift divides you. And for you, dear girl, I see upset. Don't let opportunities slip through your fingers. You need to overcome your fears. Be brave."

Martha couldn't have got this situation more right if she'd tried! Allie was beginning to feel physically sick. Why the hell did Zach Hudson have to turn up in their village? Sitting back down, Rory seemed a tad uncomfortable as Zach and Drew kept talking excitedly. Allie sipped her drink, trying to hide her thoughts, as Isla got up to hug Rory. 'Wow! A famous friend. Huge congratulations. So, when is all this happening?'

But before Zach could answer Drew threw his arms up in the air. 'What we need is champagne, a toast to this man,' he announced, patting Rory on the back and quickly disappearing inside the farmhouse kitchen.

Isla pulled up a few more chairs and everyone settled around the table. Drew handed out the glasses. 'Not sure if it's a little early but one glass won't hurt.' He twisted and popped the cork. Allie held up her glass while Drew filled it to the top.

Once everyone had a full glass Drew cleared his throat, 'Firstly, I'd like to say well done to Isla.'

'Huh? What's this got to do with me?' she asked, looking puzzled.

'Because Zach and Sydney wouldn't be here, staying at our farm, if it wasn't for you hiring out those vintage vans of yours! And secondly to Rory. We always said you were destined for greater things than Heartcross … Fame at last!'

Listening to the conversation Allie felt a little surprised at Drew's words and the idea of Rory being destined for greater things than Heartcross. Had people always thought this? Why had this thought passed her by? Judging by the reception Drew's words were getting from the group it was obviously a big possibility that there were greater things on the horizon for Rory, and it made her feel scared and nervous about their future.

'It's only a TV show!' exclaimed Rory, snagging a quick look towards Allie.

'Listen to him, "It's only a TV show"! I suppose you have us lot to keep you grounded, so the fame doesn't go to your head,' teased Drew.

Isla noticed Allie was looking more and more uncomfortable by the second and had adopted a sullen look. She took over the toast. 'Here's to Rory, here's to success!' she said, holding up her glass and clinking it against all the others.

'Thank you, but I'm treating it as a bit of fun. Just another day at the office,' said Rory, taking a sip from his glass, but Allie knew that sparkle in his eyes. Rory was excited about what was happening, and why shouldn't he be? But she couldn't suppress her own feelings. She wanted to be sitting here sipping champagne for a totally different reason: she wanted to be toasting them moving in together.

'So, when does the filming start?' asked Isla.

Zach raised an eyebrow and waggled his phone, which was lying on the table. 'I'm literally waiting for the call. The TV crew were set to follow us' – he gave Sydney an affectionate look – 'up the mountain starting tomorrow.' Sydney rested her head on Zach's knee and looked up at him with the most adorable eyes. 'But thank God you are still here to tell the tale.' He ruffled the top of the dog's head. 'I think it's possible they'll use the same crew and get your new show on the road. From what I can gather it'll be whoever walks in off the street and they'll film all day then slot the footage into five episodes.'

'How exciting! I bet you'll have them queuing down the lane to book an appointment with the surgery. And how's Stuart going to react?' asked Isla.

'I think as much as he might grumble at first about the upheaval, he'll secretly be pleased by the attention ... It's just a shame there's hardly room to swing a cat in the surgery.'

Just at that second Zach's phone rang out. He picked it up and walked over to the fence while he was on the call. As he hung up he turned around with a huge beam on his face. 'We are on!'

'Really?' answered Rory, surprised it was as easy as that.

'Really!' replied Zach. 'Sometimes you just have to be in the right place at the right time.'

Rory glanced across at Allie and held her eyes for a second. Her heart beat anxiously. Everyone was so excited about Rory being on TV, but Allie couldn't shake off the feeling that this was the beginning for him but the end for her. Usually she would have been the first person Rory told about any exciting news but at this moment she felt like they were worlds apart.

'This is brilliant news, isn't it, Allie?' said Drew, filling up Allie's glass with a smidgen of champagne that was left. She looked around at the other glasses, which were still three quarters full, and realised she'd necked the whole drink in a matter of seconds.

'Yes, just brilliant.' There was an edge to her voice that she hoped went unnoticed.

'Will the show be scripted?' asked Rory, rubbing the back of his neck and suddenly sounding nervous.

'No, it'll be off the cuff, so to speak. They'll film a day in the life of Supervet Rory Scott, starting with you opening up the surgery doors to when you close them, and then they edit it for all the best bits.'

'But this is Heartcross. Nothing exciting ever happens

here. It's either fat cats that need to go on a diet or dogs that need castrating. I'm not actually sure it's going to make riveting TV.'

'Nonsense. It's all about living in your shoes, the way you interact with your community. Honestly, people can't get enough of this kind of viewing and before you know it you'll be off on tour – a travelling vet opening up drop-in centres all around the country, with a bestselling book at the top of the charts.'

'It sounds like this is going to be the making of you – the making of you both.' Isla turned towards Allie and gave her a reassuring smile.

'Oh, and I nearly forgot.' Drew turned towards Isla. 'Rory's got to be out of his house, so I've offered him the spare room, if that's okay with you?'

Isla looked towards Allie, whose posture suddenly stiffened. Allie shifted her gaze towards Rory. Moving in with Isla and Drew was news to her, another unexpected turn of events. She had taken it for granted that he'd just move into the pub with her.

'I did say I'd run it past you first,' Drew quickly added.

Isla was put on the spot. She didn't want to draw attention to Allie but she'd registered her friend's crushing disappointment.

'As long as you don't mind Martha's singing in the morning or screaming children when they're tired?' The baby monitor crackled. 'Talking of which, that's Angus waking up; he'll need a feed.'

'I'll go and get him,' offered Allie, needing a moment. 'Is that okay?'

'Of course,' replied Isla, knowing her friend needed time out from the stresses and strains of her morning.

As Allie climbed the stairs in disbelief her chest heaved. She blotted away a rogue tear that had rolled down her cheek. What was going on with Rory? Sitting there listening to his plans she felt like an outsider, and intruding on Isla's family was not ideal. Maybe she was over-reacting and reading too much into the situation but to Allie this felt like a massive deal.

Still feeling out of the loop Allie focused her attention on Angus. Scooping him out of the cot she blew a noisy raspberry on his cheek, leaving him giggling away.

'Well, little fellow, today isn't turning out as well as I hoped,' Allie said, taking a quick whiff of Angus and laying him down on his changing mat. 'So what are we going to do? A lot seems to have happened in the space of a few hours. A few thousand followers and Uncle Rory thinks he's the next big thing. We had a chance to build our forever home and what does he do? He storms off in a tantrum chasing … actually I don't know what dreams he's chasing today. You know what, Angus, I've come to the conclusion he's never satisfied. Maybe he's hit the mid-life-crisis point early … If he wants to think he's going to be the next Zach Hudson then let him,' she huffed, knowing she was being unreasonable but feeling a little better for getting it all off her chest. She smiled down at Angus, who didn't seem to have a care in the world. She picked him up and hoisted him onto her hip. 'You are getting heavy,' she said, popping a kiss on his cheek and feeling apprehensive about joining the others downstairs once more.

She walked back outside to a deadly silence. All eyes were staring in her direction. She looked between them all and noticed an empty seat: Rory's.

Isla was fiddling with her watchstrap then looked up through her fringe and nodded towards the windowsill. For a second Allie was flummoxed, then she saw it: the baby monitor flashing away.

Shit.

Everyone had heard her conversation when she was changing Angus.

'Where's Rory?' she asked, feeling a flush creeping up her chest, her voice shaky. 'He heard everything, didn't he?'

Isla could only manage a nod.

Allie exhaled and quickly handed over Angus.

'I think you'd best go and find him, Allie.'

Allie nodded. Feeling physically sick, she accelerated from a walk into a sprint. She had always been steadfastly loyal to Rory and had never meant to show him up like that in front of their friends. If only she could turn back time.

Why did everything suddenly feel as though it was falling apart?

Chapter 8

'Bloody hell,' panted Allie through gasps of breath. At the bottom of Love Heart Lane she slowed her pace, realising how unfit she was. Taking a breather, she watched the hikers clambering over the stile at the top of the lane next to the teashop, all bursting with energy and looking forward to the climb ahead.

Allie was still cursing the baby monitor. Another fine mess she'd got herself in to. Surely Rory was going to understand? It wasn't as though she'd said it openly in front of everyone. She had been caught out. But Allie was aware Rory had been in a funny mood lately. She racked her brains and pinned it down to the night his parents had gifted them the cottage. That was when it had all seemed to change. She couldn't quite put her finger on what had actually happened, but her gut feeling was telling her something had and she didn't like it.

She knew she needed a proper conversation with him and it wasn't one she was looking forward to. If settling down wasn't for him then he needed to be truthful with himself and with her.

As Allie walked up Love Heart Lane, she thought back to the morning's conversation. If she was being honest with herself she didn't know exactly how she was feeling about Rory being catapulted into fame. It made her think more deeply about her own life. A TV show was a fantastic opportunity and who knew what it would lead to. It all sounded incredibly exciting and made her begin to question if she was actually happy plodding along. She wondered what the alternative could be for her; perhaps a career away from Heartcross? Had working in the pub just become habit, with her falling into a routine that had just become the norm – the easy option? *Was* there more out there for her?

And if the show became popular, what next for Rory? Would girls be sending him private messages and would he be tempted to answer? Would she just become part of his distant past? Maybe she was running ahead of herself; maybe this was a little bit of fun for him. But she couldn't help feeling anxious. She liked the fact that they'd always been a team and discussed everything together. But she was sorry that Rory had overheard her outburst and she knew he wasn't going to be at all happy.

Allie pressed her lips tightly together as she pushed open the gate and rapped lightly on Rory's front door. She didn't wait for him to answer but turned the handle and did what she always did, let herself in, trying to keep everything as normal as possible. Rory was sitting on the floor in the living room surrounded by cardboard boxes. He was carefully wrapping the framed photos from the sideboard in tissue and stacking them in a box.

'Oh, it's you.' He barely looked up and carried on what he was doing.

'I'm sorry,' she said softly, though she knew it was going to take more than an apology to put this right.

Rory didn't look up.

'You okay?' She perched on the arm of the chair.

'Fine.'

There was that word, 'fine'. People only used the word 'fine' when they were not fine. Allie could see Rory was far from fine. He wouldn't even make eye contact with her.

She acknowledged to herself that it was stupid to think she was going to walk in here, apologise and they'd skip off to the pub for Sunday lunch. 'I didn't mean to upset you,' she said, touching his arm, but Rory carried on what he was doing,

'Will you stop what you are doing? We need to talk about this.' Allie's tone was firm.

Immediately Rory stopped what he was doing then carried on again.

'Rory! Now who's being ridiculous? Honestly, it's like dealing with a child sometimes,' she said, frustrated.

Rory turned towards her and frowned hard, 'How do you expect me to act?' His voice was unusually sharp. 'How do you think I felt sitting there, surrounded by our friends, as you said those things? Can you imagine what Zach thought? It was embarrassing, Allie!'

'And I am sorry, but put yourself in my shoes for just a minute, Rory. You announced your new TV show without even mentioning it to me! Everything seems to be changing. I feel like I'm losing you.' Allie took a deep sigh before continuing. 'At Clover Cottage, you actually made me feel like I wasn't good enough for you. That being a barmaid wasn't a fulfilling enough job. But isn't that my choice? And then you tell me that setting up home together is all too much for you, all too soon. How do you expect me to feel? You storm off and before I know it you've made a new life for yourself, TV shows, book deals or whatever, and all these plans don't appear to include me.' Allie's voice wobbled, and she knew she was on the verge of tears.

Rory raked his hand through his hair and finally stopped what he was doing. He sat on the edge of the coffee table and faced her.

Allie took a moment and swallowed. 'What if you do end up being the next Zach Hudson?' The second the words left Allie's mouth she knew they sounded lame.

'And what if I do? Why exactly would that be a problem? For one thing, what opportunities would that provide for both of us? Not to mention the financial security.'

Taking a step back and processing her thoughts, Allie realised that Rory's words actually sounded quite rational.

What if he did become successful? What was wrong with that? Why wouldn't she be happy for him?

'There's more to life than just work, Allie. And getting married and having babies will come for us.' Rory's words cut through the air. 'But why can't we live a little first? Enjoy being us? There's plenty of time for us to do everything else.'

Allie looked at him. Hearing Rory talk like this was a shock to the system but she was beginning to really listen to what he was saying.

Maybe he did actually have a point. Was she hellbent on setting up home and having a family because that was what was expected of her and her duty to her parents, or was it because of her own insecurities? Allie knew since they'd found their home in Heartcross she'd felt settled and compelled to do anything she could to make her parents stay. She'd always carried the fear that her parents might up sticks again one day and they'd be back on the road, looking for a new place to call home. Was her desire to create her own family just a way to force her parents to finally put down roots?

They stared at each other.

'But I thought you wanted the happy-ever-after? They were your words, Rory,' said Allie, trying to clarify what Rory was wanting and thinking.

'And I meant it. I still mean it.'

'But ...'

Rory stood up. 'I'll put the kettle on.'

The last thing Allie wanted was a cup of tea. All she wanted was Rory to be honest with her, but her gut feeling was telling her that there was more going on here.

Whilst she waited for him to reappear, she grabbed a handful of tissue paper and began wrapping the next ornament that was on the floor before placing it carefully into the cardboard box.

Rory returned with two mugs in his hands. Allie spoke up the second he walked into the room. 'And why move in with Drew and Isla? I just don't get it.'

Rory exhaled. 'Okay, that wasn't planned. After leaving the cottage Drew and Zach spotted me walking along the lane. They were off to collect Sydney so I went with them. That's when Zach told me all about the TV show. I literally found out about half an hour before you did and of course I was going to come and find you when I got back. Then they asked me what I was doing for the rest of the day, and I said I was packing up the house, and that's when Drew kindly offered me the spare room or one of the vans. That was it, there was nothing sinister about it.'

'But you didn't say no,' said Allie sulkily.

'I know you want me to move into the pub, Allie, but realistically that isn't going to work for me, is it? The pub gets so busy and noisy and sometimes you don't get to bed until the early hours. I can't go operating on animals when I'm exhausted. That's when mistakes happen. When I clock off I just want to chill.' Rory's tone was sincere and he softened for a moment.

Allie acknowledged what he was saying. 'But you can't stay at Isla and Drew's for ever. You need a permanent place to stay. That's where Clover Cottage would be perfect.'

Rory was quiet.

'What aren't you telling me, Rory?' Allie had known him a long time and she knew he was holding something back. 'Just be honest with me. Surely I deserve that at least.'

'You're right,' he finally admitted, taking a deep breath. 'There is something else.'

He reached for his laptop and balanced it on his knee as he sat on the sofa. 'Come and sit here.' He nodded to the space next to him, his tone guarded.

Allie knew there had been something bothering him, but now she felt her heart beginning to race as she waited for him to explain.

After he finished typing on the keyboard he spun the laptop towards her and Allie cast a glance over the screen.

Africa.

There staring back at her was a website with bold headlines, '*We want a future where animals thrive in the wild … join the movement to stop lion farming and hunting.*'

'I don't understand. Why are you showing me this?' Then the penny dropped, and the tingling in her chest and stomach signalled dread. This could only mean one thing. Rory was going to Africa.

'You are leaving me, aren't you?' she said, her heart sinking to a new level.

She realised this was the real reason Rory was suddenly

unsettled and explained why he was so reluctant to commit to Clover Cottage.

'I've supported this cause since university. It's a massive part of who I am, part of the reason I wanted to become a vet. I want to help and make a difference.' Rory was speaking so fast he was tripping over his words. Allie could hear the enthusiasm in his voice as he outlined his dream.

'Last time, it was my parents who kiboshed my plans. They put pressure on me to become a partner in the business straight after uni and I didn't want to let them down. They'd financed my university place, they'd supported everything I did, and it was my dad's dream for me to become a partner. I put them first, Allie – but I'm passionate about this stuff. I want to do this.'

There was a long pause.

'And you think I'm going to stop you?'

Rory swallowed, placed the laptop on the table and turned towards Allie. 'I know you aren't going to be happy about it.'

Allie was on the verge of tears and Rory took her hands in his. Taking a deep breath he explained about Zach's trip to Africa and the work he was going to do out there. 'How lucky am I?'

'Lucky,' Allie repeated solemnly.

'It took me by surprise when he spoke about his next trip, the excitement that stirred in me when he suggested I could tag along in a professional capacity. Allie, he's just confirmed I'll get paid to work alongside him presenting the documentary and I'll get paid for my expertise whilst I'm out there ... It's a win–win situation.'

'And what about the surgery?'

'I'm sure Molly and her team will be able to cover for me but I need to talk to Dad first.'

'It looks like you have it all planned out.'

Rory stayed calm. 'The next twelve months will fly by.'

'Twelve months? You are going for twelve months?' Allie's eyes narrowed in confusion. She gave him a sideways glance while keeping her head still. She couldn't believe what she was hearing.

Feeling a quiver in her stomach she stood up and turned slowly towards the door. She needed to leave, needed time to think, time to get her head around it all.

'Where are you going?' Rory asked with unease. 'Don't go – stay. We need to talk about this.'

Allie held up her hands up in a defensive gesture. 'I just need some fresh air,' she replied, walking towards the living-room door.

As soon as the front door shut behind her Allie took a deep breath. This wasn't what she had been expecting when she woke up this morning. She'd had it all planned out and now she had no clue what the future held. Just like when she was a little girl, feelings of uncertainty rushed to the surface and she didn't like it. As a child, time after time she had left a town, her home, her friends, forced to start again from scratch some place new. But this time she was losing Rory; a year away from him seemed like a lifetime. She felt helpless.

Taking a moment to calm her thumping heart, Allie began walking down Love Heart Lane. She made no attempt to wipe the tears off her cheeks. This was a wakeup call for her. She'd thought everything in her life was hunky-dory and running smoothly. She'd always relied on Rory, trusted him, and now she felt as though her picture-perfect life was crumbling all around her and she couldn't stop any of it.

Five minutes later she found herself back outside Clover Cottage. She had to admit the ramshackle old place had been eye-opening this morning. Now, looking at some of the decaying brickwork, she wasn't even sure if the place was watertight.

Pushing open the back door, she stepped inside again. The kitchen looked like it had never been cleaned in its lifetime. It was difficult to be sure which were damp patches, the walls were generally so grubby, or what colour the worktops were under the layers of grime. She stared at the open fireplace, the large oak beam above littered with ornaments and a burnt-out candle, probably once a focal point of the room. The kitchen was quirky and had character and Allie visualised herself baking cakes or tending to the family meal. Even though this place was run down it had a good feeling about it.

Of course, she knew her wage at the pub didn't set the world on fire, and they would struggle to invest heavily in this place, but wasn't that half the fun? Weekends and spare time working together on the project, ripping off the wallpaper and sanding down floors.

Allie rubbed the dirt from the window to look out over the spectacular scenery and heaved a huge sigh. What the hell was happening? What direction was her life going in? After rolling up her sleeves and turning on the leaky tap she watched the cold water slosh into the bowl in the sink, drowning a cloth that had seen better days. Fighting the musty smell she leant forward and struggled to open the window. Eventually it unjammed and she breathed in the fresh air. Taking a moment she squeezed out the excess water from the cloth then wiped it across the window pane, dirty water dripping on to the sill. All she could think about was Rory.

After the initial shock of his wanting to leave for Africa for twelve months she'd managed to calm herself down. She knew things were on the up for Rory so why wasn't she feeling happy that he wanted to follow his dreams? Because selfishly she knew she would miss him. She loved him and never in a million years had she contemplated this scenario. Maybe she had been taking life and him for granted; maybe she had just been merrily plodding along, taking the steps that were expected of her. She thought about Rory's words regarding what she wanted from life – was working at the pub her burning ambition or was it just an easy route she'd taken? As she scrubbed the windows clean, she began to think more about her own aspirations.

What did she want in life? Undoubtedly she wanted to be a mother and have a family, but was there more for her to achieve before she settled for that? Deep down Allie knew that although she'd defended her position as a barmaid, if she was free to follow her heart without the guilt of letting her parents down, she would never have chosen a career working in the pub. Maybe Rory had a point, and her dreams had been stifled to help out her parents?

Allie thought about her parents' marriage. In the early days her mum hadn't had a career of her own either, and had worked dead-end jobs for pin money. As a family, they had relied heavily on her dad's employment, meaning they moved around a lot so he could find a job with a decent wage. Maybe Allie had become too reliant on her simple life in Heartcross? She didn't want to have to rely on Rory, simply as his wife – that was a position she never wanted to find herself in. Deep down she knew Rory's parents had railroaded him into taking the partnership at the time, but he'd never mentioned anything about Africa since.

As the window gleamed in front of her, Allie knew she needed to face facts. She'd been wearing rose-tinted glasses and now real life had smacked her right between the eyes. Rory had dreams and maybe his plan didn't fit with her ideal, but she loved Rory with all her heart and was determined not to stand in his way, even if that meant letting him go.

Losing count of the number of dirty bowls of water she'd swilled down the sink, she filled it up once more.

She checked the cupboards and discovered some washing-up liquid and a half-empty bottle of disinfectant. Pouring both into the bowl she began to clean down the worktop. She was amazed to discover that it was a pale oak colour, not the dark brown it seemed at first glance.

She was still deep in thought when a bang made her jump and her pulse race.

'Hello, who's there?' she called out, bolder than she felt.

'It's only me.'

Bringing a hand up to her beating heart, Allie smiled at Felicity as she walked through the door. 'You frightened the life out of me. What are you doing here?'

'A little birdy told me you might be in need of a friend,' she said warmly, holding up a flask of tea and a paper bag of delicious pastries.

'That little birdy may just be right,' said Allie thankfully, squeezing out a wobbly smile.

Chapter 9

Allie peeped inside the paper bag then watched as Felicity's eyes scanned the cottage.

'This place looks condemned but my God, it's got potential,' said Felicity, looking out through the now gleaming kitchen window at the rolling hills beyond. 'Amazing view. Imagine waking up to that every morning,' she exclaimed.

'Well, that was my plan.'

'Until Babymonitorgate ... Only you!' chuckled Felicity.

Allie knew Felicity would already know about what had happened that morning – not because Isla was a gossip, far from it, but because all of their friendships were tight, and they looked after each other.

'It's not funny!' said Allie, with a stern face.

'It's fairly funny,' replied Felicity, still laughing.

Allie's face broke into a smile as she rolled her eyes. 'Those monitors are lethal. I could have said anything.'

'You did from what I've heard!'

'Fair point ... It could only happen to me,' she sighed, mortified everyone had heard her ramblings. 'How long have you got now?'

'About an hour,' replied Felicity glancing at her watch. Allie nodded. 'Mum is having Sunday lunch at the pub with Bill. They seem to be getting on very well and Polly is out with Alfie and moving out too.'

'Moving out – really? Is she going back to London?'

Felicity shook her head. 'No, not back to London. I think we've converted her into a country bumpkin. Alfie's managed to get her a job at the council, and she's moving in with him. I'll miss her around the house. We've all got used to her being here. It's funny how she only came for a holiday and never went back, but meeting Alfie rocked her little world. I'm so happy for her.'

'Me too ... but see, even Polly has moved in with Alfie, why can't that be me?'

'Because you don't fancy Alfie?'

'You know what I mean!' replied Allie shaking her head slightly with a slight smile. 'Do you want to have a look around?'

'Of course, I do! I've always wondered what this place was like inside. It's definitely in need of some TLC.'

As they walked from room to room Allie divulged the further developments after the aftermath of Babymonitorgate.

Felicity stopped in her tracks at the bottom of the old rickety staircase. 'TV shows, trips to Africa ... How amazing is that? And all because Zach Hudson rocked up in our small village. It just shows you never know what's around the corner. I bet you are so proud,' she enthused, putting her foot on the bottom stair. 'Is this staircase actually safe?' she asked nervously, looking up to the landing then back at Allie. Then she narrowed her eyes. 'I know that look. You don't think it's amazing, do you?'

'Would it be terrible of me if I said I think it's amazing, but it makes me feel nervous?'

'Nervous?'

'Twelve months is such a long time, Flick. What if it's out of sight, out of mind ...? Am I sounding needy and insecure?' Allie looked sullen.

'It will fly by! And he'll be back before you know it,' Felicity reassured her.

'Or maybe not ... Who knows what all these opportunities will lead to? Look at Zach – he travels all over the world and barely ever goes home. Of course I want Rory to go and fulfil his dreams. I want him to be happy. But where does that leave us? I love this man but—'

'But what?' interrupted Felicity.

'But it's making me think about my own self-worth. When was the last time I did something for myself? Put me first? Maybe I've be relying on him too much, taking everything for granted.'

'You believe in your relationship, don't you?' probed Felicity, climbing the rickety staircase.

'Of course, but sometimes things happen, and you have no control over it. I mean, look at this place.'

'I'm looking.' Felicity had lost count of the number of cobwebs she'd seen but despite its current state she could definitely see the potential. 'It is a fabulous little place.'

'So why can't Rory see that?' Allie sighed.

'Of course he can see it, he's not an idiot.'

'So why doesn't he want to do anything about it? He's not even shown any enthusiasm; there's absolutely no commitment from him about our future ... zilch.' Allie could feel the tears filling her eyes. Once more those old feelings of uncertainty swirled in the pit of her stomach, making her feel slightly nauseous. 'He's never asked me to move in with him or even hinted about marriage, and yet everyone is always saying how we are destined to be together, even you.'

'And I'm in no doubt that you are destined to be together.' Felicity opened the bathroom door and stared. 'But it's all about timing, Allie. Sometimes people just can't be rushed, they get there in their own time, and you never know – Rory may be scared to ask anyone again. You never know what anyone is feeling. He was hurt when his last girlfriend left him. Maybe he's frightened to make that commitment in case it happens again. You just never know. And stop and think about it for a second – what is the rush? This place isn't going anywhere.' Felicity wrinkled her nose, peered into the bath then shuddered. 'I'm not sure I'd climb in there any time soon.'

Allie peered over her shoulder. 'All this does need modernising.'

'And think about it rationally, what difference does a year make if Rory gets it out of his system then decides he's ready to settle down? There's nothing worse than having regrets.' Felicity carried on towards the next room and pushed open the door. 'Excellent nursery,' she said, staring around the room then through the window at the view.

Allie's shoulders slumped. 'They were my words exactly. You are meant to be cheering me up.' She lifted her gaze towards Felicity. 'Why am I feeling like this?'

'Because Rory's thoughts have totally taken you by surprise. Of course, it's a shock to think you aren't going to see him for a year, but we do have those things that fly in the sky, you know. Save up, have a holiday and go and see him. Experience what he's going to experience for yourself. I'd be planning my trip already.'

Allie mulled over what Felicity was saying. For the first time she felt an inkling of excitement. She'd never travelled and maybe this was the perfect time for a trip, with Rory waiting at the other end for her.

'Make it about you too. He's going to see amazing things, meet amazing people, and you think the minute he steps on that plane he's going to forget all about you.'

'Something like that.'

'So don't let that happen. You are in charge of your own destiny.'

'That's exactly what Martha said!'

'Ha! If Martha could predict the future, we would all be betting on that winning lottery ticket.'

'But,' Allie interrupted, 'she was spot on.'

'For the love of God ... She said to everyone that walked into the tent, including me, "You are in charge of your own destiny." Come on, Allie, you're the headstrong one out of the three of us so don't let Martha's words play on your mind. Just go and talk it over with Rory. He wants a partner who encourages him, supports him to be the best he can – just like you deserve the same from him. It's his time now, and if that means twelve months away then you have to try and embrace it. Or face the fact that you might push him away.'

Feeling subdued, Allie replied, 'I know you're right.'

'I'm always right. It annoys Fergus terribly,' she said with a laugh. 'But if life was all plain sailing it would be a boring existence.'

'It would that,' said Allie, hitching a slight smile on her face.

'And this TV show is a fantastic opportunity for both of you! Get involved, stand by his side and make sure it's known he's already taken. It's simple. Treat it as a bit of fun. I expect that's what Rory is thinking.'

Allie was grateful Felicity's words were sinking in. Sometimes all that was needed was for someone else to spell it out clearly.

'And about this place. You both need to want the same things at the same time for it to work. If you push him too hard and he doesn't want to be pushed, you will end up on the losing side.'

Felicity's words struck a chord.

'Right, now, after you've shown me around those outbuildings and we've devoured those delicious pastries I've brought, get yourself back over to his and talk it over with him. And I'll see you in the pub in around an hour.'

'Thank you,' said Allie, giving her friend a quick hug. 'I will do just that.'

Half an hour later Allie left Felicity taking the path towards the pub whilst she sauntered back towards Rory's house.

She hoped she hadn't upset him too much by walking out earlier but it was hard to keep her feelings in check after the possibility of losing him for a year.

Soon enough his whitewashed terrace house was in view. Just as she was about to knock on the door, she recognised Zach's voice filtering out through the open window. Taking a peep through the window she saw Rory and Zach staring at the laptop in front of them.

Zach was pointing to the screen and Rory was smiling.

'It's all coming together,' exclaimed Zach.

'It all sounds great,' came Rory's reply. They were buzzing, full of energy.

Allie felt herself being left out once more, and, needing to get her feelings under control, she made tracks back to the pub. There was no point descending on Rory now.

They needed to talk but with Zach there it wasn't the right time. With the pub in sight she didn't have much choice except to paint a smile on her face, but once her shift was over she would go and put things right with Rory and make up for her earlier crabbiness.

Chapter 10

Allie managed to slip through the back door without being noticed. She couldn't face a barrage of questions from her parents about Clover Cottage. Reaching her bedroom she closed the door quietly and tentatively stared at her face before climbing into the shower. Tilting her head upwards she let the warm water run over her body. Everything was very much playing on her mind.

Had she relied on Rory too much? Had she fallen into a routine when actually there was more out there in the big wide world for her to discover?

She thought back to early childhood, a maelstrom of memories flooding her mind. Life had been a struggle for her parents, especially in the early days when they'd barely had the money to muddle through. She couldn't remember ever going on holiday with them or spending any quality time with them; they always seemed to be working. Her mum took any jobs she could to make ends meet, and she remembered at one point her dad had moved away from them for six months, taking a job at the other end of the country to earn a higher wage, leaving her and her mum alone in a tiny one-bedroom apartment.

Even though Allie had great respect for her parents' work ethic, she knew one thing about her future that would be different: when the time came to have children she didn't want them to be moved from pillar to post; she wanted a stable home for them right from the start. This is where she'd thought Clover Cottage would be perfect in every sense, but she knew the cost of making it their own could escalate to a huge pot of money and she'd barely saved anything from her wages at the pub. She didn't want to just rely on Rory to be the provider. She was beginning to realise she too would have to take some responsibility. She couldn't leave it all to Rory; it was all about being a team, and maybe it was time she thought about searching for a better job, so that she could contribute equally.

Ten minutes later, wearing a strappy sundress and comfy ballet shoes, Allie put the finishing touches to her make-up and wandered downstairs. Her mind was still very much on Rory.

She did her best to look happy and breathe normally as she walked into the busy dining area of the pub, where there were already lots of familiar faces – that was the way it was in Heartcross. Rona, Bill and Martha were nearby chatting amongst themselves whilst Alfie and Polly were tucking into a hearty roast dinner prepared by her mum.

Allie walked over towards them and placed her hand

on Polly's back. 'I believe congratulations are in order. You pair are moving in together, I hear?'

Alfie's beam was wide, and he looked like the cat that had got the cream.

Polly smiled. 'Yes! Thank you. I only came here on a whim and now look, I've met the man of my dreams. It all happens for a reason.'

'And a new job too!' added Allie.

'Yes, thanks to this one,' said Polly, grinning across the table at Alfie.

The pair of them were still in the first throes of their relationship, and you could see how happy they were – the way they still held hands, the way they finished each other's sentences, and that special glint in their eyes. Anyone could see they were besotted with each other.

'And huge congratulations to Rory,' trilled Polly. 'How fantastic! A TV superstar. You must be so proud. Wait until you're walking down that red carpet on his arm. You must suggest to your mum and dad to put it on the TV in here when it's aired so we can all watch it together.'

Allie was taken aback for a second. It seemed Rory's news was spreading fast around the village. 'What a marvellous idea,' she replied, smiling at Polly.

Returning to the bar she felt a tear crowd her eye and took a deep breath. The shift would soon be over and she could go and sort things out with Rory. Hopefully she would be kept busy so she wouldn't have time to dwell on things too much. After tying her apron around her waist and scribbling on her notepad to check her pen was working she caught her mum's eye. Both of her parents were standing in front of her, strangely beaming away.

'What's the matter? What are you looking at me like that for?' Allie asked, bewildered.

Meredith dug Fraser lightly in the ribs. 'We do have a clever girl on our hands.'

'You are beginning to worry me now,' said Allie, in a low whisper, still confused and feeling a little uncomfortable. 'Tell me.'

'We've had a phone call ... well, you've had a phone call.' The excitement was written all over Meredith's face.

Fraser bent down and retrieved a copy of a newspaper from behind the bar. 'As soon as the call came, your mum was straight over to Hamish's to buy a copy. Well, more than a copy – we bought the lot!'

Allie was mystified as she took the newspaper from her dad's hand. 'The Scottish *Daily Mail* – why have you bought so many copies?' Allie laid the paper down on the bar.

'Turn to page four. Go on,' her mum urged.

Allie flicked to page four and her jaw fell somewhere below her knees. 'That's – that's my photograph.'

Allie stared at the article, which was a write-up about Rory saving Sydney's life. Next to it was the photograph she'd taken of Rory, Zach and Sydney at the summer fair.

'Photo credit to Allie Macdonald,' Allie read out loud, excited at seeing her photo in the national press.

'In the national paper! We are so proud of you,' said Meredith, giving her daughter a suffocating hug.

'What did you say about a call? I'm sure you said something about a call?'

Meredith nodded. 'Here, I've written it down,' she said, scrabbling for a piece of paper at the side of the till. 'You need to call Caitlin Macleod on this number.'

'Who's Caitlin Macleod?' asked Allie, taking the slip of paper from her mum's hand.

'The editor of the newspaper. She was adamant you phone her back.'

'On a Sunday?'

'Yes! On a Sunday,' said Meredith nodding and grinning broadly. 'Now go and ring,' she said, gently pushing her daughter back towards the living quarters of the pub.

As she clutched the piece of paper, Allie's emotions were all over the place. Why would Caitlin Macleod from a national paper want to speak with her?

Allie perched on the bottom stair and stared at the number. With a shaky hand, she dialled, and her heart felt like it was going to jump out of her chest at any second as soon as the call connected.

'Can I speak with Caitlin Macleod, please?' she asked, suddenly feeling nervous.

'Who's calling, please?'

'It's Allie Macdonald. I'm returning your call.'

'Allie! I'm so glad you got back to me. Can I just say what a fantastic photo of Zach Hudson and Rory Scott you took! The second we uploaded the photograph along-side the article the views online were off the scale. It's the most viewed photograph so far this year, which I know may be down to Zach's following, but you've caught the moment perfectly; you have a talent.' Caitlin was friendly and put Allie at ease immediately.

Allie was dumbfounded, the words 'the most viewed photograph online' whizzing around her head.

'I don't know what to say.' Allie still couldn't take it in.

'We see that you are working freelance for your local paper and I hope you don't mind but we gave them a ring. Their praise for you is utterly outstanding and we've been viewing your work all morning.'

Allie couldn't believe what she was hearing. They had been viewing her work all morning ... on a Sunday?

'Anyway, you're probably wondering why the call at the weekend, so I'll cut to the chase. We would like to offer you an interview.'

'An interview?'

'Yes! We have a six-month vacancy for a photographer, to cover maternity leave.'

Allie couldn't believe her ears. This was extraordinary. It was turning into a day of extreme highs and lows. It was exhilarating, a chance for her to become a photographer working on a national paper. What an opportunity!

Her thoughts tumbled quickly over each other. It was a chance of a lifetime, but what about her parents? They needed her to help out in the pub, and she couldn't let them down.

More often than not Allie took over the early morning starts so her parents could rest after the continuous late nights, and they weren't getting any younger. She didn't want to see them struggling ... and then there was Rory too. But this wasn't just any old newspaper, this was a national newspaper, the Scottish *Daily Mail* offering her an interview. Wow! Thousands of copies were in circulation every day.

'Caitlin, I don't know what to say! Can I just ask, out of curiosity, where did you get my photo from?' asked Allie, intrigued how they'd stumbled across it in the first place.

'Rory Scott emailed it to us alongside the article about Zach Hudson from your local newspaper,' Caitlin confirmed.

After bringing the conversation to a close, Allie still couldn't get her head around Caitlin's offer. The job was full-time for six months, working alongside a particular journalist that Caitlin spoke very highly of. They would be a team, covering all the national headlines. As Allie stood up, she bit down on her smile. Could she actually do this? She wanted to scream from the rooftops that a national paper wanted her photographs. The adrenalin was pumping inside her and she knew her mum and dad would be eagerly waiting on the other side of the door to find out what the call was all about.

Allie had mixed emotions. Obviously an interview didn't guarantee her the position, but Caitlin had spoken very highly of her work. But she still felt a sense of duty towards her parents. She knew how hard both of them worked and how would they feel if she left them in lurch.

'Stop over-thinking it, you haven't even got the job yet. It's only an interview,' she muttered to herself, but she knew this was a fantastic opportunity. She had always had a passion for photography, but for that passion to actually become her job? But that wasn't all: the headquarters of the newspaper were in Glasgow, and taking the job would mean moving, as she couldn't commute the three-hour journey every day; she'd have to relocate for six months. Moving away from Heartcross, if only for a short time, made her feel anxious. She thought back to the moving around she'd done as a child: how it had affected her self-esteem and confidence and how she couldn't imagine not seeing her friends and family on a daily basis.

Allie felt excited, terrified and simply confused.

Only a few hours earlier she'd been convinced her destiny was to build her forever home with Rory at Clover Cottage – until he'd shared his dreams of Africa with her. And now, suddenly, she wasn't so sure. If he was travelling halfway across the world for over twelve months, could she actually take the job – if she was successful at the interview – and follow her own new path? Not only would she gain valuable experience, but the extra money would come in very handy too.

Allie had watched the majority of her friends go off to university but at the time she'd had no desire to do the same. Now this new opportunity had given her food for thought. Surely, if they'd gone out of their way to headhunt her, they must really think she was up to the job?

Walking back into the pub she noticed her mum ferrying plates of scrumptious-looking roast beef towards a table on the far side of the room. Allie snuck back behind the bar and looked over the orders before heading towards the kitchen to bring out the rest of the meals, the interview with Caitlin still very much on her mind.

'Not so fast, young lady.' Fraser stood in front of his daughter. 'Meredith, Allie's finished on the phone,' he called out, beckoning his wife over. She hurried towards them, her gaze firmly fixed on Allie.

'Well – what did she want?'

Allie sucked in a breath. 'You are not going to believe this.'

Meredith narrowed her eyes. 'What is it?' she asked grabbing her daughter's arm. 'I can see it's good news.'

'They've offered me an interview for a job on the paper,' said Allie beaming with pride. 'A six-month position to cover maternity leave.'

'That is brilliant, absolutely brilliant!' Meredith kissed her on both cheeks. 'You clever girl.'

'Mum, get off me! You're showing me up; I'm not twelve,' she exclaimed, wiping her cheeks, but Meredith didn't care about Allie's embarrassment.

'I knew it, I knew it!' she said, slapping Fraser on his chest. 'Our lass is destined for better things. An interview!

And if they've rung you on a Sunday, they must want you – it's in the bag!'

'It's just an interview and they will be interviewing other people; it won't be just me.'

But Meredith wasn't listening. She'd already turned and clapped her hands loudly. Every head in the pub looked over in their direction.

'Mum! What are you doing? It's only an interview and—' But before Allie could finish her sentence Meredith had everyone's attention.

'Our Allie has an interview for this national newspaper!' Meredith waved the paper in the air.

There were nods and mumblings of congratulations all around the pub, followed by cheers. Felicity was up out of her seat and heading towards her friend. 'Oh my God, what's all this? An interview? What did we say only this morning? You never know what's around the corner. This is fantastic news,' she said, flinging her arms around Allie.

'Will everyone just calm down and remember it's only an interview?'

'When is it?' asked Meredith, wanting to know everything. 'And good pay, I expect.'

'I've no idea. They are ringing me next week to confirm all the details, but the job isn't freelance – I will have to live in Glasgow for six months. And if they offer me the position, I can't just up and leave.'

'Why not?' asked Meredith. 'Of course you can. What's stopping you?'

'Because I have my job here, working with you and Dad ... and there's Rory and my friends,' Allie said, despondently.

'Don't be daft, you can't stay just for us,' answered Meredith, frowning. 'Allie, you have to follow your heart.'

'Timing is everything, and this timing couldn't be more perfect!' said Felicity, giving Allie a knowing look. 'And you'd be brilliant.'

Allie didn't know whether to feel upset that everyone seemed to be trying to get rid of her at the drop of a hat or chuffed that they believed in her ability so much.

'I can't believe they think I'm even worthy.'

'Worthy? Of course you're worthy! Surely you're going to give it some serious thought?' urged Felicity. 'Glasgow! What I'd give for six months of shopping and fantastic nightlife.'

With all the commotion Allie hadn't noticed Rory walk into the pub.

'Glasgow? Who's going to Glasgow?' asked Rory.

Allie spun round. Rory had changed from his morning attire and was wearing black jeans and her favourite pale grey shirt with the sleeves rolled up. He was looking directly at her, waiting for an answer. Zach, standing by his side, looked just as intrigued.

'Allie's had some fantastic news. Go on, tell him,' urged Meredith. 'She's been offered an interview for a job on a national newspaper,' Meredith finished, too excited to wait for Allie to fill in the gaps.

'Mum! A little privacy wouldn't go amiss.' Allie raised her eyebrows. 'It's my news.'

'Okay, okay, I'm sorry, we'll leave you to talk, and well done you on your new TV fame,' said Meredith, still brimming with pride. She touched Rory's arm lightly before kissing Allie once more on the cheek and retrieving the empty glasses from a nearby table.

Rory's expression was earnest. 'Really? A national newspaper? This is amazing. Come here,' he said, throwing his arms around her and giving her a heartfelt hug.

Allie felt guilty. Rory seemed genuinely pleased for her, and yet when he'd told her his good news all she could think about was how it affected her. 'It's just an interview – and it appears I need to thank you for that.'

'Me?' asked Rory perplexed, resting his keys and wallet on the bar. 'Why me?'

'You sent a copy of the local article to the Scottish *Daily Mail* and they uploaded my photograph of you and Zach – it's had a staggering amount of hits, apparently.'

Rory was taken aback. 'Brilliant! And they've offered you an interview for a job?'

'Six months working as a photographer in Glasgow.'

Rory let out a low whistle. 'My girlfriend, the famous photographer.'

'I wouldn't go that far,' said Allie, taking a newspaper from the pile stacked on the bar and opening it.

'Wow! Doesn't that look good?' Rory took the paper from Allie's hand then twisted it towards Zach, who agreed.

'Apparently it's the most viewed photograph this year online, which led to the editor checking out my other work with the local paper.'

Rory's mouth hitched into a huge smile and he immediately put the newspaper down on the bar while not letting go of her gaze. He thrust out his arms, unexpectedly swooped her off her feet and spun her round. Once her feet were firmly back on the ground, he took her face in his hands and kissed her.

'I'm proud of you, Allie. I really am,' he said pulling away. 'It's amazing. I told you this one was destined for great things.' He beamed as he turned towards Zach.

'He did too,' answered Zach, leaning across the bar and ordering two pints from Fraser, who was still smiling like a Cheshire cat.

'It's only an interview and it may be great, but everyone seems to be forgetting the job is based in Glasgow and I live here.' Allie knew she was testing the water, but she wanted to see some sort of reaction from Rory that if she was successful he would miss her ... but nothing.

'Six months in Glasgow will fly by, and you'll be working alongside other journalists, having your photographs splashed all over the national press. Heartcross is going nowhere. This is what you are about, Allie – photography. A national paper has recognised your talent, the ability to take the best photos. Who knows what this might lead to? It's just fantastic.'

'You're talking as though I've already got the job. I've

not even decided whether I'm going for the interview yet.'

Rory looked astounded, 'Why would you even contemplate not going for the interview? What have you got to lose?'

'That's exactly what we think,' chipped in Fraser from across the bar whilst handing over Zach's change.

Allie's mood slumped a little. It felt like everyone was overlooking the fact this job opportunity meant she would have to move three hours away. It seemed no one was going to miss her at all.

'It sounds like you are trying to get rid of me. In fact it sounds like everyone is trying to get rid of me.' Allie's voice faltered. 'Is no one going to miss me?'

'Don't be daft, of course everyone is going to miss you, but it's six months and only three hours away. Look at Zach, you make it work, don't you? And he travels all over the world,' added Rory.

'But that's different,' argued Allie, not letting Zach answer. 'My guess is Zach can be flown home at the drop of a hat by a private jet whilst I'd be sitting night after night in a hotel room all by myself, not knowing a soul.'

'Sounds like bliss to me,' cut in Meredith, passing with a handful of steaming hot dinners.

'Allie.' Rory took her by the hand and sat her down on a bar stool. 'Surely you are going to go for the interview? This could be the making of you. Step out of your comfort zone and grasp the opportunity with both hands. Do something amazing for you.'

Allie looked into his eyes.

'It's not for ever and what's the worst that can happen? If you really don't like it, you can just come home. You are stronger than you think. And I'm sure Fraser won't have rented your room out.' Rory tipped a wink at Fraser, who chuckled.

'I'm drafting the advert right this second,' he replied, grinning at his daughter.

'Dad!'

'You have to go, Allie. It's a national paper, a great wage, living in the city. Get your name out there.' Rory's huge brown eyes were clear as he willed her to attend the interview and give it everything she had.

And even though Allie was in turmoil she felt excited, too. She was used to the safety of living in Heartcross, but on the other hand why shouldn't she have a piece of the big wide world? But it would mean losing her support mechanism, the one thing that was constant in her life, and Rory. But with him going to Africa wouldn't this happen anyway? She was used to him being there by her side, holding her hand, but this time she would be all by herself. Could she actually do it?

Rory was always going to carve out a successful career for himself. A partner in a practice, he didn't even have to leave the village to be handed his own TV show. Maybe this was her chance to become more of an equal partner in their relationship, to hold her own and be successful in her own right.

'You make it sound so tempting, but I think you are all forgetting I'm a country girl at heart.' Allie turned towards Felicity, who was still standing by her side, 'Even you struggled in the city, Flick, and look, Polly's escaped from the big smoke too.'

'But this is different,' said Felicity.

Allie thought Felicity would understand how she was feeling, but it looked like even she was willing her to go.

'You have nothing to lose by just going for the interview. Then make your mind up. It's simple,' continued Felicity.

'And I second that. I think you'd be mad not to go,' chipped in Rory.

'And I third it,' added Zach.

'And we fourth it,' continued Fraser.

Allie suddenly felt overwhelmed. 'Right,' she said, taking control, 'who knows what will happen? All I know is I need to get back to work as this is my actual job at the moment and people are going to go hungry.' She jumped down from the bar stool.

Just as Allie was about to turn away, Rory touched her arm lightly. 'But we do need to talk,' he whispered.

Allie stopped in her tracks, knowing she couldn't put off this conversation for much longer. She took a deep breath to mask her nervous laughter. 'Go on.'

'I've got more details about Africa. Allie, we can talk later if you like? In private?'

Allie nodded. Since talking to Felicity she'd been

mentally preparing for this conversation, but still wasn't quite ready.

'Great. Can we grab a couple of roast dinners from you? Zach is going to run me through the schedule for tomorrow. The film crew are arriving by 6am – is that what you said, Zach?'

'Yes, bright and early,' Zach confirmed.

Allie scribbled down their orders and immediately disappeared through to the kitchen. Securing an interview for a national newspaper should be one of her happiest moments, but she felt far from happy, and had no wish to shout the news from the rooftops. Rory was being the perfect boyfriend, supporting and encouraging her to go for the interview, and she should be doing the same for him, but she knew she was going to miss him terribly.

Armed with two roast dinners Allie stopped by the kitchen door. She looked around the pub, the place that was her home, the place she'd come to love. There was the welcoming chatter of her friends and family sitting around enjoying their Sunday afternoon together. This place was such a comfort; she wasn't sure if she wanted to leave, even if only for six months. But she could see Felicity and Rory's point of view: what would be the harm in attending the interview?

Chapter 11

Beep … beep …

After a sleepless night Allie's spirits took a nosedive as the alarm clock sounded. *Surely it couldn't be time to get up just yet?* she thought, smacking the alarm and pulling the duvet back firmly over her head. She'd finally fallen asleep just after 4am and now it was quarter past six. She was shattered; every muscle in her body ached, not to mention the soles of her feet. The pub had been busy almost up until closing time, and everyone in the village seemed excited about Rory and Zach's big day today. The buzz around the pub last night had brought both men a lot of attention, and Allie had spent the whole night forcing a smile. This morning it felt like her face muscles had participated in some mad extreme sport for hours on end.

Hearing a quiet rap on the door she reluctantly pushed back the duvet and sat up in bed.

'Yes,' she answered wearily, wishing she could have sloped back off to sleep.

'I've brought you a cup of tea,' said Meredith, placing the mug on the bedside cabinet.

'Thanks. You're up early. I thought I was doing the early shift today?'

'We're expecting another full day with the film crew arriving, and the kitchen is going to be busy. I just need to make sure everything is prepped and ready to go. Apparently word has got out exactly where Zach Hudson has been staying, which has caused a few problems up at Foxglove Farm.'

'Why, what's happened?' asked Allie propping her pillow behind her and clasping the warm mug of tea close to her.

'Apparently busloads of Zach's fans arrived in the village late last night and descended on the farm, all wanting to get a glimpse of him.'

'They'll be disappointed then – he stayed at Rory's last night.'

'Thankfully, he did. But Isla and Drew had to call in the police to remove some of the more crazed fans.'

'It was that bad? You wouldn't think one person could cause so much chaos,' said Allie, taking a sip of her tea and wondering if this would become the norm for Rory too.

'And that's not all. Your dad has already been out walking Nell and reported the surgery has metal fencing erected all around it to stop fans from trampling all over Stuart's front garden. We all know how seriously he takes his gardening.' Meredith gave her daughter a knowing look. 'So with all this palaver going on I'm just making sure we have extra provisions in the fridge. No doubt the teashop will be run off its feet too. Chaos has descended once more on our little village,' she exclaimed in a dramatic tone.

'I'm here to help all day so we should be fine.'

'Here? Why aren't you at the surgery? Surely you want to be in on the act?'

Allie shrugged. Rory hadn't even invited her along to the filming, he'd been so wrapped up with Zach last night.

'I don't want to get in the way.'

Meredith looked at her daughter and perched on the end of the bed. 'Why would you be in the way?'

Allie shrugged again.

'Come on, what's the matter?' Meredith's tone was gentle.

Allie blew out a breath and placed her mug back on the bedside cabinet. 'Rory's thinking of leaving for Africa.'

'Rory's leaving for Africa?' Meredith gave her daughter an inquisitive stare. 'What are you talking about?'

Allie explained all about the charity Rory had supported since university and the fact that it was still something he was passionate about.

'Zach has offered him a fantastic opportunity, which I know he would be mad not to take up, but it's for twelve months.'

'Twelve months,' repeated Meredith, now realising why Allie was so subdued. 'And I'm assuming you aren't feeling too happy about it?'

'Yes ... no ... I don't know. I'm scared, Mum. I'm scared it's going to catapult us both in different directions.'

Meredith paused before she spoke next, knowing exactly how her daughter was feeling, 'Look at me and your dad. All those years ago, before we settled here, your dad had to take a job at the other end of the country and we were separated for a short time because we were locked into the contract on the place we rented. Your dad bunked in with a mate whilst I felt like a single mother. It was hard being apart for over six months, but it's all about trust and believing in your relationship.'

Allie nodded. She knew exactly what her mum was saying and that things had been tough for them, but they were the strongest couple she knew.

'It just feels like everything is changing fast.'

'It can feel that way at times, but that's life, Allie. So strap yourself in and embrace the ride and look for the positives.'

Meredith knew that moving around and dragging Allie from pillar to post in her early childhood had caused her anxieties. She hadn't been a confident child and her self-esteem had taken a hit because of the constant moving of school and the pressure of making new friends.

But since working in the pub Allie had grown much stronger. She was self-assured and fun to be around, because she was familiar with the environment and felt comfortable surrounded by people she knew.

'Are you going to go for this interview in Glasgow?' Meredith asked.

Allie finished her tea. She didn't know what to do.

Everyone was willing her to go, to succeed, but the thought of being on her own in a strange city frightened the life out of her.

'I will, but if I'm being honest, I'm nervous, Mum. What if I'm not as confident as the other candidates? What if they have more experience?'

'How are you ever going to feel confident in different situations if you don't experience them first-hand?' challenged Meredith. 'And as far as Rory is concerned, he's a good, genuine guy. Relationships are funny things and as people you grow at different rates. Some people grow apart, but Rory was so supportive of you last night. He wants you to achieve, to accomplish your own dreams and grab this interview with both hands. He was brimming with pride yesterday, anyone could see that. And don't forget the old saying: absence makes the heart grow fonder.'

'I know,' Allie admitted. Her mum was talking some sense.

'And how was the cottage? We didn't even get a chance to chat about that yesterday.'

'That's another thing. Rory just doesn't seem to be excited by it. He's says it's too soon for us,' Allie said, sounding exasperated.

'You know what I've learnt all the way through my married life? Men take a little longer to make decisions; they aren't impulsive like us. When we see something we want it right that very second but men take their time. The key is to let him make the decision in his own time and then you know he knows it's the right decision. Trust me.'

'You sound like you know what you are talking about.' Allie managed a smile.

'I do, I've put up with your dad for many years,' Meredith said with a chuckle. 'Now get yourself showered and over to the surgery, be a part of it all. Support Rory, you might find you enjoy it.'

Allie pulled back the duvet and swung her legs to the ground. 'And what do you really feel about this interview, Mum? You know you'll never manage without me here,' she joked, but she knew she was testing the water and checking how her mum really felt about her moving away if she was successful at the interview. 'Could you really manage without me?' She gave a sly sideways grin at her mum.

'Get yourself to the interview. I'll come with you. I quite fancy a day in the city – cocktails, a little shopping. Do you really see this place as your future?' Meredith sounded forthright. 'Heartcross was mine and your dad's dream. It doesn't have to be yours. You need to do what makes you happy. Don't think about this place or us; put yourself first. We can easily get temporary staff in from the agency.'

'Am I that easily replaceable?' Allie pulled a sulky face.

'I'm not saying I won't miss you, I may even shed a tear or two, but I want the best for you, Allie, and even though you're the best at pulling pints there's a big wide world out there.'

'You sound like Rory now!'

Meredith leant over, took her daughter in her arms and hugged her tight. 'Now make a fresh, positive start to the day, and go and support Rory. We can manage here. What will be will be.'

'Okay,' agreed Allie, thinking that joining Rory for the day would actually be fun. She'd never been on a TV set before.

Almost an hour later, after a quick shower and breakfast, Allie ambled down the high street towards the village green. Once it was in sight, she paused for a second and looked around in pure amazement. Never before at this time in the morning had she seen so many people up walking their dogs. In fact she never knew Heartcross housed so many dogs. She spotted Julia and Jessica up ahead and called out to them both.

'What's going on? Why are the world and their wife walking their dogs at ridiculous o'clock?' she asked as she strolled along next to them. 'I feel like I've stumbled across a secret dog-walking group or something and am a bit miffed I'm not part of the gang,' she joked and Julia giggled. 'And why are you both dressed up to the nines at this time of the morning?' She narrowed her eyes at them both. 'What are you up to?'

'As if she doesn't know, but no doubt you have a front-row seat.'

'A front-row seat to what?'

Julia tilted her head and grinned. 'Look at you playing it all blasé.'

Then the penny dropped, 'Oh my God, you are all off to the surgery. Are all these people off to the surgery?'

'Absolutely!' said Jessica with a grin. 'We all want our fifteen minutes of fame.'

Allie couldn't believe the sight before her: there were people carrying rabbits, cats, guinea pigs … even Fergus was hurrying over to the surgery carrying a chicken – a chicken, for God's sake. There was Finn too, with Mop trotting at his side. As she approached the surgery Allie glanced around at the assembled crowd. Rory was definitely going to be busy today, she thought, amazed by the long queue of people accompanied by their animals already standing outside the surgery.

'All this effort just to get on TV?' said Allie, staring at the white transit van parked behind the metal railings in the grounds of the surgery.

There were people everywhere squashing up against the railings, girls chanting Zach's name – it reminded Allie of being in the middle of a rock concert, and she shook her head in disbelief. All this just to get a glimpse of Zach Hudson. She made her way through the crowd, only to be stopped by a girl she didn't recognise, holding a cage with a blue and yellow budgie inside.

'Hey, missus, you can't go jumping the queue,' the girl said. She was dressed in an outfit that wouldn't have looked out of place in the Eighties with its garish neon colours, and blew out a bubble with her gum.

Allie, taken aback, was just about to apologise when

she spotted Zach through the window. He immediately appeared at the entrance of the surgery looking very handsome in his blue scrubs. Within seconds the girls went wild at the sight of him. The crowd surged forward, screaming, with their arms stretched out wide waving their phones. Allie was knocked to the ground with a bump. Before any expletives could leave her lips, she was yanked to her feet by two burly arms belonging to a security guard, who pulled her through the gates to safety.

'Oh my God, this is Heartcross, not bloody Hollywood,' she muttered, brushing herself down. 'Those people are like animals.'

The screaming was unbearable. Allie watched Zach as he saluted the crowd and quickly retreated back to safety behind closed doors.

'I'm so sorry,' he said, 'are you okay?'

'Just about. If this is what it's like being famous you can give me a quiet life any day.'

'Sometimes it gets a little out of hand; people forget their manners,' he said, rolling his eyes while placing a lanyard around Allie's neck.

'What's this for?' asked Allie looking down and suddenly feeling a sense of importance.

'This is to say you are not an imposter or a crazed fan who's managed to outwit burly Carlton here and gained access to the set.'

Allie looked in Carlton's direction. He had muscles upon muscles; in fact she'd never seen muscles quite like it.

'Thank you for rescuing me,' she said, still staring at his arms then dropped her gaze to his chest. There was no denying he fitted that shirt well, very well indeed. The hours he must have put in to build a body like that.

Carlton was a man of few words. He nodded his appreciation and took his place standing by the entrance of the surgery. There was no one without a lanyard getting past him.

'How's it all going here?' asked Allie, averting her gaze to Zach.

'Mmm,' answered Zach.

'Oh no, what's that meant to mean?'

'Are you ready for your TV debut?'

'Who – me?' asked Allie, shocked, placing a hand on her chest. Her plan today had been to remain totally in the background.

But before Zach could answer, Rory appeared in the doorway. 'Thank God you're here. Do you never answer your phone?'

Allie delved into her pocket and pulled out her phone. Eight missed calls. 'Sorry, it was on silent. What's up?'

Rory began a long-winded explanation about how his mum was being difficult and couldn't go ahead playing the role of the receptionist. 'Honestly,' he said, 'all she has to do is pick up the phone and pretend she's talking to me then tell the customer to come in. It's simple.'

'What's your plan now?'

All eyes were on Allie. 'Whoa! You want me as the receptionist?'

'Yes! You'll be perfect.' Rory was looking directly as her. 'Who better to step in than you? They want to film real people and to see what makes Heartcross so unique and you'll be just the best,' he insisted, immediately handing Allie a white coat without giving her the chance to back out.

'So what have I got to do?' asked Allie, trying the coat on. It was a perfect fit.

'See, that coat was made for you. All you have to do is pretend you are on *The Apprentice*,' said Rory, pinning a name badge on to her lapel and straightening the shoulders.

'Eh?' replied Allie.

'You know, act like the receptionist on *The Apprentice* when all the contestants are sitting outside the boardroom and he rings through and she says, "Alan Sugar will see you now."'

'"Rory Scott will see you now!"' practised Allie in her best telephone voice. 'I can manage that.' She chuckled.

Rory put both his hands on her shoulders and kissed her. 'You are an absolute lifesaver. I knew I could count on you.'

Allie felt warm and content inside. Even though she knew there was still an obstacle between them and a conversation they still needed to have, she would always be there for Rory.

'Looking at the queue outside, it would seem everyone wants to get in on the act today.' Allie nodded towards the window.

The queue was so long now that it disappeared round the bend at the bottom of the road.

'Where have all these people come from?' Rory asked in alarm. 'I'm never going to get through them all in a day.'

Allie could tell he was beginning to panic slightly, his nerves obviously beginning to get the better of him.

'Oh my God, surely all those animals can't be ill?'

'My guess is not,' said Allie, grinning, noticing that Rory suddenly looked petrified. 'Most of these people just want a glimpse of you and Zach, and to have their few seconds of fame on a TV show.'

'I can't do this,' Rory stated. 'I can't do this, Allie.'

'Of course you can,' said Allie, slipping her arms around his waist and pulling him closer for a hug. 'You do this job day in, day out. Just put the film crew to the back of your mind and pretend they aren't there.' She popped a reassuring kiss on his lips. 'You've got this, okay?' Allie said as she took both of his hands in hers and gave them a little squeeze.

'Thank God you're here,' Rory said and gave Allie a heartfelt hug, already seeming a little calmer. His words made Allie's heart leap.

Zach, standing next to them, peered out of the window at the long queue. 'It's always like this with these kinds of shows,' he commented. 'What we do is film a cross section of the public. The production team will actually peruse the crowd, have a chat with different people and see whose personality shines through. Also, they will vary the different types of animals. There's no point having a show full of just dogs. Then they'll edit it to put the best ones into the programme. It's amazing how they cut a full day of filming down to five slots of thirty minutes' viewing time.'

'So those people who think they are at the front of the queue might not even been seen?' asked Allie.

'Yes, that's right, and that's when Carlton steps in to calm any disgruntled customers,' said Zach, looking down at his phone. 'Sorry, I need to take this call,' he said, silencing his phone before disappearing into the kitchen area.

Allie looked surprised. There were going to be some disappointed customers outside who'd got up at the crack of dawn to try and be the first in that queue.

Hearing dissatisfied mutterings behind her, Allie spun round and smiled. 'Good morning, Stuart.'

It was safe to say by the look on his face he wasn't overly excited about his surgery being taken over by the TV crew. Stuart didn't seem to hear Allie's greeting; either that or he was preoccupied. 'For heaven's sake, you'd think with all this palaver we were expecting a visit from the Queen, not some two-bit TV star filming – what do they call it? – a reality show. He's just like the rest of us, you know, burps and passes wind.'

Rory looked horrified and raised an eyebrow. 'Dad!'

Having finished his call, Zach was standing behind Stuart grinning, thankfully finding Stuart's comments mildly amusing.

'I'm sorry, Zach,' said Rory, trying to smooth the way, but Stuart interrupted.

'Don't you go apologising on my behalf.' He looked over his shoulder. 'I've got a headache with all their kerfuffle.' He nodded towards the main surgery room. 'They've moved all the equipment around.'

'They need to, Dad. The room is small so they need to make space for the film crew.'

But Stuart wasn't listening. 'And those girls out there ... if anyone tramples on my flowers ...' he said, wandering past Carlton and disappearing outside.

'Sincere apologies, Zach. Sometimes Dad doesn't have a filter.'

'That's the best way in this industry – say it how it is. He'd be great on camera, so dry.'

'Right, I'll nip to the bathroom,' said Allie, thinking she hadn't set eyes on Alana this morning. Maybe she'd taken refuge back in the main cottage, away from the chaos of it all. She left Rory and Zach chatting away. Thankfully Rory seemed back to his normal self with her today. There didn't seem to be any tension between them. Maybe Felicity and her mum were right, and she'd just panicked about their future. Of course they could make his trip to Africa work.

'Rory!' shouted Allie from the bathroom.

He quickly appeared at the door. 'You okay?'

'There's no toilet paper.'

'Really? That's strange. I saw Mum with the toilet rolls

about half an hour ago. She was on her way to put them in here to make sure there were enough for the film crew.'

'Well, there's none in here now.'

Rory went to look in the store cupboard behind the desk and Allie followed.

'Any in there?' she asked, looking over his shoulder.

Rory didn't answer; he was too busy wondering why the hell there were two steaks, a carrier bag full of salad and a tub of margarine sitting on the shelf full of cleaning products – obviously his parents' dinner.

'Maybe your mum just put them down in a hurry and forgot about them. I'll nip them over to the cottage and pop them into the fridge,' offered Allie, taking the bag from Rory and sensing his concern.

'Dad said she's been in a funny mood recently, in fact more than a funny mood ... like a difficult mood.'

Allie found this hard to believe because as long as she'd known Alana she'd never found her short-tempered for no real reason; she was one of the most easy-going people she'd ever come across. Always going out of her way and doing whatever she could to help others. This didn't sound like Alana at all.

'Look around you. This is all probably just a little over-whelming for her. There are people everywhere, camera crew, bodyguards. It's enough to freak anyone out.'

'Yes, you're right,' he replied. 'But that still doesn't explain what's happened to the toilet rolls.'

'Looking for these?'

They both spun round to see Zach holding up a packet.

'Where did you find them?' asked Rory, taking them from him.

'Chilling at about three degrees in the surgery fridge. Only looked inside for some milk and there they were, on the top shelf.'

Allie held Rory's eyes for a second, and he raised his eyebrows in return. 'She will just be muddled with all today's chaos. I'll pop them in the bathroom.'

Taking them from Rory, she knew exactly what he was thinking. He had recently mentioned the missed appointments in the diary, emails left unanswered or important ones deleted. Alana had been getting flustered at work and Rory was worried about her.

When Allie returned to the surgery the number of people crammed into one space seemed to have doubled. Emma, the producer, was talking to the rest of the team and Allie watched her with admiration. She was a slim, petite girl with flame-red hair that bounced on her shoulders and a string of freckles across her nose. She was conversing with the director, a short, stocky man called Hugo, who was primarily responsible for overseeing the shooting and the assembly of the programme. And now they were both chatting to Rory and Zach. Allie was grateful her mum had talked her into coming over and was quite excited by the small role she'd acquired. The only thing she wished was that she'd made more of an effort with her hair, as it was sticking up every which way with a mind of its own. Sitting down behind the desk she stretched out her legs – then jumped out of her skin as two big eyes looked up from underneath. 'Sydney! What are you doing under there? You frightened the life out of me!' she exclaimed, leaning down and patting the dog's head. 'I suppose this is just a normal day at the office for you,' she chuckled, feeling relaxed.

Sydney rested her head back on the carpet and stretched out her legs, not at all fazed by the commotion around them. Allie smiled. Taking a leaf out of Sydney's book, she too felt relaxed and not in the slightest bit nervous, which surprised her. Usually in any new situation her anxieties would flare up; she'd be dry-mouthed, nervous and often shy. But today she was feeling relatively relaxed. Maybe it was because Rory was here, or because she was used to the surgery and its surroundings and on the odd occasion had covered for Alana on reception duties when she took a day off. Fiddling with the pen on the desk she glanced at her watch. Surely it was nearly time to begin filming? She heard movement and jumped to attention when Hugo shouted, 'Calling everyone to make-up. Only thirty minutes to go until we start filming.'

Zach and Rory were now standing in front of the desk. 'Come on. I like this bit, the calm before the storm,' said Zach, patting Rory on the back. 'Time to get pampered.'

Rory cocked an eyebrow. 'Is this the part where they make me look stunning? I'm going to have the perfect brows and a pout?' he joked, pressing his lips together and sticking them out.

'Don't ever do that again,' said Allie, standing up and laughing. 'You look ridiculous.'

'To be honest, mate' – Rory looked towards Zach – 'I'm not sure I'm up for this make-up lark, the lads will rip it out of me down the pub.'

'I think that's non-negotiable,' said Allie, looking pointedly at Rory, who looked at Zach.

'Honestly, you just get used to it, there's nothing to worry about.'

The director gestured for Rory and Allie to hurry towards the makeshift tent set up in the back garden. Inside was Kirsten, the make-up artist, holding a blusher brush and a pot of powder.

'Don't worry, I'm not going to make anyone look like a clown, even though I've been tempted with this one numerous times.' She winked at Zach and pulled out a chair for him to sit down. Allie and Rory sat in chairs alongside him and stared at their reflection in the mirrors.

'All I'm going to do is take the shine off your face and enhance your features,' said Kirsten, getting to work on Zach. 'There's nothing to worry about.'

She spent as little as five minutes on him before turning to Rory, but as soon as she started to dab the powder on to his face, he let out an almighty sneeze.

'Sorry, sorry,' he muttered.

'Bless you,' said Allie, suppressing a smile, knowing how

uncomfortable Rory felt. And he looked it, as Kirsten set to work, but within ten minutes they were all fit for purpose and ushered back towards the set. Then Allie noticed his chatter had stopped. He'd suddenly gone quiet and his face had taken on a kind of puce colour. Allie wasn't sure if that was down to the blusher. There was no escaping the fact that Rory looked petrified again.

Overcome with nerves, he blew out a breath and undid the top button of his shirt. He cleared his throat, shook his hands and looked towards Allie.

'I feel sick,' he said.

'Take deep breaths. Once you start and get into it, you'll be fine,' she reassured him. 'Now loosen those shoulders – you look kind of wooden.'

Allie couldn't help smiling as Rory took a huge breath then exhaled. It reminded her of a woman trying to control her breathing whilst in labour.

'Where's Rory?' shouted the director. 'We need him in here.'

'Here we go,' said Zach, patting him on his back.

'Lights ... camera ... action,' said Allie, feeling excited and pressing a swift kiss to Rory's cheek. Even though she could feel him shaking she was enormously proud of him. This was it, Rory's big break. 'Relax and enjoy it, you'll be great,' she reassured him, gently pushing him towards the surgery door. 'You can do this!'

Rory hesitated for a millisecond outside the surgery, took yet another deep breath then disappeared inside.

Chapter 12

Allie sat down behind the desk, where a sound man was hovering beside her with a huge fluffy-looking microphone hanging over her head. He chatted away with the director before turning towards Allie. She was the first one to be filmed and her role was simple: she would welcome the client, take the pet's name and tap away on the computer for a few seconds before picking up the phone and pretending to speak to Rory.

After delivering her line, 'Rory will see you now,' Rory would come out and greet the client before taking them through to the surgery.

Allie could hear the commotion outside as the first selection of TV hopefuls were selected along with their pets. Each one would be filmed walking through the surgery door with their pet. They would be greeted by Allie before being taken through to Rory, who would introduce himself, and then they would explain to Rory what the problem was. All so very simple.

Allie watched, intrigued, as the first five people were

brought into the waiting room. All mobile phones were switched off and they sat on the blue plastic chairs looking like they had won the lottery.

Up first were a mum and daughter holding a cat carrier with a couple of guinea pigs inside. The mum was Sophia and the daughter confidently introduced herself as Paige.

'And the names of your guinea pigs?' asked Allie, smiling sweetly at the little girl.

'Belle and Daisy.'

'Belle and Daisy,' repeated Allie, tapping away on the computer, which of course wasn't switched on. The cameras didn't bother her at all, she didn't trip over her words or feel nervous in the slightest; she was taking it all in her stride and enjoying every minute of it. Once she had pretended to log the details, she asked the clients to take a seat then picked up the phone and rang through to the surgery.

Within seconds, Rory stood in the surgery doorway,

'Sophia and Paige, would you like to bring Belle and Daisy through?'

They followed Rory promptly and the first words Allie heard were Sophia's 'Oh Zach, we are huge fans of yours.'

Allie rolled her eyes; she had a feeling every client was going to go through the same routine.

Rory took the initiative and pulled the conversation back on track. Allie asked one of the production team if she could watch from the doorway, and they agreed as long as she promised not to make any sudden movements or join in the conversation.

Allie was dying to watch Rory in action and leaning against the door frame she smiled. For a split second Rory glanced over but fortunately he was professional and didn't let her presence throw him off track, though she knew he was anxious because his neck was blotchy. His hands were slightly shaking as he opened the cat carrier to pull out the first guinea pig, a plump-looking ginger one with a white furry Mohican, and place it gently on the table in front of him.

'That's Belle,' said Paige proudly.

'Welcome, Belle,' said Rory, like an animated cartoon character and Allie had to do everything in her power not to burst out laughing, as Rory's voice had risen an octave.

Next, he pulled out a shorthaired brown guinea pig. 'And this must be Daisy?'

Paige nodded enthusiastically.

Rory set Daisy down in front of Zach who cupped his hands around the small furry creature. 'What seems to be the problem?' asked Rory, looking towards Sophia.

'She's fat.'

Rory was taken back by her words. 'Most guinea pigs are a little plump.'

Sophia continued, 'These guinea pigs have always been Paige's responsibility. You know what kids are like – they mither and mither for some sort of pet and the second they have to clean out the hutch or wash out the water bottle they can't be seen for dust, but not this one.' Sophia placed her arm around her daughter's shoulder and pulled her in for a hug. 'Every morning without fail, Paige puts them out into the run. For the past couple of months she kept telling me Belle was putting on weight but I just put it down to the lush green grass and overeating. Then yesterday Paige was having a sleepover at her friend's so I got them in from the run, and Paige is right, she has huge lumps – tumours – all over her body. I can feel them.'

Paige burst into floods of tears and began to wail, taking Rory and Zach completely by surprise. They looked at each other in horror before Zach reached for the box of tissues on the shelf behind him and Rory leant forward. 'You've brought her to the best place,' he said in a soft calming tone, trying to keep some sort of order.

'It's cancer, isn't it? Mum said. 'It can only be cancer. Please save her.' Paige's tears were still coming thick and fast as she blew out a bubble of snot from her nose.

Allie, watching from the sidelines, was gripped: she'd forgotten the TV crew were present. She couldn't wait to see how Rory and Zach handled the situation.

'When you hear the word "cancer", Paige, it frightens you and you will always think the worst. But let me assure you, we treat lots of animals within this surgery and this guinea pig won't die on my watch,' Rory promised, running his hands all over Belle's body.

What the hell was Rory saying to Paige? Allie was shaking her head – you couldn't promise a little girl that her guinea pig wasn't going to die, especially if it was riddled with tumours. The cost of an operation would be way more than the cost of fifty guinea pigs, though Allie knew that wasn't the point. Paige wouldn't want another fifty guinea pigs; all she wanted was for Belle to live for ever.

There was no denying this was making excellent dramatic TV. Allie's heart went out to the little girl and she fought to stop herself stepping into the surgery and hugging Paige, who obviously loved her pets unconditionally.

'And why is Daisy here? Do you feel any lumps and bumps on her too?'

Paige shook her head. 'No, she's here for moral support. They go everywhere together.'

'It's good to have a best friend, isn't it? Do you have a best friend?' asked Rory, trying to calm Paige down. She looked up at Rory with her big teary eyes and nodded.

'Zach, can you hold Belle steady for me?' he asked, placing his stethoscope around his neck. 'I'm going to listen to her heartbeat through this. It's every vet's magical instrument.' Then he began to smile and gave a little chuckle. Allie noticed Zach cocked an eyebrow at Rory's reaction. Then Rory tapped Paige lightly on the nose and said, 'Belle doesn't have cancer.'

'Really?' Paige's eyes were wide as she held on to her mum's hand.

'My guess is—'

'My guess is Daisy is a boar,' announced Stuart, flouncing past Allie straight into the surgery like he owned the place

– which obviously he did – and grabbing a diary from the top shelf.

'Dad!' exclaimed Rory, 'you can't just come storming in.' Rory looked like he was dying on the spot. What was Stuart doing?

'Sorry,' he muttered, 'I need this.' He waved the book in the air.

'My Daisy is not boring, she's lots of fun,' fought back Paige.

Allie was impressed that Paige was standing up for herself. What a feisty little girl! She reminded Allie of herself when she was a small child.

Stuart looked down his nose and through his spectacles and thrust the book at Zach, who took it immediately. Stuart leant forward and picked up Daisy.

'Daisy is not Daisy. Daisy would be better off being called Dave.' Stuart flipped over the guinea pig to reveal the biggest pair of testicles that Allie had ever seen on such a small animal. She witnessed the exasperated look on Rory's face. For the first time, Allie had observed Stuart completely taking over a situation when Rory had it all under control. She was beginning to realise why Rory was so frustrated at working with Stuart, if he took over every situation in this way.

'Dad, will you leave the room, please?' Rory asked, but Stuart wasn't listening.

'Daisy's a boy?' Paige looked horrified.

'And this one, judging by the look of it, has a matter of

hours before she gives birth. Those aren't tumours, they are babies.' Stuart ran his hands over the guinea pig and stared up at the ceiling, 'Yes ... mmm ... my guess is four babies.'

'So she isn't going to die?' asked Paige, looking up at her mum, whose colour had instantly drained from her cheeks. She didn't know whether to laugh or cry. 'She's not going to die, she's going to have babies!'

'I suggest you separate them immediately and make Belle comfortable in a separate cage. And you should call one of those babies Stuart; it's such a good name.' With that Stuart took the book from Zach's hands and disappeared out of the surgery without another word.

'Dad is indeed correct, Daisy isn't a girl,' confirmed Rory, trying to be as professional as he could, despite his dad's interruption.

'But I like her name and she will always be a Daisy to me. Can I still call her Daisy?' Paige's eyes were wide.

Emma the producer was stuffing the sleeve of her cardigan in her mouth trying not to laugh.

'I don't think at this late stage Daisy will get confused if you carry on calling her – I mean him – Daisy. All I ask is that once the babies are born, please do bring them in to me between two to three weeks later so I can tell you whether they are boys or girls, as we don't want any further mishaps.'

Paige's face had broken out into a huge beam. 'Thank you, Mr Rory, thank you, Mr Zach,' she said, leaning across the table and shaking both their hands. 'Mum, we are going to have babies.'

'We are indeed and thank you ... I think,' said Sophia, taking the carrier from Rory.

Rory and Zach said their goodbyes and as soon as they were shown out of the building the whole production team fell into bursts of hysterics.

'Don't they say, never work with animals or children?' chuckled Emma, wiping the tears of laughter from her eyes.

'Can I add my dad to that list too?'

'Don't,' said Zach, who was holding his sides. 'Your dad is so dry. It's like he knew what was wrong with that guinea pig without even looking at it.'

'That'll be his sixth sense or years of experience. And why, oh why, would you not think to check whether Daisy had testicles?' said Rory, still shaking his head in disbelief.

Allie walked into the surgery. 'You were brilliant!'

'Despite my dad stealing my thunder,' said Rory, rolling his eyes at Allie.

'Comedy gold at its best,' commented Emma.

'Is this what your everyday life is like?' asked Zach, looking at Rory.

'Not usually as entertaining, believe me. I can't wait to see what we've got up next. Can someone keep my dad under control?' Even though everyone thought Rory was joking, Allie recognised he meant every word.

'Let's get the next one in,' said Hugo, looking at his watch, 'and then we'll take a quick coffee break.'

'Up next is Suzi and her dog, and just to give you the heads-up, apparently the dog has ticks,' said Allie, making her way back to the desk.

Today was turning out to be a lot of fun, and her uncertainty about Rory had evaporated from the pit of her stomach. Maybe she hadn't really appreciated the stress he was under with the hours he worked. Rory was definitely right about the cramped space in the surgery. She knew all those years ago when Stuart started out it would have been perfect for a one-man band in a small village, but since then the surgery's reputation had grown. Allie was beginning to understand Rory's frustration.

'Allie,' shouted Rory, 'is there a roll of paper and disinfectant spray in the desk cupboard?'

'Yes, it's here,' she said, hurrying back into the surgery and handing it over to Rory, who sterilised the table ready for the next client.

'Can you hear shouting?' he asked. His voice was low, almost a whisper, as he cocked an ear towards the door.

The production team immediately hushed and listened.

Stuart's voice came thundering down the corridor. 'The dog has peed up my leg. Allie – Allie – where are you? I need a bucket.'

'This is the best job I've ever worked,' claimed Zach who was grinning at the chaos around him.

'I told you to add my dad to that list,' said Rory, straight-faced.

Once more the production team fell about laughing but Allie could sense that Rory's patience was wearing thin. She hurried out of the surgery to clean up Stuart.

Chapter 13

The day's filming had been a success, and everyone was about to enjoy a richly deserved feed in the Grouse and Haggis. Rory, sitting among the crew, smiled up at Allie, who was walking towards them with a tray of drinks. As soon as she placed it on the table he slid his arm around her waist and pulled her into his lap and kissed her on the lips.

'I really enjoyed today,' said Allie, giving him a quick kiss back.

'It was fun, wasn't it?' replied Rory, taking a quick swig of his well-deserved pint. 'Except for Dad's interference.'

Meredith was laying down the cutlery and working her way around the table, in fits of laughter as Emma recounted the escapades of the day's filming, including the hilarious story of Suzi and her dog.

'It peed up Stuart's leg. I shouldn't laugh ... the humiliation!' Meredith was creased over, holding her sides. 'Tell me again what happened ... When is this programme being aired?'

They all listened to Emma as she began to retell the story about Suzi and her new Alsatian puppy that had been let loose into the woodlands at the back of Heartcross on the other side of the green.

'Is that the woodlands where the derelict old manor house is?' asked Fraser, collecting the empty glasses and listening in on the conversation.

'That's the one – Starcross Manor,' answered Rory. 'The rumour is it's going to be renovated into a retirement home.'

Fraser raised his eyebrows. 'Just in time for me and you then, Meredith, to bag our place. What a place to live out your last years. Spectacular views.'

'There's life left in me yet, I'll have you know – and anyway, Fraser, just listen to this story,' ordered Meredith, flapping her hand at him and encouraging Emma to continue.

'And that's telling me,' said Fraser, smiling at his wife.

'It was the puppy's first time in the woods,' Emma went on, 'and the client had let him off the lead, which all was going swimmingly well until she got the puppy home and began to brush her coat.'

'That's when she discovered the ticks,' chipped in Rory, rolling his eyes. 'I remember her coming into the surgery and purchasing a tick remover from the stand.'

'But she just couldn't quite get them with the tweezers,' carried on Emma, grinning.

'Then Dad flounces back into the surgery while the dog is lying on her back, Zach is wrestling to keep her still and

Rory has the tick remover in his hand ...' Emma looked round the table and in unison they all shouted 'Nipples!' Fraser was taken by surprise and looked embarrassed.

'Shh ...' He looked around at the other drinkers on the tables nearby, who were looking over in their direction.

'No! That's what Dad said, and he was right – again,' said Rory with a chuckle. 'The dog didn't have ticks at all – the owner was trying to pull off her nipples!' He was beginning to see why the others were finding his dad's intrusion funny.

'Oh, my days! You are kidding, right?'

'Absolutely not,' said Emma, 'It's actually been one of my favourite days at work for a very long time.' She raised her glass and the others followed suit. 'Cheers! Here's to Rory and Zach. What a brilliant day, and we know we have some superb footage.' She looked towards Hugo. 'In fact, I think you are going to find it difficult to edit! Your Dad deserves his own TV show,' she added, turning to Rory. 'He was too funny for words.' She took a breath. 'After today, maybe we should give the African job to your dad instead of you. Do you think he would be up to leaving with you and Zach next week?' She grinned and raised her glass towards Rory.

Rory shifted slightly in his seat, and Allie averted her gaze. Sitting on his lap she was swathed in emotion. Africa? Next week?

Suddenly she felt disoriented by all the jolly faces and excited chatter around her. The crew were nodding in Rory's direction and the ones close to him were patting him on his back. 'You are going to have such an experience,' contributed Emma. 'It's my second time visiting that particular sanctuary.'

Allie felt like time had slowed down and everything was happening in slow motion, as the crew all clinked their glasses together – including Rory.

'Next week?' said Allie, looking directly at Rory, who was suddenly wearing a haunted look, the colour draining from his cheeks. 'You're going next week?'

'Allie, I only found out today.'

'Blame me,' said Zach. 'Well, blame Sydney – the trip has been brought forward as the next documentary had to be postponed until she's fully recovered.'

Allie had known that at some point Rory would leave for Africa, but she hadn't anticipated it would be so soon. She thought they would have longer to discuss the implications for both of them. Needing time to compose herself, she made her excuses and left the pub by the back door.

'Allie, wait,' shouted Rory, who'd followed her, but Allie was already striding down the High Street in a daze.

'Where are you going?' Rory increased his pace and grabbed her shoulder, causing her to spin round. 'Will you hang on a minute? There's no need for all this.'

Allie's eyes were filled with tears. 'Sorry, it just all came as a bit of a shock. Next week, Rory? Next week? I didn't think it would be that soon.'

Rory draped his arm around her shoulders and pulled

her in close to his body as they began to walk slowly towards the green. 'Please don't be upset. I've not even had a chance to talk to Mum and Dad yet, which was what I was going to do tonight after I'd told you. I was hoping you would come with me for moral support.'

Allie found it difficult to speak. Of course she was going to support Rory but she already felt heartbroken that she wasn't going to see him for a year – and he hadn't even left yet.

'Just think about it this way: the sooner I go the quicker I will be home, and by the time I get back you will have had your own little adventure in Glasgow too.'

Allie took a lungful of air and bit her quivering lip. 'You're talking like I've been offered the job, Rory. And you know about my anxieties. You know I'm only comfortable in certain situations. Half of me thinks you're encouraging me to go to ease your conscience.'

'What's that meant to mean?' Rory said as he stopped dead in his tracks.

'I'm saying you seem hellbent on the idea of me going to Glasgow when you know I'm a person who needs stability, I need my family and friends. And maybe, just maybe, you are pushing me to go because you know you're going and then you won't feel as guilty.'

'Allie, I love you and I want what's best for you,' Rory said sadly, his eyes downcast as he stood opposite her. 'Africa is an amazing opportunity for me, for us, and I was hoping you could see that and support me, but obviously not.' He dropped his arm from around her shoulders and paused for a second before turning and walking away.

Allie felt bereft. She had been determined to give him her blessing but her anxieties had got the better of her once again, leaving her saying the wrong thing.

Chapter 14

'Rory, wait. Of course it's an amazing opportunity. Please stop.' Allie's voice was fraught; she didn't want to fight with him. She knew her reasons for behaving this way were selfish. 'It's just that I'll miss you.'

Rory slowed down and turned around. 'I'll miss you too, you know.' His voice was sincere. He walked back to her and took her hands in his. 'This trip to Africa is something I've wanted to do for such a long time and this way I even get paid to do it too.'

Allie could see the passion in his eyes and felt terribly guilty.

'I've got Dad to face yet, which isn't going to be easy, and I really don't want to fight with you.'

'Me either,' Allie admitted, cuddling into his chest.

'And please tell me you really don't think I'm encouraging you to go for that interview in Glasgow to ease my own conscience?' Rory held her gaze.

Tears pricked Allie's eyes. 'Of course not.'

'Good, thank God for that,' said Rory, blowing out a

breath. 'I know it's just an interview, and you'll be nervous, but just go and see what it leads to. They will see how amazing you are, just like the customers you serve every day. You stand behind that bar and you radiate warmth, confidence ... You light up the room.'

'Because that's my territory. I know my job inside and out, because I know all the customers so well and I'm comfortable with that. That's just me.'

'Okay, I do get that but look at what happened today.'

'What about today?' asked Allie, puzzled.

'You stepped up to the mark in a situation alongside not only a bunch of strangers but a film crew too. I was nervous, in fact petrified. At one point I thought I was going to throw up, but you calmed me down, told me I could do it, and I'm now telling you the same. You know what, Allie Macdonald?' Rory brushed her nose with a light kiss. 'I think you are stronger than you think. You can do this. You really can.'

Allie leant her head on his shoulder. 'But what about our future, Rory? Where does all this change leave us?'

'Look, come and sit down,' said Rory softly, nodding towards a bench.

Allie followed him and perched on the edge of the bench with her hands resting between her knees, staring at the ground.

'Going to Africa isn't about not loving you or suggesting we don't have a future together. Far from it. I want to be successful in my field, I want to sit down with my children and tell them how their dad went off to Africa to save lions. I want them to be proud of me.'

For a moment they both stared out across the River Heart in deep thought.

'Just so you know,' Allie broke the silence. 'I do think this is an amazing opportunity for you, working with Zach, co-presenting the documentary, working alongside all those magnificent creatures.'

'It is and this might be my only chance to do it, especially as I've now got to move out of my house for the next twelve months. Something is telling me the timing is perfect.'

'I know,' said Allie, even though she didn't like the thought of him not being just down the road. She didn't want to stifle anyone's dreams or aspirations, and deep down all she wanted was for Rory to be happy.

'And what's twelve months? Every time I blink it seems to be Christmas again and I'm down the forest dragging the biggest tree towards the van alongside your dad ...'

'With my mum waiting on the pub steps tutting? "What were you thinking, Fraser? That tree is way too big for the pub"?' Allie chuckled. They went through the same rigmarole every December.

Rory gripped Allie's shaky hands.

'And after you've finished your six months in Glasgow' – he bumped his shoulder lightly against hers – 'what's stopping you coming out to visit me? You can get on a plane and I'll be waiting for you at the other end.'

A smile hitched on Allie's face. 'As long as you've not been eaten by a lion,' she said jokingly.

'I'll try my best.' Rory laughed. 'And as far as our future goes that's exactly what I'm working towards. Nothing has changed on that front. But the salary I'll be earning from the documentary, being the vet at the sanctuary and so on will come in very handy. It's not as though there's going to be any *wild* nights out except with the lions.'

Allie rolled her eyes. 'Wild nights out? Your jokes get worse.'

Sitting and chatting with Rory, Allie felt more at peace with the situation. What was stopping her going out for a visit? Absolutely nothing. 'And what about your dad, Rory? When are you going to talk to him?'

'Shall we do it now? Together? Will you come with me?'

Allie nodded. 'I do understand your frustration about your dad and the surgery. Even though it was comical I did see how when you were filming it's his way or no way. It might actually do him good to manage without you.'

'Here's hoping. The practice needs more space, the technology needs updating and we need to be more accessible and look after the animals on our own premises, but as you know I'm fighting a losing battle with Dad – he doesn't like change.'

'As much as me,' Allie teased.

'As much as you,' repeated Rory.

'Don't bite my head off, but wouldn't Clover Cottage be perfect?'

'Do you think I don't agree with you? Of course it would be perfect but there's the cost. This trip will help me to put a little bit away, and now I'm going to say the same to you—'

'Eh?'

'Don't *you* bite *my* head off, but you could do the same. I'm sure working on a national paper will pay more than the pub, even if it is for only six months, then who knows what opportunities that may lead to? The extra money will come in handy, won't it? It's all about teamwork.'

'You're right, it will,' agreed Allie, understanding that Rory was looking at the bigger picture and she needed to do so too. 'But twelve months, Rory.' She came over all emotional. She held his gaze as her chin trembled.

Rory slid his arm around her shoulders and pulled her in close. He rested his chin on the top of her head then kissed her lightly. 'I do love you, I promise I do, but promise me you will give that interview your best shot. You can do this.' But before she could answer they heard muffled voices and footsteps in the distance. Trundling towards them down the lane were Martha, Isla and Aggie.

Blinking away the brimming tears, Allie could sense something was wrong by the look on Isla's face.

Rory loosened his grip on Allie. 'What is it?' he asked.

'Thank God, we've been looking for you both everywhere,' said Isla, trying to catch her breath.

Allie's eyes flitted between them. She didn't like the sound of that.

'It's your mum, Rory,' said Aggie. 'She's missing.'

Rory gave a nervous laugh then shot Allie a quizzical look. 'Missing? Why would my mum be missing?'

Aggie looked towards Martha, who gave a nod and said, 'Your mum has been a little confused lately, forgetful, and it seems to have accelerated in the last couple of months.'

'What are you trying to tell me, Aggie?' asked Rory.

Aggie touched his arm lightly. 'Your mum isn't well, Rory. She's been diagnosed with the early signs of dementia.'

Rory was taken aback. 'Diagnosed ... Dementia? You're telling me my mum has dementia?' His hazel eyes widened with shock.

Aggie nodded, and Allie slipped her hand into Rory's and gave it a squeeze. She knew that Alana had been forgetful of late but hadn't realised it was this bad.

Rory was shaking his head in disbelief, trying to take in what Aggie was saying.

'From what we understand, she had a disagreement with your father and walked out of the cottage, only dressed in her nightgown.'

Rory raised his eyebrows. 'Are you serious? My mum is wandering about in a nightdress? And where's Dad now?'

'He's out looking for her with everyone else.'

'How come I know nothing about this yet all of you seem to know what's going on?'

Allie saw the grief-stricken look on his face, but this wasn't the time to get into the whys and wherefores.

'We spend a lot of time with your mum. We are her

friends,' offered Aggie. 'We talk ... We notice things. The past couple of months your dad has been trying to hold it together,' she added.

Allie exhaled silently. She felt a pang of sadness. She couldn't believe Stuart had been coping alone with all this and hadn't reached out for help from either of them. 'We need to find her,' she said with urgency in her voice. 'Where do you want us to look?'

'Drew and Fergus have headed up the mountain pass. Meredith and Fraser are searching the outhouses, Alfie and Polly are scaling the woodlands on the far side of the green. Felicity's looking after the children up at the farm ... Everyone is out in full force. Even the TV crew are helping.'

Allie glanced up at Rory. 'So we'll take the river,' she said, thankful her voice sounded a lot calmer than she felt.

Aggie nodded. 'Perfect. She can't have gone far.' She offered Rory a reassuring smile before turning and walking away.

'How long has she been missing?' shouted Allie after them.

'Just under an hour,' came the reply.

Chapter 15

Allie met Rory's worried stare as they trawled the banks on the river. 'Dementia,' he kept muttering over and over. 'A couple of months.'

'She can't have gone far,' Allie said calmly.

When they reached the river, it was flowing swift and strong and Allie shuddered. They searched every inch of the path, shouting Alana's name.

'Would she still even know her name, if she has memory loss?' asked Rory. 'I just don't know anything about dementia.'

Allie couldn't answer. She too didn't know what to expect.

They scanned the whole area and stopped every passerby. 'Have you seen a woman in a nightdress?' Rory knew it sounded ridiculous but every person they asked shook their head. 'Sorry, no.'

Rory raked his hand through his hair, anxiety written all over his face. 'How far do we walk? Has she crossed the bridge into Glensheil?'

Allie stared across the bridge. 'Surely, if she's made her way into the town someone would have stopped her or called the police. It's not usual for a grown woman to be wandering around in a nightdress.'

'You'd hope so, wouldn't you? Where to now then?' asked Rory.

'Let's make our way back to the village. Any texts?'

Rory quickly checked his phone. Nothing.

'What about the old boathouse? Mum and Dad used to spend a lot of time there in the past. It's just round that next bend,' he suggested.

As they turned the corner, they spotted the old decrepit boathouse. Back in the day this place had been a hive of activity and once a successful business, but the boathouse now stood empty.

'There's someone over there.' Allie pointed. A light shone above the ramshackle wooden door, which was ajar.

Rory narrowed his eyes and focused. 'There's two people sitting on deck chairs and one is—'

'Your mum,' exclaimed Allie as they began to race along the narrow path.

'Mum ... Mum ... Thank God,' Rory shouted as he reached them,

Alana looked up. 'I told you he was handsome, didn't I?' She was sitting in a deckchair clasping a mug, looking like she didn't have a care in the world.

'Mum, are you okay?'

'Of course I'm okay. Why wouldn't I be okay?'

Allie and Rory looked at each other. Apart from the fact that she was sitting in her nightdress talking to a stranger, she seemed relatively fine.

'This kind man has given me a mug of the strong stuff. We are having a very nice chat, aren't we?'

Rory felt like he was in some sort of weird dream and locked eyes with the man sitting next to Alana.

'Sorry, I can't remember your name,' she said.

His wizened face was a map of wrinkles, his blue eyes framed by thick white bushy eyebrows and his stubbly chin sprouting white whiskers.

'I'm Wilbur.' He stretched out his hand and shook Rory's. Allie had no idea who he was; she'd never set eyes on him before.

'Rory, and this is Allie,' said Rory. 'How long has Mum been here?'

'I can answer for myself. I am sitting here, you know,' Alana replied sharply.

'We need to phone your dad,' said Allie, remembering Stuart and the others out searching. 'He'll be worried.' She walked over to the door of the boathouse and stood inside while she dialled the number. She could hear Rory and Wilbur chatting outside. As soon as Allie had filled Stuart in, she joined them again. Rory had taken off his jumper and wrapped it around Alana's shoulders to keep her warm.

'Stuart's on his way. He's bringing the car.'

'I hope he's bringing himself in a better mood too,' added Alana, taking a sip from the mug.

'I was going to call the police just as you arrived.' Wilbur's tone was soft and friendly.

'Why would we need the police? I'm only out for a walk,' Alana said, with a frown on her face.

'Mum, look how you are dressed.'

Alana chuckled.

'Here's a car now,' said Allie, relieved to see Stuart arrive so quickly. The car snaked up the narrow path towards them and the engine cut out as Stuart parked at the side of the boathouse.

The doors of the car flew open and Stuart and Dr Taylor strolled over towards them.

Allie noticed that Stuart looked tired and worn. Alana and Stuart were older than her own parents. Rory was an only child and he'd told Allie that his parents had been trying for a baby for many years with no luck whatsoever, then, lo and behold, when Alana had thought all hope was lost, she'd discovered that she'd finally fallen pregnant.

Stuart took a breath to calm himself. Allie noticed that Rory caught his eye, but Stuart looked away. They had a lot of talking to do.

'Love, you gave us the fright of our lives,' exclaimed Stuart, pressing a kiss on Alana's hair.

Alana flapped her hand at him. 'I don't want to take those tablets. I don't need them.'

Allie observed a look between Stuart and Dr Taylor.

'It's nothing to worry about, Alana. Let's get you home and we can talk about it there,' said Dr Taylor warmly, helping Alana to her feet.

'I'm having a lovely evening,' she said, smiling towards Wilbur. 'This kind man shared his whisky.'

'I can't thank you enough,' said Stuart, looking grateful.

'It's not everyone I share my whisky with,' replied Wilbur, shaking Stuart's hand. 'I'm Wilbur.'

'Stuart. Pleased to meet you.'

'I'm ready for my bed. It's getting a bit chilly out here now.' Alana turned towards Wilbur, 'Thank you for your hospitality. This place' – she gazed towards the boathouse – 'holds a lot of good memories for me.'

'And why's that?' asked Wilbur warmly, standing up and leaning on his cane.

Alana's mood seemed to shift instantly as she gazed lovingly towards Stuart. Her face softened and that was the Alana everyone knew. 'That rock—'

'I remember that day like it was yesterday,' Stuart interrupted, turning towards Wilbur. 'Many moons ago we owned our own little boat and in the winter we kept it here. It was nothing flash, but we loved sailing up and down the river in the summer months, on days just like today. A little further down there's a small bay. We used to enjoy many a picnic ... but that rock was where I proposed to my gorgeous lady ... for better or worse.'

'He did too, stood on that rock and shouted for the

whole world to hear' – Alana cupped her hands around her mouth – '"Alana Reid, will you marry me?"'

'And, of course, the answer was yes!' replied Stuart.

Allie could see the love that Stuart and Alana shared. Real love. For better or worse. If the news of Alana's condition was true, Allie knew life was going to get even more complicated and difficult.

'So what's the story?' asked Stuart. 'Are you the owner of this place? Even as kids we used to dive off that jetty. It's got some history about it, this place has.'

'My son – he's a property developer – he's just bought this place.'

'Is he reopening the boathouse?' asked Rory, joining in the conversation whilst linking his arm through his mother's.

'I'm not fully sure what his intention is but I know he's got a few projects on the go in the area.'

'Property developer ... your son wouldn't be Flynn Carter, would it?' asked Stuart.

'He would indeed.'

Stuart stepped forward and shook his hand once more.

'I'm Stuart, Stuart Scott. Flynn's renting the house from us on Love Heart Lane.'

'What a small world it is.'

'No doubt we will bump into each other again very soon. Thank you for looking after Alana.'

Wilbur nodded. 'My pleasure.'

Rory walked his mum to the car and once the door was safely shut, turned to his dad. 'Dad, we need to talk.'

'Not now, son. Not now. We need to get your mother home and Dr Taylor needs to make sure she's okay.'

'Has this happened before?' pushed Rory.

'I said not now, son. We can talk tomorrow.'

Rory nodded.

Unsure what to say, Allie held Rory's hand tightly as they watched Stuart drive away.

Chapter 16

Allie made endless cups of tea whilst she sat by Rory's side as he spent over three hours researching dementia on the internet. Of course, both of them had heard the term Alzheimer's, but there were different types of dementia and Rory was struggling to cope, reading all the information that was available. He was aware Alana had never liked change – they'd argued and argued regarding the booking system at the practice – and now he was feeling guilty about it all. Was he so self-absorbed with what was going on in his own life that he hadn't put two and two together over the last couple of months?

'If you didn't know all the facts then you can't be hard on yourself,' Allie said, trying to reassure him, but it didn't make him feel any better.

Finally, Allie ordered him to bed in the early hours of the morning and stayed with him. For a long time, he lay wrapped in Allie's arms with his eyes shut but not sleeping. He felt helpless and wretched. His thoughts were with his dad and what he must be going through. How was this affecting him? His wife, the woman he'd been married to for a lifetime, was going to deteriorate in front of his eyes. How did anyone cope with that?

Rory now knew he hadn't helped, putting pressure on his dad to expand the business, import new technology and put the practice on the map. No wonder his dad didn't want any more change in his life.

Thankfully, last night Allie had stopped him from tearing around to see his dad, but he had so many questions to ask and at the moment none of the answers.

He was grateful for Allie's cuddling and eventually fell asleep in her arms. He couldn't thank her enough for being there for him. He knew she hadn't had the best twenty-four hours herself – she was hurting and upset about his travels to Africa – but yet again she'd put him first.

Lying in her arms Rory began to reconsider his trip to Africa, wondering whether this would be the right thing to do now, considering everything that had happened. Was it right to put his dreams first or did it make him selfish? Putting things into perspective … family was family. Family was everything. He finally drifted off to sleep but it seemed like just minutes later Allie was waking him with tea and toast in bed before slipping out back to the pub to let the drayman in, with the promise that she'd be back later to help him pack up the rest of the house. As if he didn't have enough on his mind, Flynn Carter, the property developer, was arriving in the next few days and there was still so much to do. Rory really didn't know what he'd do without Allie.

He kissed her and thanked her for dropping everything to be by his side. It didn't matter that they'd had their own struggles in the last few days: she knew he needed her and she hadn't let him down.

Arriving at the surgery, he took a minute to stare up at his parents' cottage. The place had been their whole life, packed to the brim with memories. The bedroom curtains were still closed, and Rory wondered what type of night his dad had had. Did he find it difficult going to sleep? Was he apprehensive when waking up, not knowing whether Alana would be her old or new self that day? Rory didn't fully understand, and he couldn't imagine. With the animals he treated in his day-to-day job it was usually a physical injury, one you could see and fix, but he knew he couldn't fix his mum and it broke his heart.

He pulled out the key to the surgery door and let himself in. Just like every morning he hung up his jacket, sterilised his hands and slipped on his scrubs. The surgery was deadly silent except for the ticking of the clock in the waiting room. Usually he would turn the sign on the surgery door to 'open', but not today. This morning the surgery would remain firmly closed until he'd spoken with his dad.

He made himself a mug of coffee and sat down behind his mum's desk. Today's schedule was jam-packed with appointments. It was the usual, a few castrations, lumps and bumps that needed scanning and a dog with an eye infection. Rory sighed and shut the appointment book.

Hearing the cottage door creak, Rory sat up in the chair. He felt apprehensive. He wasn't sure how this conversation with his dad was going to pan out. Stuart looked tired as he opened the door clutching his usual mug. His eyes looked bleary and Rory noticed for the very first time that his white coat looked huge on him. He'd lost weight.

'How are you, Dad?' asked Rory, hesitantly.

'I'm okay.'

'And Mum?' Rory's voice was low.

'She's having a bath.'

Without saying another word Stuart placed his mug down on the desk and grabbed a chair from the corner of the waiting room. He sat opposite Rory and took a sip of his tea. 'I suppose you have many questions,' he said, holding Rory's gaze.

Rory could see his dad looked beat.

'I've been up most of the night researching Alzheimer's, vascular dementia, Lewy Bodies ...' Rory began to reel off all the types he'd read about last night.

'Alzheimer's,' interrupted Stuart. 'Regardless of which type of dementia is diagnosed and what part of the brain is affected, each person will experience dementia in their own unique way,' he said quite matter-of-factly.

Rory felt like his dad was quoting straight out of a textbook. 'I just don't understand. When did all this start?'

Stuart took a deep breath. 'I noticed things slightly changing a while back but in the last couple of months things became more apparent. I'd call through with an appointment and your mum had forgotten to log it. Other times she'd be confused and book people in on the wrong days with the wrong animals. On one occasion I was expecting to castrate a dog and in walked Mr Potts with his pet parrot.' Stuart gave a little chuckle. 'At first, I just thought it was because the surgery was busy, not enough hours in the day ... You know how it is.' Stuart took a breath. 'But even on the quiet days your mum found it difficult concentrating. She'd start one thing, then another without finishing the first thing. Then there were the invoices ... Your mum could knock up an invoice in her sleep. She knew where people lived, the names of their pets, the prices for absolutely everything. But then she began to find it difficult carrying out familiar daily tasks. When people paid with cash she would get flustered, and confused over the correct change.' Stuart's voice faltered. He was emotional, talking about the change in his wife. Rory saw the tears in his eyes, reached across the desk and placed his hand on his dad's shoulder.

'Why did you not tell me?' he asked. 'And how did I not see the signs myself. I'm so sorry, Dad,' he said, genuinely devastated at not recognising the signs and putting two and two together.

For a second, Stuart looked down at the table, his hands cupped tightly round his mug then he shrugged. 'Because we are married, for better or worse. Because we are your parents and I needed to get used to the changes. It was something I had to come to terms with myself first.'

'But Aggie and her friends knew?' objected Rory softly. He could see his dad was struggling talking about it. He had a downcast expression.

'Aggie and Rona also had their own concerns about your mum. They came to see me. It must have been difficult for them both, but they only confirmed what I'd been thinking myself.' He paused. 'As you know they always go to the village hall on a Wednesday to play Bingo. How long has your mum been doing that?' Stuart held Rory's gaze.

'As long as I can remember, why?'

'Because your mum became confused about the day, place and time. Then she became anxious and started to argue with them about it. She had mood swings. Now, luckily for your mum and for me, we've had friends in this village for years and years and they knew her inside and out. They could see something was wrong. She has good loyal friends ... *we* have good loyal friends. That's what I love about Heartcross, the community; we look out for each other. I know you think I'm a grumpy silly old fool ...'

'That's not quite the case,' replied Rory, feeling guilty for all the times he'd been frustrated with his dad over what now seemed like trivial things.

Stuart continued, 'And that you think I should have

retired years ago, but I needed this job, Rory. It was my own little escape, my own little world that I knew best how to cope in.' Stuart swallowed, and Rory noticed his hands slightly shaking.

'I know that now, Dad, and I'm so sorry.' His dad hadn't needed the extra pressure that he'd been putting him under to expand the surgery and update the technology, and no wonder his mum had been happy with the old-fashioned appointments diary. 'Has she seen a doctor?' he asked.

Stuart nodded. 'At first I went to see Dr Taylor for some advice.'

'And?'

'He encouraged me to make an appointment for your mum and take her along to see him, which was difficult in itself. I mean, what do you say? "Hey, Alana, you need to come with me to see a doctor because I think you're not well"? Anyway, cutting a long story short, I finally got her there and she had a physical examination. I was questioned about the changes because sometimes memory loss can be caused by other factors: depression, anxiety, thyroid problems. He took blood tests and carried out memory tests and referred us to the hospital at Glensheil, to a psychiatrist with experience of treating dementia, and a neurologist.'

'Did Mum have a brain scan?'

Stuart nodded. 'An MRI scan and a further detailed memory test.'

'And how is Mum about it all?'

'The key is routine, to keep everything the same. Some days are good days and some days can be quite worrying, especially after last night. She's never wandered off before, even after a disagreement.'

Rory tried to give his dad a comforting smile but inside he was crushed. Everyone's life had become way more complicated and he hadn't even realised. He'd been wrapped up in his own little bubble and never even considered what was going on in anyone else's life. He felt disappointed in himself over that.

'Your mum is on medication which helps to slow it down ... She's very proud of you, you know,' said Stuart, standing up. 'And I know when I do finally hang up my coat this place will be in safe hands. Clover Cottage wasn't meant to cause you and Allie problems, you know. That place has a lot of potential. Make it your own. This place' – Stuart looked round as he placed the chair back in the waiting room – 'this place has served me well. I had to convince your mum to convert this part of the cottage into a surgery. She'd argued this was the best room, and should only be allowed to be used at Christmas.' Stuart rolled his eyes, but he was smiling. 'She had her own funny ways back then, but that's what I love about her. She wore the trousers without a doubt, but I couldn't have done all this without Drew's father: he loaned me the money to convert the rooms and buy the equipment and become my own boss. And that's what I mean about good friends –

Heartcross community, we look out for each other, and I know I'm not on my own now with your mum. Our friends will help us through this.'

Rory was listening and taking in everything his dad was saying. It was only now the penny had dropped that he realised exactly how Allie saw things. To her, Heartcross was her security, where she felt safe surrounded by the people she knew and could rely on – exactly like his father. Rory exhaled. Thinking about Allie he felt guilty. All he'd focused on had been what he'd wanted to do: take a year out to go travelling. And there was Allie still by his side, cuddling him all night even after he must have made her feel like she didn't know whether she was coming or going. He was sorry for that and knew he needed to put it right. It took a special kind of person to put someone else first, especially after the way he'd dropped Africa on her out of the blue. He only wished it hadn't taken his mother's illness to make him realise this.

'What can I do to help?' asked Rory, hearing the rattle of the surgery door and glancing up at the clock. It was time to open.

'Just be normal, keep everything normal,' said Stuart, placing his hand on his son's shoulder.

'I am really sorry, Dad.'

'Don't keep apologising. Sometimes you don't know what is going on in people's lives. Next week is your mum's birthday. Why don't we make it a birthday to remember? Now it's time for work.' Stuart nodded towards the diary on the desk. 'And can you book the client in? Your mum won't be in until late morning.'

Rory nodded and welcomed Mrs Stevens, who lived over the other side of the bridge, and was carrying her cat in a basket. As soon as Rory had checked her in and shown her through to his dad's surgery he glanced at his phone, which had just beeped. It was a text message from Zach. Swiping the screen, he read the text and felt deflated.

My flights are booked! You need to send your passport details ASAP so we can go on the same flight.

Rory stared at the text and swallowed. He had no clue how he felt – punctured, disappointed – but there were far more important things to be worrying about now. He couldn't just up and leave for twelve months, leaving his dad to hold the fort. The timing for Africa was now far from perfect; it just wasn't his time. Feeling the pressure, he typed out a text to Zach, apologising that due to personal circumstances he'd have to cancel the trip. He knew Zach had put his neck on the line to get him on board and he felt dreadful letting him down at the last minute, but he had no choice. He deleted the text and typed out another, but he just couldn't find the right words. It would be best to explain to him face to face.

Just as Rory was about to slide his phone into the desk drawer it pinged again.

Clover Cottage

How is everything this morning? I've the night off. I'll see you at yours around 6pm. Love A x

Perfect, see you at 6pm, replied Rory, thinking there was too much to go over in a text message; he'd catch up with Allie later and talk to her about what on earth he was going to do next.

Chapter 17

With a smile on her face Allie swung open the front door. 'Ta-dah!' she said, holding up a white carrier bag.

'Now that is a very welcome smell,' said Rory, appearing in the doorway of the living room.

'Me or the fish and chips?' teased Allie.

'Both,' said Rory walking towards her and placing a kiss on her lips. 'Got to love the fish and chip van. I'll get the plates,' he said, taking the bag from her and manoeuvring his way across the room.

Allie stood and stared at the chaos around her. She couldn't even see the carpet. It looked like she'd walked into the middle of a jumble sale. There was stuff everywhere, boxes upon boxes, clothes in piles and knick-knacks she'd never seen before.

'And where do you suggest we eat?' asked Allie, gazing at the table, which was piled high with files. She flipped the top one over and saw that it was Rory's work from university. 'You've still got loads to get through, Rory,' she said flicking through the next one.

He poked his head around the door. 'Actually that's the throwaway pile. Drew is going to pop up with his trailer and burn it at the farm. It's easier than getting a skip.'

'This is all part of your life,' she said, still perusing them.

'It is, but it's about time I let go of all that stuff. What's it doing anyway, except gathering dust? It's not as though I'm ever going to look at it again or use it.'

'It's still a shame. Look at all the work that's gone into some of these diagrams.'

Rory scrambled across the room and looked over Allie's shoulder.

'I don't need to keep these to remember the blood, sweat and tears that went into those studies; it's etched on my brain. I've got my memories.' He pushed the files to one side and cleared a spot on the table so they could eat.

'A glass of wine?' he asked, returning to the kitchen and reappearing with two plates of fish and chips.

'Lovely, thanks.' The smell of the food was making her stomach grumble.

Rory poured wine and, as usual, he soaked his chips in vinegar. Allie smiled to herself. If those chips were alive, they'd need a life jacket to stand any chance of survival swimming around his plate.

'Would you like some chips with your vinegar?' she joked, stabbing her fork into her own chips and shovelling them into her mouth. 'Mmm, delicious but hot,' she said, flapping her hand in front of her mouth.

Rory had managed to have a quick chat with Allie at lunchtime about his mum. They'd met up at the bench on the green and Allie had brought him a sandwich from the pub for his lunch. She was devastated to learn about Alana and she could see the distress in Rory's eyes and hear it in his voice. He'd stared vacantly ahead into the distance.

'How could I have been so blinkered?' Rory had barely been able to take a bite of his sandwich as he turned towards Allie, recollecting the conversation he'd had with his father that morning. 'What sort of son am I not to even mention it to Dad when I noticed missed appointments and deleted emails?'

'Because people get forgetful if they are busy. We are only human, we make mistakes,' Allie had said, trying to soothe his emotions.

'I feel disappointed in myself, moaning about the equipment, the lack of space in the surgery, when all the time they had greater things to worry about. Their struggles are far worse than my future career, and the way I've treated Dad, I feel ashamed ...' Rory had sucked in a breath. 'I've been short-tempered with him, frustrated, all I've done is make life more difficult for him.'

'It's not your fault. You can only react to what you know at the time. Now we both know we will be there for them, every step of the way.'

'I'm really struggling with it all,' Rory had admitted. It didn't matter what Allie said, he was still cut up about the way he'd acted towards his dad and the way he'd judged him.

Allie had felt sorry for both men. Stuart had been struggling alone while being responsible for Rory as a father and as a partner in the business, and Rory hadn't understood the bigger picture and was blaming himself for the extra pressure he'd put on his dad about the surgery's working conditions.

'So, where has all this stuff come from? I've never see half of it before.' Allie gave another glance around the room.

'The loft. It's mad, isn't it? All this stuff is from my old bedroom at home, all what I accumulated from living at university. You just pile everything into a box to tidy it away and don't realise one day you have to go through it all. Most of it should have been thrown away at the time. I've even got a box of programmes from all the football matches my dad took me to as a kid. I mean, will I ever look at them again?'

'Collectors' items for some mad footie fan,' said Allie.

'My loft was a fireman's worst nightmare with all that paper jammed up in the roof. There's tickets from every gig I ever went to, and Mum has even kept pictures I drew at primary school. Why?'

'Because that's what parents do! They are proud of their children from the moment they arrive in this mad world of ours.'

For a second there was a lull in the conversation and Allie noticed that Rory had gone quiet. She saw tears in his eyes. Reaching towards him she squeezed his hand. 'The good thing is Alana has us all. We will all look out and care for her.'

Rory couldn't speak; he wiped his eyes on his sleeve and took a moment.

'It's okay to cry, Rory. It's all come as a shock to you.'

Rory swallowed and put down his knife and fork. 'I'm so sorry, Allie.'

'What for?'

'I was putting what I wanted first without giving a second thought to anyone else. You were right about your job offer. Maybe I was encouraging you to go for the interview to make it easier for me to travel for a year without giving your feelings a second thought.'

'Ha, see, I'm always right.' Allie gave a small smile to try and lighten the mood. 'But it's okay. Relationships are difficult at the best of times. When they are good, they are good, but when you disagree, that's when you realise how strong you are. It's all about compromise.'

'It was unfair of me. Please forgive me.'

Allie bent across the table and pecked him on the cheek. 'You're forgiven. But—'

'But what?' Rory looked alarmed.

'I've been thinking about it and even though I'm happy with my life, maybe there is more to Allie MacDonald than just being a barmaid. You've given me food for thought,

Rory, and created a little bit of fire in my belly. I'm going to go for the interview because if nothing else it's all experience and if I do happen to get the job I can make a decision then – keep my options open.'

'Wow, I wasn't expecting that,' exclaimed Rory, taken by surprise. 'Right decision! Go Allie! I'm so proud of you and we both know your interview will be successful and you'll get the job.'

'If that's the case then I'll be able to save some of my salary and visit you in Africa. Win–win.'

Allie watched as Rory took a piece of bread, loaded it with the last few chips and swirled it around his plate, soaking up the vinegar. She could tell he was deep in thought because his brow had furrowed. As soon as he finished eating, he leant back in the chair with his hands resting on his stomach. He looked troubled.

'What are you thinking?' she asked, placing the knife and fork back on her empty plate and holding Rory's gaze. 'You suddenly look glum again.'

He exhaled. 'Just thinking about Mum and all our lives. It saddens me the most that when I have children they won't know their grandmother like I did, like we did. You take them for granted, that they are always going to be around, and you never think about them getting old.'

Allie could see Rory was emotional. She moved her chair back and sat on his knee, hugging him tight. She didn't like seeing him upset and only wished she could change the situation.

'We just need to make sure that we are here for both of them.'

Rory nodded. 'I know. It's frustrating when you have no control and you wish with all your might that things were different.' He rested his chin on Allie's shoulder for a second. 'Allie, I can't go to Africa and leave Dad coping with everything. I just need to tell Zach and Emma. The sooner the better.'

Allie could see he was visibly upset, his eyes still teary.

'Rory, don't make any decisions tonight. Talk to your dad, tell him about the trip and see what he says.'

'How can I, Allie? He needs the pressure taken off him at the surgery. I couldn't place that extra burden on him. And I've been thinking: I'm going to stay at their cottage, in my old bedroom. I know they are going to drive me insane, but I just need to be close to them and to the surgery.'

Allie knew this decision must have been difficult for Rory. On one hand she was ecstatic at the thought of him staying in Heartcross, but on the other she was worried about how this might affect him later. His emotions were all over the place with working out what would be the right thing to do. She knew the decision had to be his, but she was also in two minds about what would be the best thing – should he follow his dreams or stay for his parents' sake? Rory looked worn out, devastated by the whole situation. All she could do was be there for him.

'You don't need to do anything tonight. Let's just carry

on packing up your stuff and see how you feel in the morning.'

'I've made up my mind, Allie.'

Kissing the top of his head, she stood up and cleared the table whilst Rory let out a huge sigh. 'One day I'll get to Africa.'

'You will.'

For the next hour they studiously wrapped breakable items and placed them in boxes. Allie tried to keep the conversation light, chatting cheerfully to keep Rory's spirits up, even though he was clearly trying to deal with the revelations of the last twenty-four hours.

'Ha! Remember this?' chuckled Allie, holding up a framed photo of the gang when they left school. 'Look at Isla's hair ... and what is Fergus wearing? He'd be arrested by the fashion police if he wore that these days!'

She passed the photograph to Rory, who grinned. 'Never mind Isla's hair, look at mine! It's way out of control!'

'I remember we couldn't wait to be rid of that uniform and when the school bus dropped us off this side of the bridge, we all ran up to the old boathouse.'

'Poohsticks!' exclaimed Rory. 'We tied our school ties around the sticks and lobbed them from the rock outside the boathouse.'

'To this day Fergus is adamant that his stick passed under Heartcross Bridge first, but Drew isn't having any of it,' said Allie, still chuckling at the memory.

'All the sticks looked the same! The good old days. When

we didn't have a care in the world.' Rory passed the photograph back to Allie. 'Obviously that goes in the "keep me" pile – but look who isn't in the picture.' He cocked an eyebrow in Allie's direction.

'That's because I took the picture. This was years before selfies were even heard of.' She knew full well she'd always preferred to be behind the lens rather than in front of it.

She wrapped the photo frame in tissue paper and placed it carefully in a 'keep me' box. There were all sorts in these boxes, memories aplenty – everything from old football trophies Rory had won at primary school to plaster casts of dinosaurs he'd painted at school. There was even a collection of comics.

'Keep or go?' asked Allie, thinking the comics were definitely collectors' items.

'Keep the comics. I'll take them to that quirky bookstore over in Glensheil, the one on the corner. I've often seen boxes of comics outside.'

'Good idea,' replied Allie, pulling a red cardboard box towards her and flipping open the lid. She stared at a pile of letters wrapped up in a red velvet ribbon. These were handwritten letters to Rory in the smallest, neatest handwriting Allie had ever seen. Immediately Rory noticed she'd gone quiet and looked over. 'What've you got there?'

Allie looked down at the letters again and turned them over. '"Your forever love Clare,"' Allie read out loud, her heart hammering against her chest. 'Love letters ... you've kept love letters from Clare?' she said, putting them back into the box. In that little bundle tied with red velvet ribbon was an intimate exchange of words between Rory and his first love, and Allie felt a pang of jealousy. Of course, she knew Rory had had other relationships before her but this one in her eyes was a little different. He'd asked Clare to marry him, He'd never asked Allie.

Rory stopped talking and stared. 'You've got that look about you.'

'What look?'

'That look.'

'No, I haven't,' she said sulkily.

'Yes, you have,' he challenged.

'I just don't get it – why would you keep this stuff?'

'It's just part of my past, Allie. It's moulded me into who I am today, steered me towards this path with you.'

Allie looked up. The intensity of his gaze made her shiver in anticipation.

'I wouldn't change this path for the world so put those in the "must go" pile.'

'Are you sure?'

'Absolutely sure. I don't need to think about that twice,' he said forcefully, leaning over and planting a huge kiss on her lips. 'And I hope you weren't about to get jealous on me, were you?'

Allie began to object, but Rory silenced her with another kiss, sending a thousand fireflies fluttering around her stomach.

'You are amazing, gorgeous and funny, and my life would

not be the same without you in it,' he murmured as he pulled away gently. 'In fact, it would definitely not be the same without you in it ... more peaceful and calm, I'd say.' He gave her a sheepish grin and Allie swiped his arm playfully.

'I do love you,' he said, lowering his lips to hers. She grasped his hair and pulled him towards her, kissing him harder. Rory rolled on top of her and Allie screamed, 'Ouch! What's that? There's something sharp digging in my back.'

Rory pulled her up and opened the bag she'd fallen on. 'Ha! It's my rosette for winning the best Easter bonnet competition at school,' he said with a grin. 'It all kicked off when I won because Jarrod Braithwaite's mum had spent what looked like the whole weekend conjuring up a bonnet that no way on this earth could any child our age could have made, and mine was stuck together with animal hair, feathers and anything I could put my hands on from the surgery.'

Rory secured the pin at the back of the rosette and placed it on the arm of the settee while Allie took a closer look inside the bag. 'What are all these?' she asked, intrigued. There were ten jam jars with dated labels. She pulled one out of the bag and saw it was packed full of strips of paper.

'Ha! Those are my memory jars. Those five are from primary school and those five are from my time at high school.'

'And these?' she asked, pulling out numerous photographs in clear plastic wallets.

'Those are the photographs from my childhood. Look, there's one here from the day I was born. Mum and Dad standing on the hospital steps with me in their arms. They must have thought they were royalty, the way they are posing.'

Allie turned the first one over and howled with laughter. 'Oh my God, Rory, look at those trousers and that jumper! And your hair swept to one side like a combover.'

Rory cringed. 'Apparently that was called being on trend, and my mother used to lick her hand and try to straighten down the sticky-up bits. It was so embarrassing.' He shook his head. 'I would never dress our children that way or ever comb their hair that way. Please tell me you won't either.'

'So, we are going to have children?' Allie couldn't help but smile.

'One day a whole football team,' he said, grinning. 'Family is important.'

'A whole football team? We need serious words ... Maybe two,' she argued playfully, unscrewing the lid of one of the memory jars and pulling out a slip of paper. '"I was allowed to stay up past 8pm on a school night,"' she read out loud, turning the paper over and looking at the date on the front of the jar.

Rory grinned and poured them both a glass of wine. 'For ten years of my life this was part of my bedtime routine.

250

Mum would cut the little strips of paper and each night after she'd read me a story she'd encourage me to write a good memory about my day. Then we would place it in the jar and by the end of the year I would have three hundred and sixty-five memories.'

'This is so cute. What a brilliant idea.' Allie kept reading the little slips of paper. '"Today was a good day, I beat Drew Allaway in the 100m sprint at sports day."'

Rory laughed. 'That *was* a good day! We all know how competitive Drew was and still is!'

'"I helped Dad to bake my mum a birthday cake. Happy birthday, Mum!"' Allie read out before taking a sip of her wine. 'These shouldn't be stored away in an attic. These should be out on a shelf and every time you are having a bad day you can read one of them.'

'It's probably best not to read the jar from my last year of high school. That will make for interesting reading. It all went on then!'

Allie noticed the mischievous glint in his eye and dived towards the jar. Rory did the same and they play-wrestled on the floor until they were doubled over laughing. The jar safely in Rory's hands, he held it high. 'It's just like you girls writing diaries, we wouldn't dream of reading what's inside.'

'Who're you trying to kid? There is no way on this earth if you came across a diary you wouldn't read what's written inside. Curiosity would always get the better of you.'

'I can neither confirm nor deny,' he said, chuckling, while unscrewing the lid of the jam jar and spreading the memories out on the floor. 'This was my life as a sixteen-year-old boy.' Allie began to pick up the random pieces of paper and read them out loud. They spent the next hour laughing heartily at Rory's memories as a sixteen-year-old. Most of the time Rory was suitably embarrassed but he took it all in good humour.

Even though the evening had begun on a sad note, Allie felt like her relationship with Rory was back on track. This was how it had always been, full of laugher.

'Look at the time, doesn't it fly when—'

'When you're making fun of me,' interrupted Rory.

'But you know it's not done with any malice. I think these jars are brilliant and it would be something I would encourage our children to do.' Allie emphasized the 'our'. 'I wish I'd done something similar. Fabulous keepsake.'

Rory began to stack the jars back in the bag and placed it in the 'keep' pile. The room was still in chaos, but more organised chaos.

'Okay,' said Rory taking control, 'this pile goes out to the trailer, this pile will be going into storage and those bits can go back to Mum and Dad's with me.'

Box by box they began to haul the unwanted pile out to the trailer and it was full to the brim in no time. When the last file was thrown in, Rory slipped his arms around Allie's waist and they took in the magnificent view in front of them: Heartcross Mountain reaching for the sky, the burnt orange meadow flowers dancing amongst the purple heather. It all looked so peaceful.

Over at Foxglove Farm the herd of alpacas could be seen grazing in the field next to the old vintage campervans that Isla had successfully transformed into a camping site. Luckily for her Zach's fan club seemed to have dwindled for the time being.

Allie swung her glance towards Bonnie's Teashop, where through the window she could see Rona, busy cleaning the ovens, while Felicity mopped the floors. She caught Felicity's eye and waved at them both.

They watched a joyous group of ramblers heading towards them, singing songs. No doubt a well-earned pint was in order before climbing into bed.

'I can't believe tomorrow is my last night in this house.' Rory turned towards the whitewashed terrace that he'd grown very fond of. 'I'm not sure why they are kicking me out and renting it to a stranger, when I could have paid the rent.'

Allie shrugged. 'We don't know anything about anything. People have reasons for their actions, like we've just discovered.'

'I suppose the bottom line is it's their property and they can do what they want. Maybe they need the money to help with Mum's future care.'

'That could well be the case,' agreed Allie, snuggling into his chest.

'But I will need to have a chat with Zach sooner rather

than later and let him know about Africa.' Rory sounded subdued. 'It just isn't my time.'

Allie gave him a squeeze. 'You'll get your time,' she said, meaning every word. 'We'll make sure you get your time.'

They stared at the view in quiet contemplation before Allie broke the silence.

'What's going to happen to your mum, Rory? Will she be allowed to stay at home?' Allie looked up and caught his eye.

'It's early days. Dad said she has a care plan that includes doing the things that are important for as long as possible, but there will come a time when things will get too difficult.'

Allie nodded. 'I'm just thinking out loud ... about your mum's birthday – no doubt everyone will gather in the pub as usual, with music and food, and it wouldn't be a birthday without Hamish playing his fiddle, but how about making it more of a personal affair?'

'Meaning?' Rory held her gaze.

'Those photos, those memory jars ...'

'What about them?'

'I'm thinking, let's turn those photos into a slideshow. Let's pass round our own memory jar. Each of us can add our own memory of Alana and we can share them with her on her birthday. It will be good for everyone, a memory of memories ... what do you think?'

Rory's eyes brightened. 'I think that's a genius idea,' he exclaimed, pulling Allie in for an extra tight hug.

'We can use the little room at the back of the pub. Shall we run it by your dad?'

'I can do that it in the morning but for now I've got other ideas.'

'And what would they be?'

The wicked glint in Rory's eye said it all and Allie's body began to tremble with desire. He tugged at her shirt, pulled her lightly back up the path and they stumbled through the front door. Allie's heart was beating fast as she leant against the wall and lifted her hand to stroke his stubble. Their eyes stayed locked upon each other as Rory pressed his mouth against hers and her body exploded with goose-bumps. Allie grasped his hair and kissed him hard, the electricity flying. Still kissing, they clambered over the boxes and chaos that littered the stairs, tugging at each other's clothes, until they fell into bed together.

It was early morning and the sun was shining through a gap in the curtains. Allie was still lying in bed entwined in Rory's arms, an overwhelming feeling of happiness surging through her body. Luckily, she was on the late shift today, unlike Rory, who she knew would need to be up and awake in the next hour to make it in time for morning surgery.

She tilted her head, kissed him lightly on the lips and murmured, 'Wake up, sleepy head. I'll make you a cup of tea. I'll be back in a second.'

Grabbing Rory's sloppy sweatshirt she pulled it over

her head and carefully stepped down the stairs, avoiding all the clutter, which she knew would be gone by the end of the day. They hadn't really had a chance to talk about Rory's long-term living arrangements, but with everything that was going on at the moment it was easier to take each day as it came. As she flicked on the kettle she smiled at the newspaper lying on the kitchen table. It was open at the article featuring Rory and Sydney. The TV crew had wrapped up in the village and were off to their next filming, while Zach had decided to stay around and enjoy a few days of leisure time with Sydney before he jetted off to Africa, leaving his faithful friend behind.

Staring at the photograph, she thought again about the job interview in Glasgow. What would happen if she did get the job? How would she feel if Rory was now staying in Heartcross and she was the one leaving him behind? This roller-coaster of life was throwing her emotions in every possible direction.

'Take one day at a time,' she murmured to herself. 'No decisions need to be made today. Wait and see what happens first.'

Closing the newspaper, she was distracted by a van revving its engine outside. It was probably Drew coming to pick up the trailer, she thought, reflecting that Rory's stuff was going to make one hell of a bonfire. There was movement outside the front window followed by a knock on the door.

'Coming, Drew!' she shouted, placing the key in the

lock. 'The kettle's on if you want a quick coffee.' She opened the door to discover it wasn't Drew but a tall slim man, immaculately dressed. For a second she was mesmerised by his thick neat eyebrows, symmetrical lips and high cheekbones. With his streaks of grey hair at the temples and his designer stubble Allie could imagine him breaking all the rules in the book.

As he swept his hair out of his eyes she noticed the veins on his hand, suggesting strength and stamina, Feeling self-conscious dressed in her PJs and Rory's sweatshirt, and embarrassed by her bed hair, which must have resembled some kind of bird's nest, Allie said apologetically, 'Sorry, I thought you were someone else. Can I help you?'

The man looked down at the papers in his hand. 'Is this number 10, Love Heart Lane?'

'Yes, but we aren't expecting a delivery. Are you expecting a delivery?' Allie shouted over her shoulder to Rory upstairs.

'I'm not here to deliver anything. According to these papers I'm moving in today, but I was expecting to find the property empty.'

Allie took the papers from his hand and the penny dropped. 'Flynn Carter,' she said perplexed. 'Sorry, Flynn, I've forgotten my manners. I'm Allie.' He gave her a nod of the head. 'But we weren't expecting you until tomorrow,' she continued.

'Who is it?' shouted Rory from the top of the stairs.

'It's Flynn – Flynn Carter, the new tenant.'

Allie could hear some kerfuffle upstairs then Rory's footsteps bounding down. Smiling to herself, she noticed that Rory had pulled his joggers on back to front, but she didn't like to point it out in front of company.

Arriving at the bottom of the stairs he stretched out his hand. 'Pleased to meet you. I'm Rory, this is Allie. I just heard you say you're moving in today. We thought it was tomorrow, hence we are still very much in a state.' He cast a glance at the boxes piled high.

Now it was Flynn's turn to look perplexed. He juggled the papers and looked at the agreement in his hand. 'I'm sure Alana Scott told me it was today' – he perused the paperwork – 'but I have to say the date doesn't correspond to the day ...'

Rory stared down at the rental agreement Flynn was holding in his hand. He was indeed correct, 'Well, if we go by the day it's today, if we go by the date it's tomorrow,' said Rory, looking towards Allie, who was thinking exactly the same as he was: it might just be a simple mistake or Alana could have been confused.

'But whichever it is, don't stand on the doorstep. Come on in so we can sort out a plan of action,' insisted Rory, holding open the door.

'Honestly, I don't want to intrude. I've just passed a B&B. I can see if I can get a room there for the night.'

'Nonsense, we can work it out.' Rory waved him into the living room.

'You do know you've got your joggers on back to front,'

Allie whispered, chuckling as she pinged the elastic in the back of Rory's trousers. In return he gave her the kind of look that silenced a person and made them behave straight-away.

'Take a seat if you can find one.' Allie quickly cleared a space on the sofa and Flynn sat down and rested his papers on his knee.

'Tea or coffee?' asked Rory, hovering by the kitchen door.

'Coffee, one sugar. Thanks.'

Allie risked a tentative look in the mirror and really wished she hadn't. Her hair was matted and yesterday's make-up was smudged under her eyes.

Allie could hear Rory on the phone in the kitchen and she stood in the doorway and listened. He was talking to his dad and from how the conversation was panning out it seemed that Stuart was also under the impression that Flynn would be arriving tomorrow. But they soon managed to shuffle Rory's morning appointments around to give him some extra time to get his stuff moved.

'Honestly, I can keep all my belongings in the van and hunt down a bed for the night, it's no problem,' insisted Flynn as soon as Rory walked back into the living room.

'It's not a problem. I just need to move this stuff to various places and this place is all yours.'

'Have you come far?' asked Allie, intrigued by the dark brooding man sitting in front of her. She'd already noted the lack of wedding ring and the contemporary scent that lingered around him. He reminded Allie of a warrior who waged war, peace and romance with equal skill.

'About forty miles,' Flynn answered, not giving much away.

'And Dad mentioned you were a property developer. What brings you to Heartcross?' asked Rory, taking a sip of his drink.

'Tourism. Since the bridge collapsed this village seems to be constantly in the news.' Flynn stared at Rory, 'I recognize you from the newspaper. The vet who saved Zach Hudson's dog ... I bet your business is suddenly booming with your celebrity status.'

Allie couldn't help but think that was a swift change of conversation. Flynn Carter was giving nothing away about himself.

'It's had its moments,' answered Rory.

'Are you looking to invest in the area?' asked Allie, bringing the conversation back round to Flynn.

'Maybe,' he answered, still being evasive.

'Your dad mentioned you'd bought the old boathouse. What're the plans for that place?'

Flynn raised his eyebrows. 'Amongst other things, water-sports: kayaking, rowing boats, speedboat hire.'

Rory gave Allie an approving nod. 'We'd definitely be up for hiring a speedboat, wouldn't we?'

'Absolutely,' replied Allie. She already had visions of them cruising up the River Heart, stopping at the bay for a picnic.

'The old manor house has been standing empty for years too,' chipped in Allie. 'There's rumours flying around the village that the old place is going to be converted into retirement flats.'

'Starcross Manor,' added Rory. 'Magnificent place.'

Starcross was indeed magnificent, thought Allie. The Georgian manor was set in a hundred acres of park incorporating formal gardens, a private deer park, wild-flower meadow and woodlands. She thought back to the last time she was there, walking Nell through the grounds. The old place was abandoned and closed down and ivy clung to the walls of the building. As a child Allie had been impressed by the large double oak doors within a broad porch of stone pillars. The driveway was grand, sweeping in a wide circle, with an ornate fountain in the centre. Allie had remembered she used to stand behind the oak tree alongside her mum as they watched all the extravagant weddings and dreamt one day that it would be her stepping out with horse and carriage to marry her happy-ever-after.

One afternoon, back when they were in their late teens, Allie and the rest of the gang had sneaked a couple of ciders from the pub and found themselves in the woodlands at the back of the green. They'd followed Drew towards the manor house and found a door unlocked. Once inside the main reception room they had been amazed by the vast space and the staircase that twisted in a perfect spiral before their eyes. Each stair was walnut, with a thick, undisturbed layer of dust. An owl had hooted and the whole gang had screamed and scampered.

Allie had passed through the grounds a couple of weeks back and felt saddened by the house standing there growing old and tattered. She'd noticed the odd window was broken and some of the bricks were crumbling but it was still a thing of beauty.

Rory continued, 'Do you know anything about the retirement homes?'

'I'm afraid not,' replied Flynn, draining the drink from his mug then standing up. 'I'll let you pair get on. It looks like you are going to have a busy day ahead. Thanks for the drink,' he said, handing Rory his card. 'My number. Please let me know when I can move in.'

'Don't fret, we'll be out today,' confirmed Allie, thinking of the mammoth task ahead.

Flynn nodded his appreciation and once the front door had shut behind him Allie wandered over to the window.

'What do you think about him?' Allie asked, watching Flynn linger by the side of the van. He was staring across towards the teashop and looked like he was heading that way but then stopped. He glanced down at his phone before swiftly changing direction and walking back towards the van.

'He seemed a nice sort ... Expensive shoes, I noticed.'

'Hmmm.' Allie continued to stare out of the window.

'You're not convinced?'

'He seemed guarded.' He was keeping his cards way too close to his chest for Allie's liking.

'Give the man a break – he's only just arrived here and discovered we haven't moved out yet. In the circumstances I thought he was very accommodating.'

'There's something about him, you mark my words.' She gave Rory a knowing look. 'You heard it here first,' she added, turning back towards the window and watching the van disappear out of sight. 'There is something about Flynn Carter ...'

Chapter 18

'Why the bonfire? It's not November,' asked Finn, stuffing his face with marshmallows and sharing them with Esme as they watched the orange flames dance before their eyes.'

'Just so we could roast marshmallows,' answered Drew, ruffling his son's hair. 'Now take those inside with Esme and great-granny Martha will pop a film on for you both. Make sure you tell her there's some of her favourite chocolate in the bottom of the fridge.'

They all watched as Finn and Esme raced towards the back door of the farmhouse, clutching the bag of marshmallows, their bright yellow wellies clomping on the ground.

'So cute,' exclaimed Allie. 'I wish we could stay that age for ever. I'm feeling exhausted after spending most of the day shifting Rory's stuff.' Thankfully now they were sitting in camping chairs alongside their friends, huddled around the fire, clutching a well-earned beer while watching all of Rory's old university files go up in flames.

'How are you feeling?' Allie asked Rory.

'I've never known anyone accumulate so much crap,' said Fergus, laughing as he threw the next bin bag full of stuff on to the fire.

'I think that's one of the reasons I never want to move,' chipped in Isla. 'Can you imagine what's up in our loft?' She rolled her eyes at Drew.

'"Shove it in the loft,"' he said, mimicking her. '"You never know when you'll need it."'

'You behave or I'll shove you in the loft,' she joked.

Watching the banter between his friends Rory reached over to Allie, who was sitting next to him, and took her hand. 'Considering I thought this would be my last night sleeping in my house in Love Heart Lane, I'm actually feeling a little sad.' His eyes were fixed on the fire, the flames rising boldly. They all listened to the crackling, and the air was filled with the woody fragrance of smoke.

'Don't feel sad,' insisted Felicity, who was sitting next to Fergus. 'Just think of it as new beginnings. There's something better to come.' She smiled and raised her can of beer. 'Cheers,' she said and the others followed suit.

Rory managed a smile and reached down to stroke Sydney's fur. She was lying at Zach's feet. 'She's one hell of a dog.'

'She is indeed,' Zach answered, taking a swig of his beer.

'I'm sorry to let you down, Zach,' said Rory.

Allie thought she heard his voice wobble slightly, but she knew the only way to know there were better days ahead was to endure the present anguish. They'd get through it together.

'Let me down?' Zach looked towards Rory.

'Africa ... I'm sorry I can't come but with everything going on now at home ...' Rory had called round to the camper van early that evening to have a chat with Zach about the expedition to Africa. He'd had so much fun on the TV show working alongside Zach, and was devastated to turn down such a fantastic opportunity, but he knew it was the right thing to do.

'I understand, family is family and you are lucky to have so many people who care about you.' Zach looked unhappy. 'You lot'– he looked round at them all – 'you have made me feel so welcome. It's a very special place you have here. Those quaint little camping vans, the best pub I've ever had the pleasure of drinking in, the delicious breakfast in Bonnie's Teashop, and the most awesome vet who saved Sydney's life ... I hope you'll all welcome me back at any time.'

'Absolutely,' they chorused, holding their beer cans in the air.

'I actually don't want to go home. This place has captured my heart and I'm quite jealous you have all these wonderful friendships. Look at you all, throwing Rory's life on a bonfire and swigging beer, all together ... yes, jealous indeed,' he admitted.

'I happen to agree with all that,' chipped in Fergus, raising his can. 'I couldn't imagine or want to be anywhere else. Here's to good friends.'

'Here's to good friends,' everyone joined in.

'You must have some good friends though, Zach,' probed Allie. 'I mean, you *are* Zach Hudson.'

'And that's exactly where the problem lies.'

All eyes were on Zach.

'You can't stop there,' urged Isla. 'Come on.' She looked towards him for an explanation.

Zach took a deep breath. His stare unblinking, he revealed how he'd grown up in a small town feeling different from his friends at school, who didn't have the same interests. Going to drama school had made him feel happy at first. He'd thought he'd made friends there and had spent four years perfecting his craft before landing his very first job on TV. But that was when it all changed. People had stabbed him in the back, turned away from him, all because he had landed the part. They weren't his real friends, not people you could rely on in a crisis or sit round a bonfire with.

'And then when people do recognise who you are, they immediately want to be your new best friend.'

'It sounds like it must be quite a lonely life,' mused Allie.

'Sometimes it can be. But then I arrived in Heartcross.' His face lit up. 'Honestly, guys, apart from the invasion of fans at the summer fair and those who camped outside the surgery, I actually feel this place ...' Zach looked beyond the burning fire towards Heartcross Mountain, then towards the alpacas grazing in the field. 'I actually feel at home. Moving around from place to place, hotel to hotel – it's okay to begin with but believe me it gets tiresome.' He took a breath. 'I could only dream of having this. This is what you call proper friendship, friendship that has built up over the years. In my industry, you certainly find out who your real friends are. There, speech over!'

'I feel the need to applaud,' joked Isla. 'But you know what, slushy moment alert ...'

Everyone groaned.

Isla rolled her eyes, ignored them and continued, 'I couldn't ask for a better group of friends and I agree we are a very lucky bunch of humans.'

'Hear, hear,' agreed Drew, snapping back the ring pull on a can of beer and handing it to Zach.

'Maybe we could commission a show about friends,' said Felicity with a grin.

Isla let out a laugh. 'I think someone might have already beaten you to that idea!'

'Oh, yeah,' said Felicity, and giggled.

Allie felt sad listening to Zach. She could relate what he was saying to her own childhood. She'd felt lonely at times and had found it difficult to make friends. Living your life as an international superstar was clearly not what it was cracked up to be and she wholeheartedly agreed with him as her thoughts turned back towards the job interview for the Glasgow newspaper. She couldn't imagine being so far away from her friends. Zach was right: good friends were hard to come by, and these were people Allie knew she could rely on, if her life depended on it. She couldn't imagine not having her support network so close to her, and felt sad that others didn't have that in their life.

Hearing the crackle of the baby monitor by Isla's feet, Allie gave a chuckle. 'At least I'm not broadcasting on the other end of it this time.' She squeezed Rory's leg.

'Thank God,' he replied with a lopsided grin.

Over the airwaves they could hear Angus stretching in his cot and beginning to murmur.

'Martha's there, she'll see to him,' whispered Isla, holding the monitor in her hand. 'And why am I whispering? It's not as though he can hear me.'

They all listened in silence to Angus gurgling, then they heard him chuckle.

Allie brought her hand up to her chest. 'So adorable.'

Isla put her finger to her lips as they heard faint singing in the background. 'Listen.'

Martha began to sing an ancient Scottish lullaby. Her voice was angelic and everyone listening was transfixed.

> *I left my baby lying here,*
> *Lying here, lying here,*
> *I left my baby lying here,*
> *To go and gather blaeberries.*
> *Hovan, Hovan Gorry og O*
> *I've lost my darling baby, O!*

'Are you smiling at me? Are you?' Martha's lovable voice filtered through the monitor. 'Let's get you changed and give you a quick feed,' she said.

They heard Martha scooping Angus up and leaving the bedroom.

'I've said it before and I'll say it again, she's worth her weight in gold, that one.'

Drew nodded in agreement.

'I just want to stay for ever,' sighed Zach. 'How much for a long-term rental of a van?'

'This one never went home.' Felicity nodded towards Alfie and Polly, who were strolling down the long drive of Foxglove Farm hand in hand, swinging a carrier bag and laughing. 'Look at them. Young love.'

The pair of them were ambling along without a care in the world, their eyes locked on each other, sharing kisses as they walked.

'Over here,' shouted Drew, and Alfie held up the bag. 'We've brought supplies!'

Slung across their backs were their camping chairs. They unpacked them and sat down with everyone.

'So what's the fire in aid of?' asked Alfie, noticing the pieces of handwritten paper floating in the air like confetti.

'My life ... university papers, all the useless stuff I've been hoarding,' said Rory.

'It's your last night in Love Heart Lane, isn't it?' Alfie passed a gin in a tin over to Polly.

Rory shook his head. 'Should have been tonight but it

271

was actually last night. I'm officially living back with the parents – well, for now anyway.'

'Have you met the guy who's rented it out?'

Allie and Rory gave each a look.

'We will leave you to make your own mind up. Never judge someone on someone else's opinion,' Allie announced in a serious tone, taking everyone by surprise.

'Whoa, whoa, whoa, stop right there!' Felicity held up her hand like an overzealous traffic warden and looked towards Allie. 'There's definitely a story there. We know that look. What's he done to upset you?'

'Nothing, just call it a woman's intuition.'

'The poor guy has done absolutely nothing. He's okay,' added Rory.

'Maybe he's a politician as well as a property developer, as he avoided questions at all costs. We found out zilch about him.'

'Maybe he's just a private person and feels he doesn't need to share his life history with someone he's only just met,' responded Rory.

'Guarded is what he is.' Allie was convinced that Flynn Carter was going to be a force to be reckoned with.

They continued to throw Rory's belongings into the fire as they sat around chatting about anything and everything. Zach was amazed to hear about the collapse of the bridge last year, cutting Heartcross off from civilisation until they raised enough money to help fund a temporary bridge.

'What's it like where you live, Zach?' asked Fergus, imagining he lived in a mansion with a swimming pool and its own gym.

'It's just a flat. Extortionate rent due to location, not enough room to swing a cat and I've no idea who any of my neighbours are.'

'I couldn't imagine walking down the street and not knowing someone. We all know everyone. As kids we moved from house to house raiding everyone's biscuit tin.' Isla chuckled, thinking about the days when life was simple.

'Scrumping in Hamish's orchard,' chipped in Fergus.

'We used to throw the apples down the line and chuck them in the old wicker basket and eat them in the hideout up the mountain pass.'

'I feel like I'm in the middle of a *Famous Five* book,' said Zach with a laugh. 'You'll be telling me there were lashings of ginger beer next.'

'Africa next for you then, mate, wrestling lions,' said Drew, looking towards Zach, who nodded.

As Zach began to talk about his upcoming documentary and his trip to Africa, Allie noticed that Rory looked a tad upset, which was not surprising. One minute he was going, the next he wasn't. She squeezed his knee and he attempted to hitch a smile on his face, but he couldn't hide his disappointment. Allie had to admit that sitting there listening to Zach she too was deeply disappointed for Rory.

'You're going too, aren't you, mate?' asked Alfie, unaware that Rory had changed his plans.

Rory reluctantly shook his head. 'With Mum's diagnosis

I'm not sure how quickly things are going to change. Being away for twelve months was too long to leave Dad coping with the surgery and Mum,' he said, unable to hide the disappointment in his voice. 'But mark my words, I'll become just like one of Zach's superfans, stalking him on Instagram every day.'

'When are you leaving, Zach?' asked Allie.

'Early next week, but in the meantime I'm just enjoying chilling in the van with this one' – he ruffled Sydney's head – 'before I have to venture out into the real world. The lack of phone signal is absolutely bliss, I have to say.'

'You wouldn't think that if you lived here,' chorused everyone. The lack of phone signal drove them all insane daily.

'Who's this coming up the drive now?' asked Isla, narrowing her eyes to take a better look.

Everyone looked over.

Rona and Aggie, dressed in hiking gear, swayed up the gravel. Their arms were linked, their faces flushed, and they were singing at the tops of their voices.

> *Just got in from the Isle of Skye,*
> *I'm not very big and I'm awfully shy,*
> *The ladies shout as I go by,*
> *Donald, where's your troosers?*
> *Let the winds blow high, Let the winds blow low,*
> *Down the street in my kilt I go,*
> *And all the ladies say hello,*
> *Donald, where's your troosers?*

'This is so embarrassing,' said Felicity, watching her mum and Aggie dance around each other. 'It's their new keep fit regime, *let's start walking to lose a bit of flab,* they said, but to me it looks like they've been in the pub, all the gear and no idea.'

Zach couldn't take his eyes off the two women as they carried on like they didn't have a care in the world. They danced and twirled, jigged their knees up and down with less rhythm than a spider on a trampoline, limbs all over the place, but they were exhilarated, giddy and, by the looks of things, a little tipsy. It was infectious to watch.

Suddenly, Zach launched himself off his feet, and pulled Isla to hers. 'What are you doing, you loon?' she said, laughing, and they all joined in singing the Scottish song. Allie and Rory followed suit and before they knew it everyone was dancing around the dying flames of the bonfire.

'This is contagious,' bellowed Zach over the singing, He was enjoying every second. Sydney opened one eye and immediately closed it again; she wasn't for moving. 'This place just captures magic.'

Within seconds Aggie and Rona had spotted them and hurried over to join the circle. 'That's it, I'm done,' said Felicity, laughing and flapping a hand in front of her face, and she sat down again.

'Call yourself youngsters? Look at you, all out of breath.' Aggie put her hands on her hips and danced a short sharp burst of some kind of jig. They all watched with amusement. She stopped when she set eyes on Zach. 'You do look much more handsome in real life,' she said with a glint in her eye.

'Mum, don't embarrass the poor man,' said Fergus, rolling his eyes in jest. 'And anyway, I thought you were going for a walk, not' – he leant forward and wrinkled his nose – 'going to the pub.'

'For your information we have been for a walk *and* to the pub and now we've come to keep Martha company while you lot are putting the world to rights.'

'Oh, and we think the idea behind your mum's birthday is an excellent one, Rory. We have so many photographs and lots of memories to put in the jar,' said Rona, looking straight at Rory.

'What's this about a jar?' asked Fergus.

'Mum's birthday,' said Rory. 'We were thinking of doing a slideshow full of old photographs and putting a memory jar together with things that we can read out to embarrass her. Something low-key but meaningful for us all. So we all have memories of memories. How do you know about it already?'

'We just bumped into your dad on our walk,' answered Aggie, pinching a peanut from the bag Drew had just opened. 'We've been everywhere.' Aggie rattled on with the details of their route, along the river to the old boat-house, then left over the hillside until they reached the green. They'd taken the path at the back of the green through the woodlands and the grounds of Starcross

Manor, over the fields, past Clover Cottage and back along the river.

Aggie fiddled with the new-fangled watch she was wearing. 'Over 10,000 steps – today's target is met,' she stated triumphantly. 'And your dad was with a very dashing young man. We've not seen him around these parts before, have we, Rona?' She looked at Rona and carried on fiddling with her watch.

'Dark and brooding he was,' said Rona. 'Man of few words,' she added.

'Flynn Carter.' Allie filled in the name.

Rona pointed at her. 'That's it, Flynn Carter. His suit wouldn't look out of place on Savile Row and that aftershave, mark my words, was not your average Aramis.'

Rory was far from interested in Flynn Carter's dress sense or what aftershave he was wearing. 'Flynn Carter was with my dad?'

'Yes, up at Clover Cottage. There was some sort of heated discussion going on. Have to say Stuart looked a little rattled,' admitted Aggie.

Rory looked towards Allie. 'I told you there was something about him.'

Allie didn't have a good feeling about this at all and by the look on Rory's face he was thinking exactly the same.

Why the hell was Flynn Carter up at Clover Cottage?

Chapter 19

With a thumping heart Allie followed Rory back to his parents' cottage.

'Rory, slow down,' cried Allie. 'We don't know why they were up at Clover Cottage.' But Rory carried on striding. He knew his parents usually went to bed around this time but was hoping to catch his dad.

He sighed as he approached the cottage. 'Damn.' The whole house was in darkness. He'd have to wait until tomorrow to investigate why his dad had been with Flynn Carter, even though he could probably make an accurate guess.

'Just don't go waking anyone up or crashing around inside,' insisted Allie, following Rory quietly into the hallway, but both stopped dead when they heard the clunk of a glass being placed on a table. Rory looked towards Allie. 'Come on, someone is up. Dad, is that you?' he asked, pushing open the living-room door. 'Why are you sitting in the dark?'

His dad didn't answer but picked up his glass and swirled the amber liquid before draining it.

'Shall I go?' whispered Allie, not wanting to intrude.

'No, Allie, stay, you're family,' insisted Stuart.

Switching on the table lamp Rory couldn't help noticing that his dad looked exhausted. His eyes were heavy and bloodshot and he'd been crying.

Rory didn't know what to think except the worst-case scenario. 'What's happened? Is it Mum?' he asked, sliding on to the sofa next to his dad. Allie perched on the wingback leather chair next to the fire.

Stuart shook his head and patted Rory's knee like he was a small child. 'No, your mum is sleeping. Ignore me. I'm just being a silly old fool.'

Rory felt a churning in his stomach. 'Dad, you're sitting in the dark drinking whisky. Has this got something to do with Flynn Carter and the reason why you were up at Clover Cottage tonight?'

Stuart exhaled, and topped up the whisky in his glass then locked eyes with Rory.

'Dad, what is it?' asked Rory, feeling his heartbeat quicken, 'You are beginning to worry me now.'

Stuart turned and stared into his glass. 'The past has a way of catching up with you when you least expect it.'

Rory noticed his dad bite his lip to stop it trembling. Stuart pointed to two envelopes lying on the table, which Rory hadn't noticed. Leaning forward, he picked up the envelope nearest to Rory and handed it to him. Taking it, Rory looked towards Allie, who simply shrugged. He didn't have a clue what was inside. With an uneasy feeling swirling in the pit of his stomach, he opened the envelope and took out the contents: a letter and an old black-and-white photograph of two small boys sitting on the steps of a huge stone building. He showed them to Allie.

'I don't get it. Who are the boys in the photograph?' asked Rory, looking at his dad.

'That is me, five years old.' Stuart pointed to the boy on the left.

'And where are you? It looks like some sort of castle.'

Stuart swallowed. 'Far from a castle,' he said, and took a second to compose himself. 'That place, Rory, is Birkhill Care Home for Boys – my home for two years.'

Rory felt like he'd been hit by a high-speed train. He was dumbfounded. He saw shock on Allie's face too. This was the first he'd ever heard of his dad being in care.

'I don't understand. Why would you be in a care home? Granny and Grandad thought the world of you,' he asked softly, treading carefully. Rory could see the distress this conversation was causing his dad.

'You'd best pour yourself a whisky, son, and you too, Allie.'

Rory did as he was told, gave them both a good measure and sat back down. He was experiencing every emotion possible as his dad resumed speaking.

'Granny and Grandad were not my biological parents.'

Rory blew out a breath and raked a hand through his hair. Even though the words registered he just didn't understand any of it. Why was he only finding this out now? Allie got up from her chair and settled on the arm of the settee, resting her hand reassuringly on Rory's shoulder.

Stuart carried on. 'I was born to Florence Smith, who was only seventeen at the time. She must have been a gutsy girl because even though she was a single parent she fought to keep me even when her parents disowned her.'

Rory didn't understand. 'Did she struggle to look after you?'

'No, not from what I was told. Even though we lived in a dingy flat in one of the less salubrious areas of Glasgow. I was only young and don't have vivid concrete memories but ...' Rory watched his dad screw his eyes up like he was trying to remember. 'I can remember a room with a double bed. I remember waking up to noise pounding above my head. I remember hearing arguments through the wafer-thin walls and a woman who I'm assuming was my mother sitting at a sewing machine in the corner of the room making clothes. I remember there was a rail with everything she'd made hanging up, with home-made price tags attached. I have no idea where she sold them, maybe down the market. That is the only recollection I have.'

Stuart took a breath and a swig of his drink then carried on.

'The only thing I remember after that is arriving at Birkhill Boys' Home. I don't recall how I got there, who took me ... I've just no idea. The only thing I had with me was a small brown case, two changes of clothes and Eddy.'

'Eddy?' asked Rory.

'My teddy bear.' Stuart smiled fondly. 'And this too.'

He reached for his wallet on the dresser and took out

an old battered photograph. He passed it to Rory who then showed Allie. The photograph was of a baby cradled in a woman's arm.

'Apparently that's me, my mother and Eddy.' He pointed to the teddy bear that he was clutching. 'My adoptive parents gave me the photograph. It must have been with my stuff when they picked me up and took me home. They never hid the fact I was adopted. I knew from an early age. And Emmeline and George gave me their world, I couldn't have asked for more loving parents, or grandparents for you. I always felt like that was where I was meant to be. I couldn't have asked for a better life.'

'How did you end up in the home in the first place?' asked Allie, softly.

'My mum passed. Pneumonia, it states on her death certificate. I was one of the lucky ones. My time in the boys' home passed quickly and I was adopted by the most wonderful of couples.'

Once more Stuart looked down at the photograph and dabbed his eyes. 'The sad thing about it all is that my mother Florence was a strong, determined woman. She put up such a fight to keep me; she chose me and lost her family because of the outcry and embarrassment of being a single mother, and then passed away with pneumonia. Her death was tragic; she was taken way too soon. Things could have been so different for me.'

They sat in silence, lost in their own thoughts. Rory thought back to his grandparents, Granny Emmy and

Grandpa George. They were originally from Glasgow but ended up living in a house on the edge of Glensheil. George too had been a vet but worked for a practice in the town. In the holidays his granny had taught him to bake while his grandpa had set up a train track in the loft space and taught him to fish in the River Heart. He had the fondest of memories and was full of love for both of them. He would never have known or had any suspicion that they weren't his biological grandparents.

'How are you feeling?' asked Stuart, looking at his son.

Rory's wondering gaze kept moving between the photograph and his dad. 'Shocked,' he said, blowing out a breath. 'I just wasn't expecting this.' He was so sorry to hear about the tragic death of Florence. If his grandparents hadn't adopted his dad and rescued him from the care system, life most probably would be very different today.

'Florence sounds like a very brave lady,' said Allie, still staring at the photograph.

'I think she was,' agreed Stuart.

'So what's this?' asked Rory, holding up the folded letter. 'And who's that? Who's the other boy in the photograph?'

For a second, Stuart remained silent, but his eyes were earnest. He dabbed them once more with his handkerchief and looked like he was swallowing down a lump in his throat. When he spoke, his voice was shaky. 'The other boy in the photograph is James Kerr. The man who left me Clover Cottage.'

Chapter 20

Rory's jaw dropped. His head was spinning with that information. 'You were in the same boys' home as James Kerr?' he asked, still trying to get his head around his father's words.

'I was, according to that letter you have in your hand. It was given to me when I was summoned to the solicitors. I was told to bring two forms of identification. I had no idea why and your mum suggested it must be some sort of hoax. But after receiving a signed letter to remind me of the appointment I thought I'd better attend and see what it was all about and that's when I discovered the boy who was my only friend in that care home was James.'

'And you've been neighbours for all these years. You were even his vet, looking after his herds.'

'I had no idea, but he knew.' Stuart's eyes welled up with instant tears. 'Somehow he knew and now he's passed I can't ask him how he knew or why he never said anything to me. That letter is from James. He left it with the solicitor and instructed them to give it to me after he'd passed away. The solicitor claimed the letter had been logged with them for over twenty-five years.'

Rory blew out a breath. 'Unbelievable.'

'Go on, read it.'

Stuart and Allie watched as Rory unfolded the paper. He stared down at the words written on it and without another word he began to read.

Dear Stuart,

I'm struggling to know how to begin this letter and you are probably sitting there bewildered and wondering why the hell I am writing to you.

I was the boy you shared a dorm with at Birkhill Boys' Home. You thought the name James was posh so came up with the nickname Jimbob which I eventually grew very fond of.

You were like a brother to me then, and we stuck by each other through thick and thin. Each day was tough, and I was the one who always broke the rules or rebelled against the teachers.

I remember each morning we had to stand by our beds and acknowledge the rules:

– Forget the evils of your past.

– Do not leave the premises.

– Strict obedience must be paid to the superintendent matron.

Clover Cottage

– Irreverent use of God's name, vulgar language, slang words and nicknames are absolutely forbidden.

– Neatness and cleanliness are a must at all times.

I could go on …

I also remember the day you walked out with your brand new family. It was bitterly cold, a January morning, and they'd brought you a brand-new coat to wear with a bright red scarf. They looked so caring and I was truly happy for your new start. We hugged on the stairs and you told me you'd left me a present on my bed and not to worry as a beautiful family would come for me soon. As you went to climb into the car you looked over your shoulder and gave me one last wave before driving off and leaving for your new life.

I treasured the present you left me, your brown velvet jumper. I wore it until the arms were somewhere near my elbows.

Unlike you, my new family never arrived.

I have no idea how to finish this letter except to say thank you. You were a good friend in some of the toughest times of my life without even knowing it. Therefore, it would be a great honour and a comfort to me if you would take care of my herds and Clover Cottage, when the time comes.

Thank you for your kindness,
Your brother in arms,
Jimbob

Silent tears slid down Rory's and Allie's faces. She had read the letter over his shoulder.

'I really don't know what to say,' said Rory softly.

'That makes two of us,' answered Stuart, still looking at the photograph. 'To think of him staying in the care system all that time.' Stuart's voice was shaky.

'And you had no clue that James was Jimbob?'

'No clue whatsoever. What I don't know is how he knew who I was and why he didn't tell me.'

'I suppose it's one of those questions we will never find out the answer to.'

Stuart was quiet as he read over the letter again. 'The memories from back then are hazy. We arrived at the same time and were put in the dormitory together and in that place we stuck together like superglue. We always had each other's backs and it's heartbreaking to know his new family never came. He lived there with those rules and regulations and no proper parents until I suppose he was sixteen.'

'What was his story? How did he end up being in there?' asked Allie.

Stuart shrugged. 'You weren't allowed to talk about it. The past was past. The only thought that haunts me is the fact that he never got out of there. He didn't have a proper family ... no home-cooked meals, no bedtime reading, no loving parents who looked out for you. I mean, my parents could have easily chosen Jimbob to take home to be their son. How do you choose? How does it happen that one boy gets a brand-new life and one doesn't?' Stuart's voice cracked as he squeezed his eyes shut.

Rory had never ever seen his dad so distraught. He was physically shaking as he drained his glass once more. Rory tactfully moved the bottle to one side; drinking wasn't going to help the situation.

'Dad, you had no control over that. You can't beat yourself up over it.'

'I keep thinking, Mum and Dad had no other children, why couldn't they have taken both of us?'

Rory could see this had shaken his dad, that he was hurting, but he didn't have any of the answers.

'We can't change the past. What's done is done.'

'He struggled and was dealt the shitty card of life. It's so unfair. Every morning since I've received that letter I wake up and think of the rules we had to chant out loud and to think he had to carry on doing that …'

'People judged James, his alcoholism, his sons,' said Allie, tearfully, thinking of the troubled life and reputation the Kerr family had had.

'I'm afraid so, but that's what people do. But I can honestly say he never did me any harm. He had a difficult life, but that man was a survivor, not a victim. Now pass that whisky bottle. We need a toast.'

Rory didn't argue but poured a small splash into his father's glass. After leaving the bonfire he never for a moment thought he would walk into a situation as extreme as this.

'To James Jimbob Kerr.' Stuart raised his glass.

'To James Jimbob Kerr,' Rory and Allie repeated.

With a terrible sadness bleeding through the room they sat in silence, lost in their own thoughts.

Rory looked at his watch. It was getting late. He needed to be up for the morning surgery. Placing his empty glass back down on the table, he noticed the second white envelope lying there.

'So what's in that second envelope?'

Stuart exhaled and raised an eyebrow.

'Written on a piece of paper in that envelope is the sum of money that Flynn Carter believes I will accept in exchange for Clover Cottage and all the land.'

Allie did everything in her power to stifle a gasp.

Rory couldn't believe his ears. He caught his breath and slumped back in the chair. 'You're kidding me. How much is written on it?'

Stuart shrugged. 'I've no idea. It's still sealed,' he said heaving himself up and out of the chair. 'I need my bed, otherwise I'll never get up in the morning.' He went to leave the room but paused beside Rory and rested his hand on his shoulder. 'I know I don't say it as often as I should, but I do love you, son.'

'I love you too, Dad.'

Hearing his dad's footsteps peter out at the top of the stairs and the creaking of the floorboards on the landing, Rory picked up the sealed envelope and flipped it over in his hand. He was curious to see the figure that Flynn

Carter thought he could buy his dad off for. After hearing about his father's past Rory felt a little angry towards Flynn Carter.

'I think your gut instinct might have been right about that man, Allie.'

'And I was hoping I was overreacting,' answered Allie, slipping into the space next to Rory on the settee.

'Who does he think he is, waltzing into our village offering money for Clover Cottage? What do you think he wants that for?'

'My guess is, just like any property developer, he's probably looking to build a brand-new housing estate.'

Rory's eyes widened, 'No one would want hundreds of houses squeezed together with gardens as small as postage stamps, spoiling the views and polluting the roads.'

Rory was sure the villagers would be up in arms about such an idea. The village was happy just the way it was and after everything his dad had shared with the two of them, he wasn't going to let Flynn get his hands on that land just to line his own pockets. Clover Cottage belonged in their family and he was going to honour James Kerr's wishes. Clover Cottage was going to stay exactly as it was.

Chapter 21

Meet me at Clover Cottage tonight 7pm.
Allie was lying in bed intrigued by Rory's early morning text.

They'd sat in shock for a while last night, talking in hushed whispers about Stuart's past. Rory had wanted to open Flynn's envelope, but Allie had advised strongly against it and placed it behind the clock on the mantelpiece for safe keeping. She texted back:

Why Clover Cottage at 7pm?

Her phone pinged almost immediately.

Just because.

Allie had a busy morning ahead. All the girls had arranged a breakfast meeting at the pub to begin to put together Alana's very own memory jar. Martha knew she had some old photographs from as far back as Stuart and Alana's wedding, and Rona had plenty too, which would be perfect for the slideshow. Placing the phone on the bedside table, Allie plumped up her pillows and lay back thinking of Rory and how proud she was of him. The way he'd stepped up to the mark after discovering his mum's condition just showed the kind, decent, genuine man she'd fallen in love with. Powering up the laptop next to her bed she began to research dementia. She wanted to do all she could to support Rory and had felt a real sense of belonging as one of his family when Stuart had shared the news of his past with her too. She began to read all the information available to her. Rory had told her that Alana was still in the early stages, but as Allie began to read through the blogs of people whose loved ones had developed dementia, she felt utterly heart-broken.

One husband's weekly blog was informative, detailing every moment from the second his wife was diagnosed. Simon had documented their daily lives to help others, even though Allie knew this was also a way of coping. Unfortunately, after five years, the blog had ended six months ago when Simon's wife had passed away. There was a beautiful photograph of Joyce that had been published in a women's magazine with an article titled 'Simon's Story'. Allie admired how Simon and his children had shared their own experience and she was touched by the way the man had put his feelings on the line and shared all the good as well as the trying situations of the last few years. One thing was clear: he loved his wife very much, and her diagnosis had never changed those feelings.

She read on and discovered Simon's passion was photography, too, and whilst Joyce was alive he'd created a magnificent memory board for her, full of photos of their family members, their children, their pet dog and friends. The board had been pinned to the wall in the kitchen.

Allie wiped away a lonely tear and felt some sort of connection she couldn't explain. The article had totally touched her heart. Impulsively, she fired an email off to the blog with such warmth for Simon and thanked him for sharing his posts. She included a quick update about Alana's diagnosis. She wasn't expecting a reply but by the time she'd got showered and ready for work there was an email sitting in her inbox. She clicked on it and read back an appreciative response from Simon, with a genuine offer to help or advise Stuart in any way he could. Quickly writing down his details she stuffed them in her pocket. She was sure Stuart would jump at the chance to talk to someone who'd coped in similar circumstances.

Walking down the stairs and through the door into the main pub she saw a table looking very fancy in the corner, with a couple of bottles of Buck's Fizz.

'What's all this?' asked Allie, looking towards her mum, who was polishing the ornaments on the bookcase.

'Mission Alana!' Meredith smiled. 'We are expecting the

girls and grannies once the children have been dropped at school.'

'Nice touch,' said Allie, thinking about Alana and the wonderful friends she had in the village.

'And Rona's bringing across some pastries but she can't stay as she needs to mind the teashop, but Felicity will be here.'

Lost in thought, Allie nodded.

'You've gone all pensive, what's on your mind?' asked Meredith passing the new beer mats to Allie, who laid them on the tables.

'Friends, life in general.'

'That's deep for this time in the morning.' Meredith stopped and looked at her daughter.

'Life is just so unfair sometimes. Why do awful things happen to the most wonderful people? What has Alana ever done to anyone?' Allie exhaled. 'And I know I wasn't initially pleased about the idea of Rory going away to Africa for a year—'

'But ...?' Meredith interrupted.

After reading Simon's story Allie had realised how much everyone's lives were going to change as Alana's illness took hold. In the early blogs Simon had shared the key to his happiness: not only should you carry on as normal but you should be sure to live life to the fullest and tick off all those things on your bucket list before it was too late. Knowing that the speed of the disease varied with each individual made Allie think of Rory and his dream of visiting Africa. When was he ever going to get an opportunity like this again? Allie knew he was putting his own dream on hold to support his family, which made her love him that tiny bit more, if that was even possible.

'But I think he should go.' Allie took a breath. 'I think he should go while he's got the chance.'

Allie couldn't believe what she was saying, but in the last few days all her own insecurities about their relationship had been eradicated. They'd been there for each other, supporting and encouraging. They were each other's future and she was in charge of her own destiny. She felt sad about Stuart's past but admired what he'd achieved in life: a successful business, the love of a good woman. It was all about loving and looking after each other like no one else mattered. The trip to Africa wasn't about *their* relationship, it was Rory's dream, something he'd wanted to do since university, something to tell their children about.

Meredith narrowed her eyes. 'Has something happened?'

'It has.' Allie shared with her mum about Stuart's past. Meredith couldn't quite believe it and pulled out a chair to sit down.

'Stuart was in a boys' home with James Kerr and he kept that hidden for all these years?'

'He didn't know it was James until he was left Clover Cottage in James's will,' said Allie.

'What a life that poor man had, in care all his childhood. What a struggle, I just can't comprehend it. I'm shocked. Everyone judged James, his unruly kids ... You never know what secrets the past hides. It just shows he was a decent man, leaving the cottage to Stuart.'

'I agree and I'm just trying to work out the best way to make it happen for Rory to go to Africa and whether it is possible with the way things are with Alana. I've been reading people's blogs in similar situations and everyone encourages you to carry on with your life as normally as possible whilst you still have the chance. Alana is only going to deteriorate over time and that's when Rory will really need to be at home helping his parents.'

During the hours Allie had been researching dementia, she'd also been thinking more about Stuart and his past with James Kerr, which had planted the seed of an idea in her mind.

'What do you think about this, Mum?' Allie enthused, 'I've an idea.'

But before she could carry on the conversation, the door to the pub swung open and in waltzed Felicity and Rona followed by Martha, Aggie and Isla in quick succession.

'Good morning!' cried Rona, walking towards them. 'Do you smell that?'

The source of the aroma was the delicious-looking tray of breakfast pastries she was carrying.

'That is the sweet smell of caramelised sugar and cinnamon, baked with my own fair hands, and those are Nutella puffs. Now don't think about the calories.'

Allie had no intention of thinking about the calories as she pinched one off the tray and popped it into her mouth.

'Mmm, oh my God, they are A-M-A-Z-I-N-G!' she said, stringing out the word and bringing her hand up to her mouth to catch the crumbs.

Rona chuckled. 'That's years of practice.'

'Where's Angus?' asked Allie, noticing the lack of wheels in front of Isla.

'Drew's taken him to market, starting him young,' said Isla grinning, as she took off her jacket and hung it on the back of her chair.

Allie got behind a frazzled-looking Aggie, who was juggling a large cardboard box and desperately trying not to drop it whilst Martha trundled along carrying a couple of carrier bags.

'Let me help,' said Allie to a grateful Aggie.

'You pair look like you're moving in. What have you got in there?' asked Meredith, clearing a space on the table. She peeped inside. 'That looks like a whole lot of history to me.'

'That's exactly what it is. There's photographs in here that go back decades,' declared Aggie, triumphantly.

'Where did you get them from?' asked Meredith, taking a handful from the top of the box and shuffling through them. 'Oh my, I think this memory night is going to bring back memories for all of us. Some of these are just embarrassing.'

'I can imagine! Stuart gave me the box. He asked if we would select the best ones and make sure we put them in chronological order ready for Alana's birthday.'

As soon as Aggie spoke the words 'Alana's birthday', she exhaled softly and flapped a hand in front of her eyes to compose herself. Immediately Allie could see the tears welling up in her eyes, and she slipped her arm around Aggie's shoulders to comfort her. Aggie gratefully placed her hand on top of Allie's and gave it a little squeeze. 'Thanks, love. Sometimes the emotion gets too much for me.'

'I think it's going to be a night for all of us to remember,' added Rona, giving her a friend a warm smile. 'I need to get back to the teashop. There's a full house at the B&B and Julia has ordered packed lunches for the hikers.'

'Talking of Julia,' chipped in Martha, holding up a bag, 'Mystic Martha is back out in full force.' She took out her crystal ball and placed it on the table alongside her fortune-telling outfit.

'We will have no witchcraft in here,' said Meredith, wagging her finger in Martha's direction. 'I'm already convinced there's odd goings-on in that cellar, and I promised Fraser all those years ago we wouldn't go near that Ouija board again. I don't need any kind of spirits floating around here.'

'I'm not talking to dead people, even though up at that farmhouse I feel a presence ... footsteps.' Martha glanced towards Isla, who looked up, alarmed.

'Gran! Don't say that and definitely don't say that in front of Finn, he'll never go to sleep.'

'To be fair, I think it's Drew creeping downstairs for a

cuppa in the middle of the night when he can't sleep.' She winked teasingly.

Isla brought her hand up to her chest. 'Do not do that to me.'

'And as far as the pub goes, it's already full of spirits ... Vodka, gin ...!' A broad grin spread across Martha's face.

The talk of ghosts made Allie remember when she was a little girl. Once her parents had read her a bedtime story – she'd always fallen asleep while they worked the bar – but this one evening her father had been away on pub business for the brewery when she'd woken in the middle of the night. The door from the bar to the upstairs living quarters was propped open and she could hear voices. Allie had sneaked behind the old battered purple velvet wing-back chair and witnessed Aggie, Rona and Alana huddled around one of the tables. There were cards laid out in front of them and their forefingers were firmly on the glass in the middle of the table. Allie had watched and listened as they'd begun to spell out words and sentences. She hadn't had a clue what was going on. Then, when her dad returned from his trip and they were having dinner together, she turned her empty glass over, placed her finger on the top and said, 'Is there anyone there?'

When her dad began to question what she was doing, the look of horror on her mum's face had said it all. Meredith had promised she wouldn't mess around with the spirit world ever again.

'Why does Julia need a look into the future?' questioned

Meredith, opening the Buck's Fizz and pouring everyone a glass as they settled around the table.

'Julia's getting a little anxious to say the least … Something about planning permission and an extension to the B&B. She wants me to look into my crystal ball and see what the future holds.'

'Why doesn't she just ask Alfie? Surely he could check where planning was up to at the office?'

'Because that would be the sensible option and mine is a lot more fun,' replied Martha with a chuckle, placing her crystal ball on a nearby table.

Aggie began to spill out the photographs into the middle of the table. Straightaway everyone could see there were decades of memories. Some photographs were in black and white, some in colour. There was a sudden silence while they began to look through them.

'It's like that TV programme *This Is Your Life*, when you look back on all the occasions and all the people who made your life so special. Then they give you that big red book at the end,' said Allie. She heard her mum sniffle. She looked over and her mum was gently weeping. 'I just had that very same thought. One thing I always remember about that programme …' Her voice faltered.

Allie knew exactly what her mum was thinking. The people whose lives they chose to celebrate were near the end of their career and possibly their life.

'I can't bear to think of any one of us suffering or losing each other. I know this is very selfish of me and I can't believe I'm saying this, but I've always wanted to go first because I just don't think I could cope without any of you.' Meredith was tearful and Allie attempted to rescue the situation by picking up her glass.

'We, the community of Heartcross,' she said in a very formal, posh voice, like she was the mayor or the prime minister, 'are very lucky to have each other and look out for each other. I for one love our little community, and this, Alana's birthday, is a time of celebration. I know we don't know what to expect.' Allie took a breath. 'But we are going to make the evening one to remember.'

'Hear, hear,' chorused everyone, clinking their glasses.

They took a sip of their drink and reflected on Allie's words. The community bond in Heartcross was unbreakable. It didn't matter which generation you belonged to.

Martha gave a friendly thump on the table before leaning across and grabbing a cinnamon swirl.

'Now let's have a look through these photographs and place them into piles,' she said with authority. 'This pile is a definite for the slide show, a "maybe" pile and a "definitely not" pile, and then we can narrow it down and put them in some sort of order.'

For the next hour they sorted through the photographs and reminisced. They laughed and dabbed away happy tears. The "definite" pile consisted of Stuart and Alana's very first car, the opening of the surgery, their wedding day and the birth of Rory. Allie couldn't help but laugh at the photographs before the digital age; in half of them people had their eyes closed or their heads cut off, often both.

'There was none of this deleting a photo and taking it again or these new-fangled things – what do they call them? – filters?' said Aggie. 'This is what you call a proper photograph.' Aggie held up a picture and everyone laughed. 'Goodness knows whose shoes those are.'

'The camera must have been pointing to the ground,' said Felicity. 'Can you imagine sending your photographs off to be developed and waiting for the postman to deliver them only to discover everyone had no head or you'd taken photographs of the ground?'

'It was like winning the lottery if you were all looking the right way, with your eyes open and your head fully intact,' said Martha, grinning.

'I know exactly whose those shoes are,' announced Aggie. 'Those shoes' – she pointed at the photograph – 'were Stuart's winkle-pickers.'

'Winkle ... what?' Allie cocked an eyebrow. 'It sounds painful.'

'Winkle-pickers,' said Aggie. 'Shoe fashion back in the day. They all thought they were rock 'n' roll stars wearing those.'

After another twenty minutes and lots of discussion all of the photographs were sorted into piles, then Martha dealt them out into lines like she was performing some sort of card trick. Once they'd agreed on the definite ones for the slide show, Meredith placed them in an envelope for Stuart to look over, then disappeared behind the bar. She brought out an old jar and small pieces of cream-coloured paper cut up into rectangles. 'Now for the memories, the more humorous the better,' she said, passing the paper around the table. 'We don't all want to be crying unless it's with laughter. Hamish has already been out collecting some,' she said, popping the ones he'd gathered into the jar.

They set to work writing their memories on the pieces of paper while Allie had them in fits of laughter telling them some of the stuff that Rory had written as a sixteen-year-old boy for his own jar.

'I think this is a brilliant idea,' said Isla. 'I'm going to start this with Finn and Angus – obviously not just yet with Angus. It'll make for a great family evening looking over the past year.'

'Agreed! Esme will love this too, it's a great idea,' enthused Felicity.

After another ten minutes and with all the pastries devoured, they declared themselves finished.

'A lifetime of memories.' Allie said and everyone was full of mixed emotions. No one knew how quickly Alana's disease would progress but what everyone did know was that they would all be there for each other.

Julia arrived just as they were finished and popped her own memory in the box.

'Right, I'll get myself changed and we can look into your future,' said Martha, reaching for her bag of clothes.

'Don't tell me you're going to say Julia is going to meet a tall handsome man and fall in love,' teased Felicity.

But before Martha could reply the pub door swung open and in walked Flynn Carter. Felicity gave Martha an 'I told you so' look.

'Another ten minutes until opening time,' announced Meredith, tapping her watch but with a smile on her face.

'Sorry, sorry,' said Flynn, all apologetic. 'Is it possible I could use your bathroom?' He thrust his hand forward towards Meredith. 'I'm Flynn, I've just rented the house on Love Heart Lane.'

As soon as Flynn introduced himself Allie noticed Julia narrow her eyes and bristle. She was staring straight at him with a stony face.

'As you are going to be a regular in this establishment then yes, the toilets are that way.' Meredith nodded towards the door in the corner.

'Thank you, thank you,' he said, glancing round at everyone before hurrying in the direction of the bathroom.

'Very sultry. Did you see those eyebrows? All dark and mysterious,' said Meredith, nodding with approval as soon as Flynn was out of sight. 'He is a man who looks after himself.' She raised her nose and took in the woody fragrance. 'And that's not cheap aftershave.'

'Are you trading Fraser in for a younger model?' teased Martha.

'He's not your cup of tea, is he, Allie?' joined in Felicity, reminding Allie of her reservations the night before.

'What was going on at Clover Cottage last night? Did you find out?' asked Aggie in a hushed whisper. 'Why the heated discussion with Stuart?' She raised her eyebrows then pressed her lips into a fine line.

Allie wasn't going to go into that now and it seemed she didn't have to when Julia spoke up: 'That man can't be trusted.' Julia's voice was low and everyone spun round to look at her but before she could be questioned any more the bathroom door swung open and Julia stared towards Flynn.

'Thank you, ladies,' said Flynn, his voice full of charm and his smile as bright as a toothpaste advert.

'You're welcome,' said Meredith politely. 'Can we get you anything else?'

'I'll be back later for a spot of lunch.' And with that Flynn walked out of the pub leaving everyone turning towards Julia once more.

Felicity was first to ask the question that was on everyone's lips. 'And why can't that man be trusted?'

'How do you know him?' added Aggie with curiosity.

A stunned-looking Julia scuttled over to the window, looking like an international spy as she gave an incredulous stare out on to the street to make sure he was nowhere in sight.

'That really was Flynn Carter, wasn't it?' she said touching her throat whilst still staring out of the window. She turned back round. 'That was the man who left my schoolfriend standing at the altar. That is the man who promised her the earth and stripped her of her dignity on her wedding day. That man broke her heart then disappeared off the face of the earth. Her parents lost thousands of pounds from the wedding. I can't believe he's here in Heartcross.'

Everyone gasped.

'Drinks all round, Allie,' ordered Meredith. 'Tell us more. We want the full story about this Flynn Carter.'

Chapter 22

It was a couple of hours until Allie was due to meet Rory at Clover Cottage. He was being very cloak-and-dagger about the whole affair and his continual texting throughout the day, reminding her not to be late, indicated he was definitely up to something.

She strode towards the top of the hill on Love Heart Lane, thinking how the small incline never seemed to get any easier, and she paused and caught her breath at the gate of Bonnie's Teashop, taking in the view. The magnificent mountain of Heartcross towered above her.

The old-fashioned bell tinkled above her head as Allie stepped inside the vintage teashop. She immediately noticed Stuart sitting in his favourite spot in the window and waved before heading towards the counter. Eyeing up the scrumptious-looking cakes under the glass domes, she didn't know which one she was going to devour.

'I know I should try something different, but it's always—'

'Lemon drizzle cake for you,' chorused Rona and Felicity together with a chuckle.

'You know me so well!'

Felicity slid a plate over the counter with the biggest slice Allie had set eyes on. 'I'll give it a go and take one for the team,' Allie said with a grin, ordering a pot of tea and looking over in the direction of Stuart, who already had a drink and a slice of cherry Bakewell tart.

'I'll bring it over,' said Felicity, placing a small pot of tea on a tray and following Allie to the table.

Stuart looked up, smiled and pointed to the slice of cake on his plate. 'This is our little secret. Alana already thinks my waistline is expanding but at my age if you can't have a little of what you fancy there's no hope.'

'I won't tell a soul,' Allie said, placing the envelope of photographs on the table and sitting down opposite him. 'How is Alana today?'

'Today has been a very good day. It's like everything is just normal and there is nothing wrong.'

'That's good then,' said Allie reassuringly, seeing the relief on Stuart's face. She took a breath. 'I've been reading up on the diagnosis,' she said tentatively, 'and there are some wonderful, inspiring blogs on the internet written by people in your position. They didn't know what to expect and how it was going to change their life, but one man's story I just couldn't stop reading. It was so positive and uplifting.'

Stuart nodded. 'I've read through a couple of blogs. Everyone's story is different.'

Allie rummaged inside her bag, then and slid a piece of paper across the table.

'What's this?' asked Stuart, taking his glasses from their case and peering through them.

'This is the email and the phone number of a guy called Simon. I was reading his blog and ... I think you should read it. I sent him an email to tell him how much his story touched my heart and he gave me his details when I explained what our family was going through. He told me to tell you if you need someone to talk to who's been in the same situation, then don't hesitate.' Allie hoped she hadn't overstepped the mark.

Stuart nodded. 'Thank you. I might just do that,' he said appreciatively.

Allie poured her tea and watched Stuart flipping the piece of paper over in his hand before placing it carefully in the top pocket of his shirt.

'There is a lot of support out there,' she said knowingly. 'You aren't on your own.'

She saw him swallow. He leant forward over the table, cupped his hands around hers and shook them heartily. 'Our family ... I like that. You are a part of our family and you are good for Rory. Keep him on the straight and narrow for me.'

'I will, I promise,' replied Allie, meaning every word.

'I'm scared,' admitted Stuart, then he hesitated. 'I don't want to let my good lady down.'

'That's understandable and you won't, but talk to Simon;

he's been in this situation. It will be good to have some outside support too.'

'I will, I will. Thank you, Allie.'

'You, Stuart, are one in a million, one of the good guys, just like Rory, and you won't be on your own. We will all be here for you both.'

Stuart picked up the envelope of photographs. 'We are going to make this a night to remember.'

'You'd better believe it! If you want to write the captions for each of the photographs, I'll sort out the slideshow.'

'And of course, I'll be making the cake,' chipped in Rona, passing with a handful of dirty plates she'd collected from a nearby table. 'And no charge, before you ask.'

'Perfect! Thanks, Rona.'

For the next five minutes they devoured their cake and watched the weary hikers climb over the stile and fall into the teashop. Rona always baked a fresh tray of sausage rolls just before the teashop was due to close. With all the hungry walkers spilling back down the mountain, she knew there wouldn't be enough to go round otherwise, and within a matter of minutes of the oven-timer pinging, she was proved right.

'Am I too late? Is there anything left?' asked a worried-looking Zach, coming through the door followed by Sydney.

Felicity was wiping down the counter and looked up 'Still half an hour to go before we shut up shop. What do you fancy?'

'Any of your homemade lasagna left? With a little salad and a coffee?' he asked hopefully.

'One serving left with your name right on it,' said Felicity. 'Go and sit down and I'll bring it over.'

'Thanks,' said Zach, turning round and smiling at Allie, who was waving at him.

'Come and join us,' she said, pulling out the chair next to her.

'I'm not intruding, am I?' He looked between Stuart and Allie.

'Not at all,' confirmed Stuart, devouring the last of his Bakewell tart.

'My final supper,' said Zach, thanking Felicity, who'd brought his coffee over.

'Are you all packed and ready to go?' asked Allie, thinking she'd got quite used to seeing Zach around the place.

'I have to say I'm packed but not ready to go. I've grown quite fond of this place. There's something about this little Scottish village hidden away in the mountains.' Zach took a sip of his coffee. 'And when I get home I've got to say goodbye to this one.' He bent down under the table and gave Sydney a pat. 'It's the hardest thing, leaving her behind, but I've managed to secure a few weeks off here and there so I'll be on the first flight home.'

Rona appeared at the side of the table. 'One lasagna with salad and a special slice of Victoria sponge for dessert, on the house.'

'Thank you, Rona. You've all been so welcoming, I actually don't want to leave.'

'You know you are welcome back any time and I'm sure Isla and Drew will always have a van available for you.'

'I hope so!' he replied, picking up his knife and fork and tucking into his food.

'And it's a shame you'll be on the other side of the world when the TV show is aired. We are planning a night of it here.'

'It is an absolute shame, but I'll get to watch it somehow.'

'So it's Africa for you next?' asked Stuart.

'It is, a place I've always wanted to go and a documentary I can't wait to make.'

'Very David Attenborough,' teased Allie.

'He was a massive idol of mine when I was a child, still is. I'd sit for hours watching those wildlife programmes. My guess is Rory would have loved this trip. It's right up his street. It's a shame he's no longer coming ... I'm sorry to hear about Alana.'

Allie looked between Zach and Stuart, knowing that Stuart knew nothing about Rory accompanying Zach on the trip to Africa.

Zach continued, 'I really enjoyed working with him and it's not often someone fits in with the crew as easily as he did.'

'Rory ... Africa? No longer going?' questioned Stuart, looking down his glasses, which were perched on the bridge of his nose, straight at Zach.

Allie dithered for a moment, her stomach twisting in a thousand knots. 'Rory had the opportunity to travel with

Zach for twelve months, to work with the lions in Africa, but he's decided not to go,' she said, trying to play it down.

'And this is the first I know about this? Why isn't he going?'

Allie looked at Zach.

'Sorry, sorry. I hope I've not said anything I shouldn't have,' said Zach, looking embarrassed.

Stuart, still looking bewildered, scratched his head. 'Why hasn't he said anything? It sounds like an amazing opportunity.'

Allie took a deep breath. 'Because there's no way Rory is leaving you to manage everything – the surgery, the family – for twelve months. That's just way too much pressure to put on anyone.'

'Nonsense! We can easily get Molly to cover the surgery. She loves working with me. I mean, who wouldn't? Easygoing, good-humoured ...' He tipped Allie a wink. 'Will he be making the documentary with you?'

'Yes, joint presenters,' Zach confirmed. 'Well, that was the plan. Apparently we have that on-screen chemistry and to have a vet on site would be an absolute bonus.'

Stuart pushed his empty plate to the side and folded his arms on the table.

'He must go. I'd give anything to have had an opportunity like that at the start of my career.'

'He's made up his mind, Stuart. With everything going on, he doesn't want to leave Heartcross for twelve months.'

'But this is the best time for him to go and accomplish

his dreams. Alana will be so proud of him, watching him and following his journey.'

'But he doesn't want to leave her or you,' said Allie.

Stuart scratched his head. 'He can't put his life on hold just for us. This is something he's always wanted to do, a cause he's always supported. What's your take on it?' He held Allie's gaze.

She took a breath. 'If I'm truly honest, I wasn't all for it at the start, for my own selfish reasons. I had us moved into Clover Cottage, married, children, but I know that can only happen when both of us are ready, not just one of us. Rory wants to do this. He wants to work alongside Zach and see these wild animals up close and personal. But in the grand scheme of things, to be committed for twelve months now, under the circumstances …'

'He'll regret that decision,' said Stuart. 'Mark my words.'

'I agree. Could you cope at the surgery?' queried Allie.

'It's twelve months, not a lifetime. A year flies by. I feel like I'm always dragging those Christmas decorations out of that blooming loft.'

For a moment they sat in silence while Allie mulled over an idea in her head. Suddenly, she had a lightbulb moment. A fleeting smile played across her lips, but first she needed to run it by Zach to see if what she was thinking was at all possible.

'Zach, I've got an idea,' Allie said enthusiastically, keeping her fingers crossed behind her back.

Zach and Stuart were all ears.

Chapter 23

A text from Rory pinged.

Don't be late.

Allie bit her lip and smiled. She had no clue what he was up to, but after continuous messages landing throughout the day there was no way she even dared to be a second late.

After her conversation with Zach and Stuart, Allie was walking on cloud nine and couldn't wait to share her idea with Rory. It took her approximately ten minutes to walk to Clover Cottage but as usual she stopped to take photographs at every opportunity. On arrival she stood and pointed the lens towards the cottage. There was definitely a good feeling about this quaint little piece of rundown paradise, but she couldn't quite put her finger on it. Taking one last snap she pushed open the gate and walked towards the front door. She twisted the knob, but the door was firmly locked. Taking the path to the back of the cottage she called out Rory's name, but there was no reply. The back door was ajar. Allie stepped inside the cottage and let out a tiny gasp. Lying on the floor was a trail of crimson paper hearts that led her through the kitchen up a step and into the living room. She couldn't believe her eyes – the entire room was swathed with twinkly fairy lights draped around the walls. In the middle of the room were two chairs facing each other on either side of a small table. The white linen tablecloth was skilfully decorated with scattered sugar-pink rose petals. Dozens of tea lights were dotted over the floor, all lit and twinkling away. It was plain to see a romantic meal was on the cards.

Allie had no idea what was going on or what this was all in aid of.

'You took your time,' said Rory, appearing in the doorway.

'What's all this?' she said, feeling a flutter of excitement.

Looking more handsome than usual, if that was even possible, Rory walked towards her and pulled her in for a hug. The scent of his aftershave made her feel dizzy; her body trembled, her heart pounded.

'This is dinner, brought to you by Little India,' said Rory as he tilted her face towards his then kissed her tenderly on the lips, making her shiver with goosebumps.

Little India was her favourite Indian restaurant, just over the bridge in Glensheil. Rory pulled out a chair and Allie sat down. Then he disappeared into the next room and returned with two steaming plates of food. 'This is the reason you couldn't be late – we have no oven to keep it warm,' he said with a grin, placing her favourite dish of lamb Rogan Josh in front on her. 'We have poppadums, chutneys, rice, naan bread and this ...' He disappeared once more and returned with two champagne flutes and a bottle of Lanson Black Label champagne. Allie couldn't contain her grin.

'Are we celebrating?' she asked, her eyes wide, still not really understanding what all this was in aid of.

'I hope so, but first tell me how it went this morning. Did you find the best photographs to suitably embarrass my parents?'

'We did our best, but I have to say it was a little emotional at times.'

'I bet.'

'In fact I've just given your dad the photos we've selected ... And how have you been after the revelations last night?' asked Allie.

'Still shocked, to tell you the truth. My dad in a boys' home, my grandparents not my biological grandparents ... but I could see how hard it had shaken Dad, finding out about James Kerr, and that he'd given him this place.'

'I know, it was all so surreal.'

Allie looked around the living room. There was no wallpaper, the plaster was hanging off the wall and there wasn't even a radiator plumbed in. All James seemed to have had was the battered old armchair next to the coal fire, which was probably the only heat in the house.

'And there's more,' said Rory tearing off a piece of naan bread and passing it over the rickety old table to Allie. 'This morning, I tried to encourage Dad to open the envelope, the one from Flynn Carter ...'

'Out of curiosity?'

Rory nodded. 'Yes, but he was having none of it. Dad took the envelope from off the mantelpiece and threw it in the fire and set it alight. "The cottage stays in this family. Over my dead body will any property developer get his hands on it. It is not for sale for any amount of money."'

'Good for him, and I can understand why, after everything that's happened. Julia's not keen on Flynn Carter either. Apparently, she knows him from years ago and he jilted an old schoolfriend at the altar!'

'It's a small world,' observed Rory.

Tucking into her food, Allie was unaware of Rory watching her. He reached over the table and put his hand on top of hers, making her jump.

'I've got something I need to tell you.' His voice was soft, his smile warm.

'I was wondering when we were getting round to the champagne moment because I've got the best news too, and you are going to love it!' Since walking into the cottage Allie had had to do everything in her power not to blurt it out. She didn't know how she'd already kept it in so long without bursting. She knew she had a wide grin on her face.

'Is that so? What are you up to? I know that look.' He narrowed his eyes and Allie laughed.

'It's all good, I promise.'

'Who's going to go first?' asked Rory, eyeing Allie closely.

'Rock, paper, scissors?' suggested Allie with a chuckle.

They exchanged looks. 'Let's just blurt it out at the same time,' proposed Allie, sitting up straight and moving her plate to one side while she rested her arms on the table.

'Okay,' agreed Rory, copying Allie's stance. 'One ... two ... three.'

'You're going to Africa!' revealed Allie.

'We're going to renovate the cottage!' declared Rory.

'Woah, woah, woah ... What do you mean, "We're going to renovate the cottage"?' asked Allie, unable to contain her excitement. She was up on her feet kissing his face and hugging him tight.

A bewildered-looking Rory pulled away. 'What do you mean, I'm going to Africa? I can't go to Africa with everything that's going on.'

'You can, you can. It's all sorted.'

'How is it all sorted?' Dazed, Rory sat down and waited for Allie to explain all. 'You know it's impossible now. I can't leave Mum and Dad for twelve months.'

'This is the good news: you don't have to go for twelve months. I've spoken to Zach and your dad and they are in favour ...'

Rory was shaking his head. 'You've spoken to Dad?'

'I have. Just listen. What if you went for three months? Molly can definitely cover the surgery for a few months, it's not too much of a burden on your dad, and your mum will be so proud watching you on TV.' She took a breath. 'Zach has cleared it with the producer and director and they are willing for you to take part in some of the series. I know it's not the full twelve months' experience but surely something is better than nothing?'

Allie noticed the corners of Rory's mouth hitching into a smile. 'And it's okay with Dad – and you?'

Allie was beaming and nodding. 'It's more than okay with your dad and it's more than okay with me too. If he had his way, he'd be packing you off for the full twelve months. And if I get the job in Glasgow it might turn out that I'm away longer than you but—'

'But what?'

'I've had another idea.'

'You are full of them today, aren't you?' Rory grinned.

'I've been thinking about James Kerr and the life he led. I want to give something back to the community, something in his memory.'

'Go on. What are you thinking?'

'There's not a lot to do around these parts, especially for kids,' continued Allie, 'and I was thinking I could combine my photography skills with my patience, as I have a lot of that, dealing with you,' she said teasingly, 'and set up a small centre for those more disadvantaged. We could start with a photography club and if I successfully land the job at the paper maybe I could persuade the editor or local businesses to help support the project, perhaps with funding. We could call it The James Kerr Centre.'

She watched Rory break out into a smile. 'I think that's a brilliant idea. You'd be perfect to run something like that. You have fantastic people skills and you are caring and I think Dad will be made up at the idea.'

'Surely there will be grants for this type of thing. I'll talk to Alfie – he'll know.'

'You never cease to amaze me, Allie Macdonald. Behind a good man is always a good woman.' Rory pulled Allie to her feet, taking her by surprise. He cupped his hands around her face and kissed her passionately, taking her breath away.

'This all sounds too good to be true,' she said, bursting with happiness.

Allie loved Rory with all her heart. This was true love: watching each other grow, supporting each other and cheering them along the way.

Rory raked a hand through his hair. He still couldn't quite believe he was actually going to Africa. 'I can't thank you enough,' he said, swooping down for another kiss.

'Now, sit down and let's finish this curry because from what I can remember you just said we were going to renovate this cottage and I want to hear more about it.'

'Where shall I start?'

'The beginning?'

'Yes, but first' – he twisted the cork and pop! It flew into the air and the champagne flowed into their glasses – 'Here's to us and Clover Cottage.'

Allie couldn't believe it. She felt giddy. She wanted to

share the news with her friends and the whole wide world. 'Are you saying you've accepted Clover Cottage and it's yours?'

'It's not mine ... it's ours! This cottage is staying in *our* family.'

Allie was thankful she was sitting down. Weak at the knees she took the glass from Rory and with a wide smile she squealed dramatically, causing Rory to laugh as she clinked her glass against his, her hand visibly shaking.

'Okay, so this morning we had a couple of no-shows in the surgery, which gave me a chance to talk to Dad about the future of the place.'

Rory had explained how disappointed he was in himself for being frustrated with Stuart's ways and he'd apologised for putting pressure on him about upgrading the surgery. Stuart had explained the reason they'd given Clover Cottage to Rory was because when his mum had received the diagnosis they'd sat down and talked and knew the time would come when Stuart would have to retire, and that was when they wanted to have their cottage back.

'Have their cottage back?' asked Allie not understanding the full picture.

'Once Dad retires, they don't want clients traipsing up to the cottage. They want to shut down the doors to the surgery.'

'End of an era ... How are you feeling about that?' asked Allie, finishing her curry and placing her knife and fork down on the empty plate.

'Sad, because that's been my dad's business for all these years. It's where Scott and Son all started. But I get it, they just want to be there by themselves. They want to enjoy the quiet life.'

'Which leaves you where, job-wise?' Allie took a sip of her champagne.

'Which leaves us here in more ways than one. Clover Cottage, the land, the outbuildings are ours. After speaking with Dad, we decided to move the surgery here. It will be up and running before we close the doors of the old one.' Rory was beaming.

'Rory, that's fantastic news!' Allie couldn't believe what she was hearing. This would be brilliant for Rory, everything on site, making his life a lot easier.

'Isn't it just! I can design the whole practice and we have the extra space to build a veterinary hospital. I won't have to transport any animals over to Molly's in Glensheil. I want a fleet of vans, staff ... This is going to be amazing.'

Allie could see Rory's enthusiasm: he was as excited about this new project as about going to Africa. His eyes shone with excitement, and he was speaking so quickly that he was tripping over his words. Allie didn't want to burst his bubble, but where was the money coming from if he wanted the new surgery up and running before the old one shut its doors?

'Have you won the lottery?' she asked, pouring them both another glass of champagne.

'I wish! Not only are Mum and Dad giving us the rent

money from Flynn Carter for the next twelve months, but this afternoon I've been to the bank.'

'You are a dark horse. All this plotting without me.'

'The bank has agreed, in principle, to lend me the money against the value of the cottage to renovate this place as well as build the surgery.'

'I can't take all of this in. This is brilliant,' exclaimed Allie, fit to burst. She stared around the room. 'I can already visualise how it's going to be. Brick fireplace, log burner, reclaimed oak-beam hearth. We can decorate this place anyway we want.'

Rory reached down under the table and brought out a pile of brochures. 'Ta-da! We have kitchen ideas, bathroom books, colour schemes, the latest copy of *Country Living* magazine for inspiration.'

'You've thought of everything,' said Allie suitably impressed, taking the pile of creative ideas from him.

'Allie ...'

She held his gaze.

'I just want you to know that building this home really does matter to me – especially after—'

'I know, you don't need to say it.' She touched his hand affectionately before flicking through the first brochure. 'Look at that layout ... oh my gosh – an Aga! Please can we have an Aga?'

Rory grinned. Allie was like a kid in a sweetshop, her eyes wide as she babbled away.

'You can have anything that makes you happy.'

Allie looked up. 'You make me happy, Rory Scott. And whilst you are off in search of your lions, tigers and bears, I'll be trying to land a job on the paper as well as drawing up plans and colour schemes.'

'That's good to hear because I'm leaving it all in your capable hands.' Rory paused for a second. 'And what you just said about James and setting up a project for disadvantaged kids ... the outbuilding at the far end of the property, adjacent to the lane, has three rooms. It's got the main area, a small kitchen and a bathroom. We can erect a gate off the road, maybe a small car park, and use that space to set up your group. And maybe I can get involved with the vet's practice, give work experience or even apprenticeships to kids that just wouldn't get the chance.' Rory took a breath and Allie could see the tears in his eyes. 'My dad was lucky to have been adopted by such a wonderful family. He was lucky to find my mum and I'm lucky to have wonderful parents ... not to mention just the best girlfriend.'

Allie was overwhelmed. That morning she had had no idea her day was going to pan out like this. Within the space of a few hours Rory was off to Africa, they were renovating their cottage and they were giving something back to the community. She couldn't wait to get started.

'I wonder if Flynn Carter still thinks he's going to get his hands on this place,' mused Allie, pointing to a racing green Aga in one of the magazines.

'He can think all he likes but sometimes money isn't

the answer to everything,' replied Rory, nodding his head towards the Aga in the magazine. 'Just being a decent person counts for a lot more and whatever was written on that piece of paper was an insult to James's memory. This place, Clover Cottage, will be perfect for the next stage of Scott and Son, thanks to James.' Rory's voice cracked, his emotions riding high. 'One of the virtues of living in a small community – we help each other.'

Allie swallowed a lump in her throat. 'You, Rory Scott, are a wonderful, caring man and I'm lucky to have you.'

He shot her the biggest grin. 'I'm really going to Africa, aren't I?'

'You really are!'

'Just promise me one thing, Allie.'

'I will if I can,' she replied, noting the seriousness in Rory's voice.

'We will always look after each other.'

'I promise,' she answered, meaning every word.

Chapter 24

'Don't cry, don't cry, hold it together,' Allie was telling herself over and over again, but it was no use, the tears welled up in her eyes. Dabbing her face for the umpteenth time, she knew she was being daft. Rory would be back in three months. The time would fly by. But it didn't stop her from feeling sad.

Trying to compose herself she stood and looked out of her bedroom window. The world appeared silent, the street outside was empty, there was no tractor in the field and not a soul walking up the High Street. She knew everyone would be getting ready for Alana's party, which was due to start within the next hour. The only movement she noticed was Isla's truck manoeuvring up the road; she'd nipped across to Glensheil to pick up the birthday balloons to decorate the room. Allie couldn't help but smile as they danced around Isla's head as she drove. She watched Isla pull up outside and hand the cluster of pink and ivory balloons to Fergus, who was waiting on the steps of the pub. They both looked in good spirits as they wrestled with the balloons before disappearing.

Watching the world go by, Allie thought about the last few days and how it was possible to have no clue what was just around the corner. She'd received an email that very morning from Caitlin Macloed, her interview was next Friday and she was already panicking about what she would wear.

Wrapping her arms around herself, Allie felt emotional, but her heart swelled with happiness. She and Rory were building their future together. Clover Cottage was their happy-ever-after home, with a brand-new, state-of-the-art surgery for him to build his new empire. Yet with all these exciting things happening in her life Allie still felt sad. The wrench in her stomach of not seeing Rory for the next three months was beginning to feel too much to bear.

Hearing a knock on her bedroom door she spun round to see Isla smiling at her. 'Your mum has sent me up to hurry you along. And why aren't you dressed yet?'

Allie was still wrapped tightly inside her dressing gown.

'I just got waylaid ... thinking, smiling and crying.'

Isla sat on the edge of the bed. 'I know you're sad that Rory is leaving but he's going to have a fantastic time and we'll get to laugh at him on the TV when he's away and honestly he'll be back before you know it.'

'I know, it's just since we've been together we've never actually spent so long apart.'

Allie knew that was what she was going to find the

most difficult: the fact that she couldn't just nip down the road to see him whenever she wanted, or grab a chat over the bar when he'd finished work. But there were going to be changes in her life too, if she landed the job in Glasgow, as well as throwing herself whole-heartedly into the James Kerr Project and overseeing the renovations at the cottage. In the past month, she felt she'd grown up and blossomed. True, she was stepping out of her comfort zone with regards to the interview, but Rory had made her think, and she realised she had no ambitions to follow in her parents' footsteps and own a pub. Her passion lay elsewhere.

'Come here,' said Isla, standing up. She gave her friend a hug. 'We are all going to miss him, and any time you feel sad or lonely, you ring or come on over.'

'I have just the best friends,' said Allie with sincerity.

'And that goes for me too,' said Isla in return.

'It's funny, looking back on the day of the summer fair. Mystic Martha seems to have got most of her predictions right,' said Allie, thinking back over that day.

'Well, don't be telling her that otherwise she'll be doubling her prices,' said Isla, chuckling as she swung open the wardrobe door. 'Now, what are you wearing?'

'I just thought I'd wear jeans and a shirt,' said Allie, flicking through the rail of clothes in front of her.

'You will not. We need something a little more memorable.'

'Need? Why do we need something a little more memorable?'

'Just trust me on this one ... What about this? It's perfect for a summer evening.'

Isla held up a beautiful rose-print dress, its flattering feminine design featuring a fitted bodice with boat neckline and a gently flared skirt with a tiered ruffle. She held it against Allie. 'Blooming gorgeous!' she said enthusiastically. 'This is the one. You'll look fantastic.'

Allie narrowed her eyes. 'What are you up to?'

'Me?' said Isla, raising her hand in mock protest. 'Absolutely nothing. Now go and get ready,' she ordered.

Allie disappeared into the bathroom, slipped on the dress and quickly reapplied her make-up before stepping back into the bedroom where Isla was still waiting.

'You look fantastic!'

Allie gave a quick spray of her perfume and declared herself ready.

'Keep smiling, no tears ... He'll be back before you know it.'

Allie nodded but she couldn't promise there weren't going to be any tears.

'Is Rory here yet?'

'Yes, the only people who aren't are you, Stuart and Alana.'

Leading the way downstairs Allie noticed Rory's suitcases stacked in the hall. He was leaving right after the party. Zach was already in Africa, but he'd arranged to send a car to pick up Rory and take him to the airport. Allie hated goodbyes, but the last thing she wanted was to wave him off at the airport and then have to drive home with tears streaming down her face. It was simpler this way.

'How's Zach getting on?' asked Isla, keeping the conversation going so Allie didn't have time to think about Rory leaving.

'His Instagram looks amazing.'

'And so will Rory's.'

'Did I hear my name?' Rory stepped into the hallway juggling an armful of presents.

'Yes, you did indeed. Do you need some help?' asked Isla, leaning forward and taking the top two presents from the pile.

'Those are for Mum, but this one's for you,' said Rory beaming at Allie.

'I'll leave you to it,' said Isla, disappearing back into the pub to give them a moment.

Rory placed the present down on the hall table and took Allie's hands in his.

'I'm going to miss that smell,' she said, leaning in and taking a whiff of his aftershave, which always made her feel weak at the knees.

'I'm going to miss you full stop.' Rory bent down and kissed her lightly.

For a second she held his gaze. 'I love you, Rory Scott.' She wrapped her arms tightly round his waist and hugged him, burying her face in his chest.

'How are you feeling?' Rory asked, tilting her face towards his.

'Happy, sad ... for me, but I honestly do want you to have a good time and experience all that wildlife.'

'I know, and even though I'm off to Africa, don't think I'm not feeling the same. I'll miss you and when I'm back we have so much to look forward to. Now open the present,' whispered Rory, leaning towards the table and picking up the small oblong box.

'What is it?'

'That's the whole idea of presents, you have to open them!'

Feeling a flutter of excitement Allie pulled on the red velvet ribbon and carefully opened the lid of the box.

Inside the burgundy silk-lined box lay a shiny silver key.

'A key?'

'Yes, indeed a key. Your key ... to our home ... Clover Cottage.'

Allie's heart began to hammer against her ribcage. She couldn't believe it. Everything was coming together.

'Rory, I don't know what to say,' she exclaimed, flabbergasted.

'Just no wild parties whilst I'm away,' he joked, grabbing her face and planting a kiss on her lips.

'I can't promise that.' She grinned, feeling all grown up. This was like a dream come true - a key to their home together.

'Come on, we'd better make an appearance, but before

we go in there can I just say how stunning you look tonight?'

'You can indeed,' said Allie, slipping her arm around his waist whilst listening to the excited chatter filtering through the door. Rory gave her a squeeze and pushed open the door. They were just in time.

'Stuart and Alana have arrived,' announced Meredith, ringing the bell behind the bar to silence the room.

Stuart walked in holding Alana's hand. They were both beaming, and Allie couldn't help thinking how much in love they still looked after all these years.

Everyone applauded as Stuart led Alana to the seat at the very front of the room. Fraser cued the music from behind the bar and everyone burst into song.

As 'Happy Birthday' played out Rory kissed his mum on the cheek and sat down next to her whilst Allie sat next to Stuart. She looked over the sea of people and came over all emotional. The room looked amazing, every table with a fresh white linen tablecloth, balloons and a bottle of champagne. An abundance of food was set out on long trestle tables at the back of the room, and taking pride of place in the centre was a magnificent cake made by Rona.

'Is it possible to say a few words?' said Stuart, blowing into the microphone.

'If you must!' called out Rory and Alana slapped his arm playfully. Everyone laughed.

'We are here tonight to celebrate my beautiful wife's birthday. I knew the second Alana walked into my life she was going to be the girl I was going to marry and be my happy-ever-after.' Stuart's voice cracked and Allie noticed Alana's eyes had welled up with tears too.

'This evening we are bringing to you, Alana, a slideshow of our greatest moments, picked and selected by all our friends in this room, followed by a jar of memories.'

Alana beamed as Rory stood up and handed his dad a glass of wine.

'But before we begin, I would like to make a toast,' he said, raising his glass. 'To my Alana. Happy Birthday.'

The whole room echoed him and raised their glasses too. Allie shot Rory a warm, loving smile. She hoped that she and Rory would still be going strong after as many years as Stuart and Alana had spent together.

The mood was jovial despite everyone knowing that upsetting and difficult times were not that far away. Allie reflected that all the people sitting in this room were a part of her life in some shape or form, people she loved and cared for, people who were there for each other no matter how difficult things got. Heartcross was a community she was proud to be a part of and she never wanted that to change.

'And secondly,' Stuart went on, 'I would like to raise another toast to our son Rory, who makes me proud every day. We all know you leave for Africa tonight on a three-month trip of a lifetime. Whilst you're off tackling lions, tigers and bears I have the pleasure of keeping everything together here until you get back.' Stuart took a breath and stared at the floor. 'But it is with great sadness that I have to tell you that Scott and Son will be shutting its doors at the cottage in the very near future.'

There were gasps from around the room.

'However, you can't get rid of us that easily! We are pleased to announce that a new state-of-the-art surgery is going to be built up at Clover Cottage – Rory and Allie's new home!'

Everyone applauded.

'I'm hanging up my scrubs and this old bugger is finally retiring to spend time with his beautiful wife.'

Whilst everyone was still clapping Stuart looked from Rory to Allie. When the applause died down he continued, 'You are both going from strength to strength, living your lives, supporting each other and loving each other. I'm sure you will all join in raising our glasses to Rory, Allie and their future at Clover Cottage.'

'Hear, hear,' everyone chorused in unison.

Allie noticed that Alana whispered something in Rory's ear then slipped something into his hand.

'Now I believe Rory would like to say a few words. Over to you, son.'

Rory stood up and Stuart stepped to one side.

Allie raised an eyebrow at Rory. 'What are you up to?' she whispered, giving a nervous laugh.

Rory held her gaze and took a deep breath.

'Here goes. As you all know, I've known Allie for most of my life. When she turned up in our village she was a shy girl ... How things have changed,' he said, grinning.

'But I'll never forget the first time I plucked up the courage to ask you out on a date. I was covered head to toe in blood after saving your dog's life, and you still said yes. I knew I was punching above my weight. In fact, even to this day the lads remind me of that.' Rory gave a swift look at Drew and Fergus, who were smirking and holding up their glasses in acknowledgement.

'Definitely punching above your weight,' shouted Fergus, but stopped heckling when Felicity gave him a stern look.

Rory turned towards Allie. 'As much as I'm excited to be going off to Africa, I'm going to miss you and can't wait to get home and build our new future together.'

Allie felt herself trembling as Rory knelt down on one knee. He held up a small red box in front of her. 'This ring was my grandmother's, and it brought her and my grandfather years and years of happiness. They had the most fantastic marriage and if we are half as happy as our own parents, we are going to be very lucky. Allie Macdonald, will you do me the greatest honour of becoming my wife?'

Allie gasped then clamped her hand to her mouth as the whole room fell silent.

'Well, say something,' whispered Rory, looking up with big, hopeful eyes.

'Yes ... yes ... YES!' she gasped, the happy tears streaming down her cheeks.

Rory's face said it all as he stood up and slipped the ring onto Allie's finger.

'The girl said YES!' he exclaimed.

'Is this really happening?' she asked, beaming down at the elegant diamond ring that sparkled on her finger.

'You'd better believe it. You are my happy-ever-after, Allie Macdonald. Now kiss me!'

Allie didn't need to be asked twice. She brushed her lips against his and melted into his arms.

Everyone was on their feet clapping. Meredith and Fraser popped the champagne corks and began to fill the glasses while Stuart and Alana joined Rory and Allie, hugging them tight.

Allie couldn't believe it. This was it, their happy-ever-after. Rory was hers and she was his and they had such exciting times ahead of them.

As Allie looked out over the sea of faces, she caught the eye of Martha, who winked straight at her. She had been right; she was in charge of her own destiny. And he was standing right beside her.

'Allie Scott ... it has a nice ring to it,' said Allie, not taking her eyes off the diamond on her finger.

'It has a perfect ring to it.'

'I love you,' said Allie, feeling on top of the world. It felt good making plans and having hope for their future together.

'I love you more ... but we do need to talk at some point ... I'm still up for having a football team!'

'Not a chance, Rory Scott, not a chance!'

THE END

A Letter from Christie

Dear Readers,

Firstly if you are reading this letter, thank you for choosing to read *Clover Cottage*.

I sincerely hope you enjoyed reading this book, if you did, I would be grateful if you'd write a review. Your recommendations can always help other readers to discover my books.

This is my TENTH BOOK, and I'm really sorry for the SHOUTY CAPITALS but I'm super proud I have ten books published. Writing for a living is truly the best job in the world and I love spending my time in a fictional land.

I'm particularly proud of this novel due to the fact I could have easily given up writing in the last eighteen months due to my health and personal circumstances but good things do happen in life when you surround yourself with kind beautiful positive people. They've taught me to dream big, work hard and stay focussed.

All the characters in the Love Heart Lane series have

been a huge part of my life in the last two years and the good news is there are still more books to come based around the little village of Heartcross in the Scottish Highlands.

Huge thanks to everyone who has been involved in this project. I truly value each and every one of you and it's an absolute joy to hear from all my readers via, Twitter, Facebook and Instagram.

Please do keep in touch!

Warm wishes,
Christie x

Acknowledgements

I'm absolutely shouting from the rooftops that my tenth book has been published, I really can't quite believe it!

It takes a great team of people to get a book over the finish line and there is truly a long list of fabulous folk to thank.

Special thanks to my fabulous gang: Emily, Jack, Roo and Mop, who are simply the best.

Woody (my mad cocker spaniel) and Nellie (my labradoodle) you are both my writing partners in crime and are always up to no good but I love you.

Endless love to Anita Redfern (BMITWE) my one true friend, who walks in when the rest of the world walks out.

I couldn't do this job alone and I want to express huge love to One More Chapter. I am beyond blessed to be working with such a fantastic team. Many thanks to the utterly beautiful Charlotte Ledger, who goes far beyond the call of duty to encourage, inspire and make the magic happen. I still can't believe you turn my stories into books ... thank you!

Christie Barlow

Big love to my frightfully brilliant editor, Emily Ruston (feelings, Barlow – we need feelings!) whose encouragement and belief throughout the year has kept me writing when times have been tricky.

Thanks to my agent Kate Nash, for your vision, energy and continuous support in me.

High fives to Bella Osborne, Erin Green, Glynis Peters, Kiren Parmar ... You rock! Writing can be a lonely job but thank you for providing continuous laughs along the way.

Team Barlow! Huge love to my merry band of supporters and friends: Sue Miller, Jenny Berry, Tammi Forbes-Owen, Annette Hannah, Claire Knight, Sarah Hardy and Joanne Robertson, whose support has never wavered from when my very first book was published. Writing can be a solitary profession but when your book flies out into the big wide world it's a team effort and I have the most amazing squad of merry supporters.

A special thank you to my technical experts Nicola Rickus and Molly Mckendrick for their wonderful veterinary knowledge when writing this story.

Biggest thank you to the fabulous bloggers, reviewers and wonderful readers for getting behind my books in such an overwhelming way. I am eternally grateful for your constant sharing of posts and your support for my writing is truly appreciated.

Finally, this book wouldn't have been written if it wasn't for my eldest daughter Emily. My awesome girl provided the little spark for this story when she took the brave deci-

sion to leave everything and everyone she knew to up sticks and leave England for a year to work in Madrid as a teacher without knowing a single word of Spanish.

Thank you so much for all your lovely messages, tweets and emails, please do keep them coming. They mean the world to me.

I have without a doubt enjoyed writing every second of this book and I hope you enjoy hanging out with Allie and Rory. Please do let me know!

Warm wishes,
Christie x